IMRE

IMRE
A MEMORANDUM

Edward Prime-Stevenson

edited by James J. Gifford

broadview literary texts

National Library of Canada Cataloguing in Publication

Prime-Stevenson, Edward, 1858-1942
    Imre : a memorandum / Edward Prime-Stevenson; edited by James J. Gifford.

(Broadview literary texts)
Includes bibliographical references.
ISBN 1-55111-358-9

I. Gifford, James J., 1946- II. Title. III. Series.

PS3525.A98614 2002   813'.52   C2002-904875-3

Broadview Press Ltd. is an independent, international publishing house, incorporated in 1985. Broadview believes in shared ownership, both with its employees and with the general public; since the year 2000 Broadview shares have traded publicly on the Toronto Venture Exchange under the symbol BDP.

We welcome comments and suggestions regarding any aspect of our publications—please feel free to contact us at the addresses below or at broadview@broadviewpress.com.

North America
PO Box 1243, Peterborough, Ontario, Canada K9J 7H5
3576 California Road, Orchard Park, NY, USA 14127
Tel: (705) 743-8990; Fax: (705) 743-8353
email: customerservice@broadviewpress.com

UK, Ireland, and continental Europe
Thomas Lyster Ltd., Units 3 & 4a, Old Boundary Way
Burscough Road, Ormskirk
Lancashire, L39 2YW
Tel: (01695) 575112; Fax: (01695) 570120
email: books@tlyster.co.uk

Australia and New Zealand
UNIREPS, University of New South Wales
Sydney, NSW, 2052
Tel: 61 2 9664 0999; Fax: 61 2 9664 5420
email: info.press@unsw.edu.au

www.broadviewpress.com

Broadview Press Ltd. gratefully acknowledges the financial support of the Government of Canada through the Book Publishing Industry Development Program for our publishing activities.

Series editor: Professor L.W. Conolly
Advisory editor for this volume: Michel Pharand

PRINTED IN CANADA

This book is made of paper from well-managed FSC® - certified forests, recycled materials, and other controlled sources.

For Paul David Stern

Contents

Contents

Acknowledgments

Not much is really known about Edward Prime-Stevenson, and much remains hidden about his secretive life, though this little book now reveals more than ever about him, I hope; and it hasn't been just my own energy that has done it—not by a long shot. My interest in *Imre* was warmly shared by "The Friends of Eddie," my European circle of Prime-Stevenson enthusiasts, whom I fortuitously found on the internet, and who have encouraged me every step of the way, as well as provided me with research and time and materials I could not possibly complete from my desk in upstate New York. Raimondo Biffi of Rome supplied me with letters and photographs of Prime-Stevenson that he had luckily acquired in a rare copy of *Long-Haired Iopas*. Jean-Claude Féray of Paris generously provided me with the results of his own painstaking research and an advance copy of his and Raimondo's excellent article on EPS as a European author.

Most generously, Tom Sargant of Brighton was a beacon of enthusiasm, and a provider of new research laboriously acquired through long hours at the British Library, liberally shared. I can never thank him enough for his time behind dusty tomes and his dogged tracking down of every possible lead. It was he, not I, who discovered what no scholar of gay studies had known before: that Stevenson had consistently lied about his age—for whatever reason—after his remove to Europe in 1900. Now countless libraries will have to go to their records to emend Edward Prime-Stevenson's date of birth from 1868 to its real one of 1858, and all because of Tom. In the midst of his own writing, Tom unfailingly offered theories, hunches, reflections, new data, and an intelligent critical eye leveled at an author whom few people know and many people should. Tom in many ways co-authors this much-needed edition of *Imre* and I remain grateful for his help and friendship.

The school where I teach is a community college, and yet it offered me every kind of support for research in a rather arcane field, giving me a grant to research in Budapest in the glorious summer of 2000, as well as providing the reassurance that what I was doing was worthwhile. Sandra Engel and John Bolton and Patty Fox were invaluable, and our president Michael Schafer signed me the monies: I thank them and Mohawk Valley Community College a thousand times. In the library Colleen Kehoe—a former student now turned colleague—helped me track down sources, and there Sherry Day earned sainthood in allowing me my way in my over-use of interlibrary loan.

Darby O'Brien of the Utica Public Library did the unheard-of: she let me take a reference work out of the building so that I could reproduce it and show you for the first time in a hundred years what Stevenson looked like.

My good friend Tim Drew, managing editor of Home magazine, showed me his versatility by helping me translate several necessary foreign articles.

I owe Mark Mitchell and David Leavitt thanks for their continued support and encouragement throughout my Prime-Stevenson research.

In Budapest, Gabriel and Jackie Angi-Dobos were my saviors. Not only did they help me find my way around and treat me to a never-to-be-forgotten dinner high in the hills of Buda, but they continued for months afterward to help me translate the formi-dable words and phrases that Stevenson so blithefully strews about his text. Dr. Géza Buzinkay, senior curator at the Kiscelli Museum in Budapest, generously gave me several hours in response to the minutest questions about the topography and history of 1900 Hungary. I grew to understand Stevenson's love of Hungary and its people because of my contacts there. And a thank-you to the learned author John Lukacs, born in Hungary and lately retired from Chestnut Hill College in Pennsylvania, for his patient interviews and valuable leads.

Burton Weiss of San Francisco helped me several years ago with *Dayneford's Library*, and he helped me again with his knowl-edge about the details of *Imre's* first and only edition.

But of course it is the unsung support at home which under-pins it all, and for this I thank as always the encouragement of my sister Barbara Gifford Lanigan, the example of perseverance through hardship of my friend John Gilbert, and most of all my partner Paul Stern, who helped me through all this, and wound up learning more about Edward Prime-Stevenson than perhaps he ever wanted to know.

EDWARD IRENAEUS PRIME-STEVENSON,

approximately 40 years old. *The Book Buyer* (May 1899).
Courtesy Utica Public Library, Utica, NY.

EDWARD IRENAEUS PRIME-STEVENSON,
51 years old, shortly after writing *Imre*. *The Musical Courier*, 12 January 1910.
Courtesy Sibley Music Library, Eastman School of Music, University of Rochester.

Introduction

The list of things Edward Prime-Stevenson's *Imre* will not do for you, his reader, is rather forbidding. It will not provide a swashbuckling tale full of mistaken identities, hidden crimes, and hairpin plot twists. It will not lead you on a physical adventure where life and limb are at stake. For those readers seeking a gay Harlequin romance superimposed upon a period representation of the past, *Imre* disappoints. In spite of its reputation as the first overtly gay American novel, there are no scenes of physical intimacy, no rollicking Tom-Jones style bedroom romps, no kisses save of the most formal and chaste kind. No subterranean visits to gay brothels or bathhouses grace its pages, though such places existed in 1906, as they probably always have. The omission of such lubricity perhaps surprises a reader approaching this book for the first time. A "homosexual novel" that does not focus on groinal activity seems odd, for many readers might wonder what else there is to say in a work whose two main characters' chief interest for us might be their sexual orientation. Though perhaps startling to a modern reader (even one appreciating Victorian reticence in such matters, gay or straight), the book's single sexual episode is oblique, and an object of shame for its perpetrator. Quite an oddity for audiences reared on the frankness of the novels of David Leavitt or films such as *Queer As Folk*. To those expecting such business to be a requirement to understanding the "gay experience," *Imre* is quaint, even curious. To hear that the author never meant his work as "entertainment" daunts one most of all.

What the novel *will* do for you, as it did for its original (small) audience, is to take you into the minds and feelings and thought-processes of people facing the world's disapprobation for feelings and desires they cannot help. Its trajectory from loneliness to fulfillment has universal appeal. Stevenson called his work "a little psychological romance," one he undertook because he felt that the English-speaking world possessed nothing like it, and in that he was right. The two men's wary roundelay as they approach each other, followed by incessant quizzing and searching, forms the crux of the romance. Gay men in 1906 seldom recognized each other on sight: their mating ritual necessitated a very measured process of disclosure—the gradual peeling away of layers of protection, or masks, that society's disapproval had required of them. *Imre* is cerebral in the best sense of the word; its word-dance is both redolent of and more honest than the works of Henry James. Corporal action is not particularly important in *Imre*, for into the void left by the physical stasis comes the dramatic motion of disclosure. Two men who are drawn to each other must reveal themselves, giving away their darkest and most dangerous secrets, so that they can find what they are looking for: each other. Their gradual unmasking is the book's chief metaphor. If this seems occasionally slow-going for a modern reader thinking "Strangers in the Night", with its more immediate gratification, it must be understood that the period demanded utter discretion when it came to such "deviant" desires. Lives could be ruined, fortunes lost, public honor brought down in disgrace, and suicide was not uncommon.

Dialogue, then, is all-important for Stevenson. "It is certainly a fundamental principle of the modern dramatic novel," he said, "... that such scenes as present vividly emotional and human situations, the play of chief personages against each other, so to say, should be carried out by dialogue between such protagonists, as far as possible. Merely the narrative, 'told historically,' without rapid and dramatic dialogue, will not serve for vital episodes. In such cases, they are likely to leave us cold to their force in the tale, relatively." [1] Talking is integral, then, to the revelation of the self. It is not so different from the earliest Greek plays, where confrontation between two characters formed the core of the drama. *Imre* is indeed "a memorandum," a statement that summarizes the terms of a contract or transaction—here, the brokering of peace and fulfillment between two people who have been isolated by "difference."

The Period

Imre is not the first American gay novel. We could list *John Brent* by Theodore Winthrop (1861) or *Joseph and His Friend* (1870) by

---

[1] "The Bride of Lammermoor," *The Times Literary Supplement*, 31 July 1919, 413.

Bayard Taylor as earlier works, and more may come to light. But *Imre's* merit—though not its only one—is its conclusion, where for the first time through an American author's agency, two homosexual characters are "allowed" the ending that has been a heterosexual commonplace for hundreds of years: the two lovers wind up together happily, facing an optimistic future. Moreover, the idea of a novel in English dealing *openly* with homosexuality in 1906—a world still reeling from the Oscar Wilde trials of 1895—was distinctly daring. What few works had appeared, according to Edward Prime-Stevenson, were covert and vague. "The field ... is virgin to the audacious!" he told Paul Elmer More, so he set about writing a tale of "a strange sincerity" with "informative purport," full of idealism and "ethical dignity" (see Appendix A). Stevenson well knew the troubles he would face in publishing such a work: "The author or publisher of a homosexual book, even if scientific, not to speak of a belles-lettres work, will not readily escape troublesome consequences. Even psychiatric works from medical publishers are hedged about with conditions as to their publication and sale" (*Intersexes* 376).

The late nineteenth century, awash in Darwin's scientific theories and the appearance of dynamic psychology, had a great desire to understand human behavior. If, as we are told, the unexamined life is not worth living, the lives in *Imre* are, if anything, over-examined. The subtitle of the book insists on a dissection and anatomization common to this period.[1]

The rise of dynamic psychiatry brought with it the notion of sexual "inversion." Religion's term "sodomite" gradually gave way to science's concept of "urning" or "uranian" or "homosexual": analysis, it felt, could explain such tendencies. In so doing, the medical establishment gave homosexuals a name, a form, and ultimately a voice.[2] The case history, psychiatry's chief analytic tool,

---

[1] Henry James subtitled works "a study" or "a sketch," for example. Henry Nash Smith discusses this love of anatomization thoroughly in *Democracy and the Novel* (New York: Oxford UP, 1978); see especially pages 145–146. Another interesting "anatomy" is Willa Cather's short story "Paul's Case: A Study in Temperament" (1905).

[2] The most general and compelling exploration of this idea remains Michel Foucault's ground-breaking work, *The History of Sexuality: An Introduction* (3 vols.) (New York: Vintage, 1976–84).

though often lurid and over-ripe with pathological "explanation" and analysis, created new categories to explain human sexuality. Richard von Krafft-Ebing's *Psychopathia Sexualis* (1886), Albert Moll's *Die conträre Sexualempfindung* (1891), and Havelock Ellis and John Addington Symonds's *Sexual Inversion* (1897) were just three such influential works. Though replacing the notion of "sinful" with "pathological," underneath such exploration there was an implied call for understanding if not outright acceptance. In recognizing their "symptoms," many men and women paradoxically found a solution to the riddle of their feelings. Several gay authors such as Stevenson assimilated the case history into their writing, employing the structure if not always the theory of difference, always stretching it in surprising directions. Not satisfied with the pathology such histories were meant to illustrate, they would transmogrify the form. In 1901 Claude Hartland published *The Story of a Life* ostensibly for the medical establishment in St. Louis; and though he employed case-history format to tell his story, he succeeded in suggesting a far more sympathetic and human portrait than the format usually tolerated. Charles Warren Stoddard's autobiographical novel *For the Pleasure of His Company* (1903) does much the same thing. Indeed, so rapidly would homosexuals adopt the case history as a means of finding a voice to tell their stories that by 1897 Havelock Ellis felt compelled to argue against such a notion in *Sexual Inversion* (see Appendix C). Edward Prime-Stevenson's disgust with the pathologizing effect of the case history led to his own monumental study, *The Intersexes* (1908), intended as a refutation of the medical establishment. Under the "anxiety of influence," as Harold Bloom might say, he re-formed the text of the homosexual's life, bringing to it a new and unashamed sympathy. *Imre*, written concurrently with *The Intersexes*, translates the same defense into belles-lettres. Such perpetual analysis risked tedium, but such territory was distinctly *terra incognita* in 1906. By presenting two men who struggle with their homosexuality but are on the whole responsible and socially well-adjusted, as well as in conformity with contemporary masculine stereotypes, *Imre* subverts the case history. Since the homosexual men in the case studies of Krafft-Ebing are most often typified as effeminate, with any "normal" masculine traits obscured or non-existent, Stevenson underscores his own heroes' masculinity. In fact, he insists on this so much that he occasionally runs the risk of misogyny, since what is feminine is often devalued in *Imre*—to the point where Oswald must insist that homosexuals are not woman-haters, but simply unaroused by them sexually. Unlike the enervated, languid, "neurasthenic" subjects of earlier case studies, Imre and Oswald are direct, aggressive men who seek partners with similar strength of character. Imre especially runs counter to Krafft-Ebing's neurotic homosexuals in his ability to be a soldier—a career that the age felt was the apotheosis of masculinity.[1] If he is accused by Oswald of lacking the necessary drive to get ahead, Imre's lassitude comes from a dislike of the military, not an inability to succeed in it. Physically, Imre is almost perfect: he can leap over a table in a single bound, take prizes in athletic contests, swim the wide and current-ridden Duna with ease. When he is accused, even playfully, of being "womanish," he bristles in anger. The only "feminine" characteristic he will admit to is that he says no when he means yes! Most importantly, by the novel's close, both Imre and Oswald's case histories reach satisfying conclusions. Any neurosis arising from repression (as Freud might later say) finds its healing in the discovery and acceptance of "the friendship which is love." Indeed, Oswald summarily rejects scientific analysis in asserting that homosexuality is at heart a "mystery." By the third edition of *Sexual Inversion* Havelock Ellis had to admit that *Imre: A Memorandum*, for all its clear usage of the case-history model turned into fiction, "embodies a notable narrative of homosexual development which is probably more or less real" (340).

The cult of Hellenism that had arisen in the 1870s—a love for Greek culture and ideas—was still popular when *Imre* was written.[2] For men "in the know" at this period, things Greek often

---

[1]   See Jackson Lears, *No Place of Grace: Antimodernism and the Transformation of American Culture 1880–1920* (New York: Pantheon, 1981).

[2]   Among others, see David M. Halperin, *One Hundred Years of Homosexuality* (New York: Routledge, 1990) and Richard Dellamora, *Masculine Desire: The Sexual Politics of Victorian Aestheticism* (Chapel Hill: U of North Carolina P, 1990). Tom Stoppard's play about the life of A.E. Housman, *The Invention of Love* (New York: Grove, 1997) is perhaps the most readable and moving exploration of this idea.

emblematized the ideal of same-sex friendship and the acceptance of homosexuality. John Addington Symonds's seminal essay, *A Problem in Greek Ethics*, written in 1873, was a work Stevenson must have known. The myth he creates around Lorand and Egon Z., the cousins memorialized in the monument that forms the backdrop of one important scene in *Imre*, recasts the Greek story of Damon and Pythias as a Hungarian ideal of friendship.

It must be mentioned too that gay literature at this period was often a case of passing a text "from hand to hand."[1] Such networking among homosexual readers was widespread, and its implications have yet to be fully explored. The text that Stevenson had printed privately in Naples early in 1906 consisted of only 500 copies, and their distribution remains unknown, though certain continental bookstores may have helped.[2] Stevenson gave copies to trusted friends (see Appendix A) but very few of them survive. *Imre* doubtless had a limited audience. Its erudition suggests well-educated readers. Paradoxically, such gay writing was often a private and elite form of literature whose proselytizing doubtless reached only "converted" readers.

Imre: A Memorandum

The choice of Budapest as the setting for *Imre* is inspired. A frequent visitor, Stevenson was quite knowledgeable about Hungary and had many acquaintances there. Indeed, he followed its politics closely.[3] (After World War I he would refuse to go back, saying that his connection was broken, his friends scattered or long gone.) He masks the locale—an interesting echo of the book's most common metaphor—by calling it Szent-Istvánhely—Saint Stephen's Place, for Hungary's patron saint. Such an exotic location hearkens back

---

[1] The phrase belongs to Mark Mitchell and David Leavitt. See the insightful Introduction to their anthology of gay writing, *Pages Passed from Hand to Hand: The Hidden Tradition of Homosexual Literature in English from 1748 to 1914* (Boston: Mariner, 1997).

[2] The second page of the also-privately-printed edition of *Her Enemy, Some Friends—and Other Personages* notes a very limited list of such bookstores.

[3] "The Political Crisis in Hungary: 1903," *The Independent* 55 (30 July 1903), was one such example.

to an earlier nineteenth-century Romantic yearning, and the melancholy, introverted quality of the Hungarian character seems utterly appropriate for a tale of repression and the crushing necessity of hiding behind a mask.[1] In situating his story as far as he had ever traveled from his homeland, Stevenson effectively erases America from his tale, to the point where Oswald, the author's alter-ego, is made an Englishman. The sole American referent is a psychiatrist whose "cure" for homosexuality is to direct Oswald to marry, perhaps suggesting Stevenson's disdainful view of the United States as backward and misguided.

Aside from its exoticism, Budapest's geography itself complements the author's theme of searching for one's soul mate. The beautiful Lánchíd or Chain Bridge that spans the wide Duna (Danube) and joins the cities of Buda and Pest becomes an appropriate space for Oswald and Imre to reach out to each other, to gradually reveal their own inner geographies, to attempt a union link by link. Their initial conversation on the bridge misfires, but the final quiet walk over the Lánchíd shows them at last united and directs them back to the shared space of Oswald's room. The word games and constant probing of each other are further links in the growing chain that draws them together. Indeed, the search for a mate (not unlike "The Noiseless Patient Spider" of Walt Whitman casting its tentative lines in endless search for Another) is echoed even in the several tables that often isolate or divide the heroes in the novel, as at the café where they first meet. In the novel's final scene, the table that Oswald keeps between them as a last barrier gets significantly pushed aside by Imre. Yet more than barriers, tables function as bargaining-sites (one recalls Nora and Helmer at the end of Ibsen's *A Doll's House*), places where the characters communicate and confront each other honestly, attempting linkage. The memorial to the Z. cousins, the sole location in the book which is probably a fiction of the author, continues this metaphor. Not only is this monument to male-male love a reflection of the two heroes' feelings for each other, it is where they join hands in the dark, an echo of the chain bridge to connect them. Likewise,

---

[1]   Prime-Stevenson discusses the image of the mask in *The Intersexes*, pp. 86–87.

artistic temperament, often discussed in *Imre*, is frequently seen as a homosexual signal.[1] Music and literature forge further connections between Imre and Oswald, their tastes often minutely catalogued. Stevenson had spent most of his life as a music critic, and felt qualified to see music as harboring a particularly homosexual relation.[2] Not surprisingly, he often notes that something is "in harmony" or "out of key" in his writing.

Did Stevenson exploit the case histories in *Imre* to tell his own story? Indeed, music and literature are not the only autobiographical details in *Imre*: Oswald's age, coyly designated as "past thirty" (Stevenson was actually 48 when *Imre* was published, though by 1906 he had subtracted ten years from his age everywhere he could get away with it); his study of languages (*Imre* is liberally peppered with foreign terms); Oswald's wealth to pursue his wanderlust; his wide travel experience, including eastern Europe; his self-proclaimed "exile" from his roots—all these particulars point to Stevenson himself. Even in Imre there are further details of the author's character: his insistence on his "masculinity"; his turn to athleticism after a sickly childhood, like Teddy Roosevelt; his dismay at watching a love-interest marry. While the book's three chapter-titles speak of the gradual disclosure of the hearts behind the masks, one cannot help but remark on the many masks that one must filter through in order to find Stevenson himself. The book is ostensibly written by Oswald, who sends the book to Xavier Mayne to edit, who in turn is the cover for Edward Prime-Stevenson—an intriguing subterfuge. One wonders in retrospect if indeed Stevenson ever met the original for such a man as Imre. Or is "Imre" an incomplete anagram for "Prime"?

Yet Imre is indeed a masturbatory figure, a hyper-masculine ideal as attractive as any of J.C. Leyendecker's Arrow Collar men: all muscle and manliness, with a dash of *noblesse* besides, the apotheosis of a gay man's desire. It matters little that much of his life is pretense (he pretends to be straight, is known as a ladies' man, acts the soldier though he does not feel it)—the point is

---

[1] This is a continual theme in *The Intersexes*. See especially pages 279 ff. and 387 ff.

[2] See Appendices C and E, as well as *The Intersexes*, pages 395–401.

that he easily "passes" for heterosexual. Ironically, the ideal of many gay men is to find someone who does not *seem* to be gay, and that is Imre's forte. By the end of the book Lieutenant Imre must learn to express what has remained hidden: his homosexual side. As "the man who knows" (Stevenson's translation of the Wildean "love that dare not speak its name") he must become "the man who speaks."

Though *Imre's* happy ending was unprecedented in a gay novel in English, it cannot escape comparison with a near-contemporary, *Maurice* by E.M. Forster. Written in 1913–1914 at the height of Forster's powers[1] but not published until 1971, *Maurice* too provides a happy conclusion for its two lovers. We see the same Hellenism, the endless analysis, the resistance and repression, the uselessness of psychiatrists to help (the American doctor's advice to marry is identical in both books!), the same upper-class backwash in the wake of the Oscar Wilde trials, the same fascination with the athletic build, a similar use of music as a gay trope, and probably much more. *Maurice*, however, is caught up as much in a class struggle as well as a gay one, something Stevenson ignores. Maurice must find happiness outside the aristocracy, whereas Oswald and Imre are both aristocrats. And where *Maurice* admittedly shows the greater art in providing a more "active" plot, *Imre* is a tale almost exclusively of the mind.

Edward Prime-Stevenson

Born on January 29, 1858, in Madison, New Jersey, Edward Irenaeus Stevenson was the youngest child in a family that had a strong literary and religious heritage. He was proud of his French, British, and Italian ancestry, and particularly of his mother's side of the family, the Primes, which boasted several writers among them. His mother's brother, Samuel Irenaeus Prime, was a strong influence, and as a literary clergyman, a

---

[1] Nonetheless, it has been a commonplace among the public as well as the critics that *Maurice* is inferior to his other fiction (see *Who's Who in Gay and Lesbian History: From Antiquity to World War II*, edited by Robert Aldrich and Garry Wotherspoon, pages 165–166).

lecturer, a world traveler, and a newspaper editor combined a quiltwork of interests that Stevenson himself would later mimic. His father, the Rev. Paul Stevenson, died when he was only twelve, but apparently the family had some wealth, perhaps from his mother's side, and he received good formal training at the Freehold Institute, where he excelled in languages, and as a member of the Clio Society, spent his Friday nights working on "composition, Declamation, and Debate." Though he entered the "University of New York" upon graduation in 1875, no record exists of his formal training after that, though he claimed to have passed the New Jersey bar exam. Ignoring the law, he began writing almost immediately for the popular magazines of his day, trying his hand at poetry and some rather melodramatic fiction before settling into the niche of music criticism. His ability to remember and assimilate all he read made him a formidable storehouse of information. By the 1890s he was working on the editorial staff for the Harper Brothers, and while he contributed regularly to *Harper's Weekly* he also founded the music department at *The Independent*, a popular periodical based in New York. His criticism favored classicism, but in focusing on opera—his forte—and the great singers of his day, his writing reveals an openness to new ideas, always firmly balanced by an appreciation for the past.

Stevenson's earliest published novels included two successful boys books, *White Cockades* (1887) and *Left to Themselves: Being the Ordeal of Philip and Gerald* (1891), both of which had multiple printings. If the books in Horatio Alger's contemporaneous and comparable series are now viewable in a homosexual light,[1] so are Stevenson's, and that by his own admission. Looking back over a dozen years later in *The Intersexes*, he admitted that an underlying subversive dynamic had been engineered into those early works. Although both feature adolescent same-sex crushes of the sort that even Freud might excuse, the author's knowing complicity invites a second glance. *Left to Themselves* forecasts *Imre* in unashamedly uniting Gerald and Philip for life by tale's end,

---

[1] *The Lost Life of Horatio Alger, Jr.* by Gary Scharnhorst with Jack Bales (Bloomington: Indiana UP, 1985) provides a creditable introduction to this aspect of Alger's writing.

and touching quietly but insistently on the boys' initial solitariness followed by a continuing love and need for each other.

While he was putting his heart into these two works, Stevenson was also busy making his name in adult fiction by aping the melodramatic novel of his day with its plot twists and love triangles and secret revelations in such works as *Janus* (1889; republished in 1896 as *A Matter of Temperament*) and his magazine stories (e.g., *Mrs. Dee's Encore; or, You Will Will You?* [1896] serialized in *Harper's Bazar*). These popular works, geared toward a women's audience, spelled success for the hard-working writer, but Stevenson continued looking for his own niche, as he attempted short dramas, poetry, and an amusing foray into cartomancy published under his first pseudonym, Robert Antrobus. It is not our place to remark here whether the means of fortune-telling espoused in *The Square of Sevens* (1897) worked, but the witty introduction (under his own name) shows his love for esoterica and a distinct pleasure in hoodwinking an audience.

Of his private life in New York City in the 1880s and 1890s we know very little, though it was during this time that he met the man who would be the love of his life, young Harry Harkness Flagler, the heir to a great oil and railroad fortune. Together they enjoyed life in the city, sharing a love for music and theater and literature. A short story called "Once: But Not Twice" probably describes the halcyon days of their first acquaintance (see Appendix E). Flagler broke off their friendship in 1893, however, and his marriage in 1894 devastated Stevenson. Though he doubtless formed other friendships, Harry continued to haunt him for the rest of his life. Several of Stevenson's works are dedicated to him.

Stevenson lived with his aging mother and sister throughout this period, shuttling back and forth between Small House, his residence in Hackensack (described in an 1899 *The Book Buyer* as "a small museum of literary and artistic curios"), and an apartment in the city. An active and social person, he was a constant figure on the theatrical and music scene. When his mother died early in 1896, he must have come into some money, and he used it for travel, leaving New York for longer and longer periods. Although as an author he had toyed with several versions of his name (E. Irenaeus Stevenson, E.I. Stevenson, Edward I. Stevenson), sometime near the new century, at what he said was family insistence—a condition of inheritance from the Primes, or emblematic of the need to find his true voice?—he officially adopted the hyphenated name that he would keep for the rest of his life. In forging this new identity, he also determined to renounce his professional career, and after 1900 he became an expatriate, adopting Europe as his permanent residence. This abrupt and radical change in his life must have been a mystery to his friends. A 1910 article in *The Musical Courier* suggested only that he "did not assimilate with the strenuousness of our life here and he retired to Europe for study of art and literature, and to give to his system the support of repose and the elegance of leisure" (23). A more logical explanation would be that his homosexual leanings were proving to be an overwhelming liability in America. Safe in Italy, he would write the young poet Leonard Bacon in 1907 about the need to "really *be oneself.* Speaking, feeling, showing, following oneself—to not even one! in a group of friends very fairly friends but still not-wholly such. Over here there's another sort of world as to that; as to so many other conditions of daily life. The clock keeps the old time, after all,— over this side.... *One has got back into the sun.* No wonder that so many of your compatriots and mine will rather live in a garret *au-deça,* than in a Commonwealth Avenue or Riverside-Drive palace *au-delà.* I know a legion of such deserters not small ... Into the sun ... into the sun!... Good God—good Sun-God!—how it shines here!" (see Appendix F).[1] Part of his new-found freedom literally made him years younger: once he was in Europe he dropped ten years in all references to his birth-date.[2] Even today libraries still keep the results of this gentle lie in their catalogues.

Stevenson traveled everywhere: England, France, Germany, Switzerland, Austria, Hungary, Italy. He became an habitué of the rented room, never settling down, eventually making a "circuit" of favorite places, dependent on the seasons for his location: the

---

[1] "Into the sun" seems to indicate an existence where one need not hide sexual orientation. The phrase recurs in the 1913 short story, "Out of the Sun," where Stevenson describes the hero's rejection by a younger lover and his resultant suicide. In a footnote, Stevenson said that this was excerpted from a longer novella called *Into the Sun,* which has not been traced.

[2] Tom Sargant unmasked Stevenson's deception in 2001.

Hotel de Russie in Rome, the Minerva in Florence, the Mirabeau in Lausanne. Annual visits to America eventually became less and less frequent. He stayed in shape by climbing mountains and frequenting gymnasiums. He studied elocution and bragged to *Who's Who* that he was master of nine languages, later reducing the number to seven. He lectured on a variety of topics and gave public readings of his works; by 1920 he was the proud owner of a first-rate phonograph and discovered further acclaim in public "auditions," where he could lecture on musical selections and then play them. One such annual series at the Hotel Minerva drew a faithful audience and was repeated for years.

But it was in writing that Stevenson gradually found the freedom he sought. Not long after moving to Europe he began a compendious study of homosexuality, gathering news clippings, assembling a sizeable library, reading foreign periodicals, meeting people from all walks of life, interviewing medical professionals. As familiar with gay meeting-places as he was with the music and literary world in European capitals, he gathered information there as well. At some point he had met Richard von Krafft-Ebing, the eminent Viennese sexologist, and it was at his urging that he assembled this knowledge into a book that he felt was his life's work: *The Intersexes: A History of Simisexualism as a Problem in Social Life* (1908). He felt it was the answer to the medical establishment's problematizing of the homosexual. In many ways it was the first strike for gay rights by an American author. Simultaneously, Stevenson was preparing a book as small as *Intersexes* was large, and in its fiction was the distillation of his argument. *Imre: A Memorandum* was as concise as *Intersexes* was sprawling: both represented the acme of his literary career. Under the name of Xavier Mayne he paid for both books' printings and supervised their distribution. Though *Intersexes* consisted of only 125 copies (quite an investment for a work well over 600 pages!) and *Imre* of 500, Stevenson probably knew where each copy went. He must have longed for a wider dissemination, though *Imre's* fame quietly spread among a homosexual audience. He was vastly amused with all the guesses he heard as to Mayne's true identity.

In 1913 he published, again privately, *Her Enemy, Some Friends—and Other Personages*, an anthology of his short fiction. Although several gay stories were included, for the first time he bravely published them under his own name. In fact, he modestly promoted his book, although with a run of only 250 copies it remained hard to get. After that, his writing was restricted to reworking stories for public readings (*Dramatic Stories to Read Aloud*, 1924), and gathering his musical essays into the splendid collection *Long-Haired Iopas: Old Chapters from Twenty-Five Years of Music-Criticism* (1927). He was surprised and gratified when the European and American musical establishment paid it considerable notice.

With the Depression his financial holdings lessened, and by the time he had reached his eighties the war and the difficulty of travel kept him sequestered in Lausanne. There he kept up with his correspondence—always considerable—and wrote several works that he told Philip Nieson Miller were "press-ready," including a family history and perhaps an autobiography. But when he died of a heart attack on July 23, 1942, at the Hotel Mirabeau, he had no literary executor. Perhaps because of the exigencies of wartime, his sole heir, a nephew then in the United States Air Force, apparently never rescued Stevenson's remaining manuscripts and papers from the warehouses in Switzerland where they were stored, and all traces of them eventually disappeared.

Stevenson's importance in the landscape of gay American literature cannot be overstated, however. In an age where a powerful medical establishment delineated the homosexual as pathological, and any gay writing seemed covert and defensive, Stevenson's *Imre* took an amazingly pro-active stance. In presenting homosexuality as an accceptable and not-uncommon extension of nature's sexual spectrum, he wanted to show that gay men were not ill or monstrous, that they could be unremarkable and contributing members of society, and, above all, that they were human. By insisting on an unprecedented happy ending for his two heroes, Stevenson—for all his flight from his native America—was also aggressively inscribing fundamental American ideals: the insistence on tolerance and the individual's right to "life, liberty, and the pursuit of happiness."

Edward Prime-Stevenson:

A Brief Chronology

1858   Born January 29, the youngest of six children, in
       Madison, New Jersey, to educators of Italian and
       French descent, Rev. Paul E. and Cornelia Prime
       Stevenson.
1870   Brother Archibald dies of pneumonia, February 10.
       Father dies of "softening of the brain," March 17.
1875   Graduates June 17 from the Freehold Institute, New
       Jersey, following a three-year Classical Course. His
       graduation essay is "Toussaint L'Ouverture." The
       school catalogue notes that he "enters the
       University of New York."
1878   First known work published, a poem called "The
       Show," in *Harper's Weekly*, July 9.
1881   Begins writing extensively for popular magazines.
1887   First novel, a juvenile adventure called *White Cockades:
       An Incident of the 'Forty-Five'*, is published. Stevenson
       later admits that the "passionate devotion from a rustic
       youth toward the prince, and its recognition are half-
       hinted as homosexual in essence."
1891   *Left to Themselves: Being the Ordeal of Philip and
       Gerald*, by Edward Irenaeus Stevenson, is published
       simultaneously in New York and Cincinnati.
       Stevenson says of this work that "The sentiment of
       uranian adolescence is more distinguishable…. [It is]
       a romantic story in which a youth in his latter teens
       is irresistibly attracted to a much younger lad: and
       becomes, *con amore*, responsible for the latter's
       personal safety, in a series of unexpected events that
       throw them together—for life."
1893   Becomes estranged from Harry Harkness Flagler,
       whom he has known and loved for several years.
1896   Mother dies. Living at Small House, Hackensack,
       New Jersey, "a small museum of literary and artistic

curios." Begins his most productive period of magazine writing as literary reviewer and musical editor for *The Independent*; and on the critical and literary staff for the Harpers where he establishes the Musical Department of *Harper's Weekly*.

1897   Under the name of Robert Antrobus, Stevenson publishes *The Square of Sevens: An Authoritative System of Cartomancy, with a Prefatory Notice by E. Irenaeus Stevenson*. Serves as translator and assistant editor of The Warner Library of the World's Best Literature.

1900   Gives up professional writing and moves to Europe to begin a nomadic life in hotels, with no permanent residence. Devotes himself to linguistics, Egyptology, literature, and to "several important studies in a special branch of sexual psychiatrics." Travels widely through England, France, Italy, Germany, and Austria-Hungary, and continues this pattern for the rest of his life. Lectures on literature, music, and drama.

1905   Spends the autumn at Capri.

1906   As Xavier Mayne, privately prints 500 copies of *Imre: A Memorandum* in Naples.

1908   *The Intersexes*, a major examination of homosexuality in European and American culture, is published. 125 copies are printed at the author's expense.

1910   Contributes to *Grove's Dictionary of Music and Musicians*.

1913   *Her Enemy, Some Friends—and Other Personages: Stories and Studies Mostly of Human Hearts* is privately published in Florence. The character Imre makes a minor appearance in the short story "Madonnesca." Several stories, including "Once—But Not Twice," feature a homosexual dynamic. Since the book is printed under his own name, this is his first public emergence as a homosexual author.

1914   Makes public appearances in Berlin and Paris as a "literary elocutionist," reading from his own works.

1916   Begins occasional correspondence in *The Times Literary Supplement* (until 1940).

1927   Last major work, a collection of his musical essays
        and criticism, *Long-Haired Iopas: Old Chapters from
        Twenty-five Years of Music-Criticism*, appears. Though
        privately published, the book receives considerable
        notice from the European musical establishment.

1929   Visits America for the first time in ten years.

1932   After years of lecturing—notably as an annual event
        at the Hotel Minerva in Florence—on symphonic
        music with "public auditions" using his Paillard
        Electric Gramophone, he publishes, at his own
        expense, *A Repertory of One Hundred Symphonic
        Programmes*.

1940   Confides to Philip Lieson Miller that he has four
        complete books and over twenty shorter pieces
        "ready for print." These and other papers stored in a
        warehouse in Lausanne are subsequently lost.

1942   Dies July 23 at 1:45 p.m. in Lausanne, Switzerland,
        at age 84 of a heart attack. Last residence: the Hotel
        Mirabeau, where he had most frequently lived in
        his last years. Is cremated two days later.

A Note on the Text

This text of *Imre: A Memorandum* is based on the 1906 edition published in Naples by The English Book-Press/R. Rispoli. Privately printed under the pseudonym Xavier Mayne in only 500 copies, this book was reprinted in facsimile form by *The Arno Series on Homosexuality* in 1975 (New York: Arno Press), and in English only one other time, in a highly altered and scurrilous state, by Masquerade Books in 1992. A *Verlag rosa Winkel* edition (Berlin, 1997), edited by Wolfram Setz, reprints a German edition ca. 1910 titled *Imre. Ein Erlebnis. Aus dem Englischen von D. G.* The novel was translated into Dutch by Hans Hakfamp for *Gay 2000: Een Jaarboek* (Amsterdam: Vassallucci, 1999). Spelling and punctuation have been modernized and obvious textual errors have been corrected. The goal of this edition is to make available for the first time an affordable version of a work currently only available in expensive facsimile copy. Brief annotations accompany the text to clarify unfamiliar terms and non-English expressions. The appendices are intended to provide the reader with historical context and further background relating to the author and topics raised by the novel.

IMRE

A MEMORANDUM

"There is a war, a chaos of the mind,
When all its elements convulsed, combined,
Like dark and jarring ..."

"The whole heart exhaled into One Want,
I found the thing I sought, and that was—thee."

★　★　★　★　★

"The Friendship which is Love—the Love which is Friendship"

Prefatory

My dear Mayne:

In these pages I give you a chapter out of my life—an episode
that at first seemed impossible to write even to you. It has lengthened under my hand, as autobiography is likely to do. My apology is that in setting forth absolute truth in which we ourselves
are concerned so deeply, the perspectives, and what painters call
the values, are not easily maintained. But I hope not to be tedious
to the reader for whom, especially, I have laid open as mysterious and profoundly personal an incident.

You know why it has been written at all for you. Now that it
lies before me, finished, I do not feel so dubious of what may be
thought of its utterly sincere course as I did when I began to put
it on paper. And as you have more than once urged me to write
something concerning just that topic which is the mainspring of
my pages I have asked myself whether, instead of some impersonal essay, I would not do best to give over to your editorial
hand all that is here? as something for other men than for you
and me only? Do with it, therefore as you please. As speaking out
to any other human heart that is throbbing on in rebellion
against the ignorances, the narrow psychologic conventions, the
false social ethics of our epoch (too many men's hearts must do
so!), as offered in a hope that some perplexed and solitary soul
may grow a little calmer, may feel itself a little less alone in our

world of mysteries—so do I give this record to you, to use it as you will. Take it as from Imre and from me.

As regards the actual narrative, I may say to you here that the dialogue is kept, word for word, faithfully as it passed, in all the more significant passages; and that the correspondence is literally translated.

I do not know what may be the exact shade of even your sympathetic judgment, as you lay down the manuscript, read. But, for myself, I put by my pen after the last lines were written, with two lines of Platen[1] in my mind that had often recurred to me during the progress of my record: as a hope, a trust, a conviction:

Ist's möglich ein Geschöpf in der Natur zu sein,
Und stets und wiederum auf falscher Spur zu sein?

Or, as the question of the poet can be put into English:

Can one created be—of Nature part—
And ever, ever trace a track that's false?

No—I do not believe it!

Faithfully yours,
Oswald
Velencze, 19—

---

1 Count August von Platen-Hallermunde (1796–1835) was a poet whose sonnets embodied the themes of Platonic love, friendship, and an unrequited love for men. His diary (*Die Tagebücher*), not published until 1896–1900, was explicitly homoerotic. EPS made Platen the object of a special study which became an appendix to his great defense of homosexuality, *The Intersexes* (1908).

"You have spoken of homosexualism, that profound problem in human nature of old or of today; noble or ignoble, outspoken or masked: never to be repressed by religions nor philosophies nor laws; which more and more is demanding the thought of all modern civilizations, however unwillingly accorded it.... Its diverse aspects bewilder me.... Homosexualism is a symphony running through a marvelous range of psychic keys, with many high and heroic (one may say divine) harmonies; but constantly relapsing to base and fantastic discords! ... Is there really now, as ages ago, a sexual aristocracy of the male? A mystic and Hellenic Brotherhood, a sort of super-virile man? A race with hearts never to be kindled by any woman; though, if once aglow, their strange fires can burn not less ardently and purely than ours? An *élite* in passion, conscious of a superior knowledge of Love, initiated into finer joys and pains than ours? —that looks down with pity and contempt on the millions of men wandering in the valleys of the sexual commonplace?" (Magyarból[1])

---

[1]   Literally, "from the Hungarian." No more specific source is listed. Perhaps EPS quotes from one of his own works, as he occasionally did in his other writings (e.g., *The Intersexes*, "Out of the Sun").

I

MASKS

Like flash toward metal, magnet sped to iron,
A Something goes—a Current, mystic, strange—
From man to man, from human breast to breast:
Yet 'tis not Beauty, Virtue, Grace, not Truth
That binds nor shall unbind, that magic tie.

—Grillparzer[1]

It was about four o'clock that summer afternoon, that I sauntered across a street in the cheerful Hungarian city of Szent-Istvánhely,[2] and turned aimlessly into the café-garden of the Erzsébet-tér,[3] where the usual vehement military-band concert was in progress. I looked about for a free table, at which to drink an iced-coffee, and to mind my own business for an hour or so. Not in a really cross-grained mood was I; but certainly dull, and preoccupied with perplexing affairs left loose in Vienna; and little inclined to observe persons and things for the mere pleasure of doing so.

The kiosque-garden was somewhat crowded. At a table, a few steps away, sat only one person: a young Hungarian officer in the pale blue-and-fawn of a lieutenant of the well-known A. Infantry Regiment. He was not reading, though at his hand lay one or two journals. Nor did he appear to be bestowing any great amount of attention on the chattering around him, in that distinctively Szent-Istvánhely manner which ignores any kind of outdoor musical entertainment as a thing to be listened to. An

---

[1] Franz Grillparzer (1791–1872), the Austrian poet and playwright, was popular in Budapest at the turn of the century. His plays were frequently presented at the National Theater.

[2] EPS calls Budapest by this name, literally Saint Stephen Place. St. Stephen was the first King of Hungary and its patron saint.

[3] Elizabeth Square, one of Budapest's large public spaces, is located on the Pest side of the Danube. As it was then, it continues to be a popular gay cruising site. EPS mentions it as such in *Intersexes* 218.

open letter was lying beside him, on a chair; but he was not heeding that. I turned his way; we exchanged the usual sacramental salutations in which attention I met the glance, by no means welcoming, of a pair of peculiarly brilliant but not shadowless hazel eyes; and I sat down for my coffee. I remember that I had a swift, general impression that my neighbor was of no ordinary beauty of physique and elegance of bearing, even in a land where such matters are normal details of personality. And somehow it was also borne in upon me promptly that his mood was rather like mine. But this was a vague concern. What was Hecuba to me?—or Priam, or Helen, or Helenus, or anybody else, when for the moment I was so out of tune with life!

Presently, however, the band began playing (with amazing calmness from any Hungarian wind-orchestra) Roth's graceful "Frau Réclame" Waltz, then a novelty, of which trifle I happen to be fond. Becoming interested in the leader, I wanted to know his name. I looked across the table at my vis-à-vis. He was pocketing the letter. With a word of apology, which turned his face to me, I put the inquiry. I met again the look, this time full, and no longer unfriendly, of as winning and sincere a countenance, a face that was withal strikingly a temperamental face, as ever is bent toward friend or stranger. And it was a Magyar voice, that characteristically seductive thing in the seductive race, which answered my query; a voice slow and low, yet so distinct, and with just that vibrant thrill lurking in it which instantly says something to a listener's heart, merely as a sound, if he be susceptible to speaking-voices. A few commonplaces followed between us, as to the band, the program, the weather—each interlocutor, for no reason that he could afterward explain, any more than can one explain thousands of such attitudes of mind during casual first meetings, taking a sort of involuntary account of the other. The commonplaces became more real exchanges of individual ideas. Evidently, this Magyar fellow-idler in the Erzsébet-tér cafe was in a social frame of mind, after all. As for myself, indifference to the world in general and to my surroundings in particular, dissipated and were forgot, my disgruntled and egotistical humor went to the limbo of all unwholesomenesses, under the charm of that musical accent, and in the frank sunlight of those manly, limpid eyes. There was soon a regular dialogue in course, between this stranger and me. From music (that open road to all sorts of mutualities on short acquaintanceships) and an art of which my neighbor showed that he knew much and felt even more than he expressed—from music, we passed to one or another aesthetic question; to literature, to social life, to human relationships, to human emotions. And thus, more and more, by unobserved advances, we came onward to our own two lives and beings. The only interruptions, as that long and clear afternoon lengthened about us, occurred when some military or civil acquaintance of my incognito passed him, and gave a greeting. I spoke of my birth-land, to which I was nowadays so much a stranger. I sketched some of the long and rather goal-less wanderings, almost always alone, that I had made in Central Europe and the Nearer East—his country growing, little by little, my special haunt. I found myself charting out to him what things I liked and what things I anything but liked, in this world where most of us must be satisfied to wish for considerably more than we receive. And in return, without any more questions from me than I had from him—each of us carried along by that irresistible undercurrent of human intercourse that is indeed, the Italian *simpatìa*, by the quick confidence that one's instinct assures him is neither lightly bestowed, after all, nor lightly taken—did I begin, during even those first hours of our coming-together, to know no small part of the inner individuality of Imre von N., *hadnagy*[1] in the A. Honvéd Regiment,[2] stationed during some years in Szent-Istvánhely.

Lieutenant Imre's concrete story was an exceedingly simple matter. It was the everyday outline of the life of nine young Magyar officers in ten. He was twenty-five; the only son of an old Transylvanian family; one poor now as never before, but evidently quite as proud as ever. He had had other notions, as a lad, of a calling. But the men of the N. line had always been in the army, ever since the days of Szigetvár and the Field of Mohács.[3] Soldiers,

---

[1]   Lieutenant (Hungarian).
[2]   An example of a local Hungarian regiment, often organized by aristocratic families.
[3]   The disastrous battle of the Field of Mohács (1526) is seminal in Hungarian historical consciousness, for the victorious Turks would occupy Hungary for the next century and a half.

soldiers! always soldiers! So he had graduated at the Military Academy. Since then? Oh, mostly routine-life, routine work, a few professional journeyings in the provinces—no advancement and poor pay, in a country where an officer must live particularly like a gentleman; if too frequently only with the aid of confidential business-interviews with Jewish usurers. He sketched his happenings in the barracks or the ménage—and his own simple, social interests, when in Szent-Istvánhely. He did not live with his people, who were in too remote a quarter of the town for his duties. I could see that even if he were rather removed from daily contact with the family-affairs, the present home atmosphere was a depressing one, weighing much on his spirits. And no wonder! In the beginning of a brilliant career, the father had become blind and was now a pensioned officer, with a shattered, irritable mind as well as body, a burden to everyone about him. The mother had been a beauty and rich. Both her beauty and riches long ago had departed, and her health with them. Two sisters were dead, and two others had married officials in modest government stations in distant cities. There were more decided shadows than lights in the picture. And there came to me, now and then, as it was sketched, certain inferences that made it a thought less promising. I guessed the speaker's own nervous distaste for a profession arbitrarily bestowed on him. I caught his something too-passionate half-sigh for the more ideal daily existence, seen always through the dust of the dull highroad that often does not seem likely ever to lead one out into the open. I noticed traces of weakness in just the ordinary armor a man needs in making the most of his environment, or in holding out against its tyrannies. I saw the irresolution, the doubts of the value of life's struggle, the sense of fatality as not only a hindrance but as excuse. Not in mere curiosity so much as in sympathy, I traced or divined such things; and then in looking at him, I partly understood why, at only about five-and-twenty, Lieutenant Imre von N.'s forehead showed those three or four lines that were incongruous with as sunny a face. Still, I found enough of the lighter vein in his autobiography to relieve it wholesomely. So I set him down for the average-situated young Hungarian soldier, as to the material side of his life or the rest; blessed with a cheerful temperament and a good appetite, and plagued by no undue faculties of melancholy or introspection. And, by the bye, merely to hear, to see Imre von N. laugh, was to forget that one's own mood a moment earlier had been grave enough, it might be. He had the charm of a child's most infectious mirth, and its current was irresistible.

★ ★ ★ ★ ★

Now, in remembering what was to come later for us two, I need record here only one incident, in itself slight, of that first afternoon's parliament. I have mentioned that Lieutenant Imre seemed to have his full share of acquaintances, at least of the comrade-class, in Szent-Istvánhely. I came to the conclusion as the afternoon went along, that he must be what is known as a distinctly "popular party." One man after another, by no means of only his particular regiment, would stop to chat with him as they entered and quit the garden, or would come over to exchange a bit of chaff with him. And in such of the meetings, came more or less—how shall I call it?—demonstrativeness, never unmanly, which is almost as racial to many *Magyarak*[1] as to the Italians and Austrians. But afterwards I remembered, as a trait not so much noticed at the time, that Lieutenant Imre did not seem to be at all a friend of such demeanor. For example, if the interlocutor laid a hand on Lieutenant Imre's shoulder, the Lieutenant quietly drew himself back a little. If a hand were put out, he did not see it at once, nor did he hold it long in the fraternal clasp. It was like a nervous habit of personal reserve; the subtlest sort of mannerism. Yet he was absolutely courteous, even cordial. His regimental friends appeared to meet him in no such merely perfunctory fashion as generally comes from the daily intercourse of the service, the army world over. One brother-officer paused to reproach him sharply for not appearing at some affair or other at a friend's quarters, on the preceding evening—"when the very cat and dog missed you." Another comrade wanted to know why he kept "out of a fellow's way, no matter how hard one tries to see something of you." An elderly civilian remained several minutes at his side,

---

[1] Hungarians.

to make sure that the young Herr Lieutenant would not forget to dine with the So-and-So family, at a birthday fête, in the course of the next few days. Again, "Seven weeks was I up there, in that damned little hole in Galizien![1] And I wrote you long letters, three letters! Not a postcard from you did I get, the whole time!" remonstrated another comrade.

Soon I remarked on this kind of dialogue.

"You have plenty of excellent friends in the world, I perceive," said I.

For the first time, that day, since one or another topic had occurred, something like scorn—or a mocking petulance—came across his face.

"I must make you a stale sort of answer, to—pardon me—a very stale little flattery," he answered. "I have acquaintances, many of them quite well enough, as far as they go—men that I see a good deal of, and willingly. But friends? Why, I have the fewest possible! I can count them on one hand! I live too much to myself, in a way, to be more fortunate, even with every Béla, János, and Ferencz reckoned in. I don't believe you have to learn that a man can be always much more alone in his life than appears his case. Much!" He paused and then added:

"And, as it chances, I have just lost, so to say, one of my friends. One of the few of them. One who has all at once gone quite out of my life, as ill-luck would have it. It has given me a downright stroke at my heart. You know how such things affect one. I have been dismal just this very afternoon, absurdly so, merely in realizing it."

"I infer that your friend is not dead?"

"Dead? No, no, not that!" He laughed. "But, all things concerned, he might as well be dead—for me. He is a marine-officer in the Royal Service. We met about four years ago. He has been doing some government engineering work here. We have been constantly together, day in, day out. Our tastes are precisely the same. For only one of them, he is almost as much a music-fiend as I am! We've never had the least difference. He is the sort of man one never tires of. Everyone likes him! I never knew a finer character, not anyone quite his equal, who could

---

[1]   Galicia was a region that is now roughly southern Poland.

count for as much in my own life. And then, besides," he continued in a more earnest tone, "he is the type to exert on such a fellow as I happen to be exactly the influences that are good for me. That I know. A man of iron resolution, strong will, energies. Nothing stops him, once he sees what is worth doing, what must be done. Not at all a dreamer, not morbid—and so on."

"Well," said I, both touched and amused by this naïveté, "and what has happened?"

"Oh, he was married last month, and ordered to China for time indefinite—a long affair for the Government. He cannot possibly return for many years, quite likely never."

"Two afflictions at once, indeed," I said, laughing a little, he joining in ruefully. "And might I know under which one of them you as his deserted Fidus Achates[1] are suffering most? I infer that you think your friend has added insult to injury."

"What? I don't understand. Ah, you mean the marriage part of it? Dear me, no! nothing of the sort! I am only too delighted that it has come about for him. His bride has gone out to Hong Kong with him, and they expect to settle down into the most complete matrimonial bliss there. Besides, she is a woman that I have always admired simply unspeakably—oh, quite platonically I beg to assure you!—as have done just about half the men in Szent-Istvánhely, year in and out, who were not as lucky as my friend. She is absolutely charming, of high rank, an old Bohemian family—beautiful, talented, with the best heart in the world, and—*Istenem!*"[2] he exclaimed in a sudden, enthusiastic retrospect, "how she sings Brahms! They are the model of a match: the handsomest couple that you could ever meet."

"Ah, is your marine friend of uncommon good looks?" He glanced across at the acacia tree opposite, as if not having heard my careless question, or else as if momentarily abstracted. I was about to make some other remark, when he replied, in an odd, vaguely-directed accent. "I beg your pardon! Oh, yes, indeed—my friend is of exceptional physique. In the service, he is called

---

[1]   Literally, "faithful Achates." Achates was the close friend of Aeneas in the *Aeneid*, and
      the expression signified intimate or romantic friendship. EPS uses it as a coded term
      for lover in *The Intersexes* (e.g., 199).

[2]   Oh God! (Hungarian).

'Hermes Karvaly' (his family name is Karvaly) though there's Sicilian blood in him too—because he looks so astonishingly like that statue, you know—the one by that Greek—Praxiteles,[1] isn't it? However, looks are just one detail of Karvaly's unusualness. And to carry out that, never was a man more head over heels in love with his own wife! Karvaly never does anything by halves."

"I beg to compliment you on your enthusiasm for your friend. Plainly one of the 'real ones' indeed," I said. For I was not a little stirred by this frank evidence of a trait that sometimes brings to its possessor about as much melancholy as it does happiness. "Or perhaps I would better congratulate Mr. Karvaly and his wife on leaving their merits in such generous care. I can understand that this separation means much to you."

He turned full upon me. It was as if he forgot wholly that I was a stranger. He threw back his head slightly and opened wide those unforgettable eyes—eyes that were, for the instant, somber troubled ones.

"Means much? Ah, ah, so very much! I daresay you think it odd, but I have never had anything—never—work upon me so! I couldn't have believed that such a thing could so upset me. I was thinking of some matters that are part of the affair, of its ridiculous effect on me, just when you came here and sat down. I have a letter from him too today, with all sorts of messages from himself and his bride, a regular turtle-dove letter. Ah, the lucky people in this world! What a good thing that there are some!" He paused reflectively. I did not break the silence ensuing. All at once "*Teremtette!*"[2] he exclaimed, with a short laugh of no particular merriment. "What must you think of me, my dear sir! Pray pardon me! To be talking along—all

---

[1] Greek statuary still epitomizes ideal beauty, but there is an underlying irony in Imre's referral to a culture that showed understanding and acceptance of homosexuality. The writings of John Addington Symonds (1840–93) in particular had advanced the connection between ancient Greek culture and homosexual tolerance (see his essay "A Problem in Greek Ethics"). The Hermes with the Infant Dionysus by Praxiteles (fl. 370–330 B.C.), found in the Heraeum, Olympia, in 1877, is the only example of an undisputed extant original by any of the greatest ancient masters. Hermes holds the child Dionysus in a display of psychological self-absorption and romantic inwardness. That Hermes / Karvaly holds Dionysus, the source for the term Dionian/ heterosexual, is not lost on EPS.

[2] This not-very-serious swear word expressing impatience is from Hungarian country life. The old meaning of the word is "has been done" or "done."

this personal, sentimental stuff—rubbish—to a perfect stranger! Idiotic!" He frowned irritably, the lines in his brow showing clear. He was looking me in the eyes with a mixture of, shall I say, antagonism and appeal; psychic counter-waves of inward query and of outward resistance. Of apprehension too. Then, again he said most formally, "I never talked this way with anyone—at least never till now. I am an idiot! I beg your pardon."

"You haven't the slightest need to beg it," I answered, "much less to feel the least discomfort in having spoken so warmly of this friendship and separation. Believe me, stranger or not—and, really, we seem to be passing quickly out of that degree of acquaintance—I happen to be able to enter thoroughly into your mood. I have a special sense of the beauty and value of friendship. It often seems a lost emotion. Certainly life is worth living only as we love our friends and are sure of their regard for us. Nobody ever can feel too much of that; and it is, in some respects, a pity that we don't say it out more. It is the best thing in the world, even if the exchange of friendship for friendship is a chemical result often not to be analyzed; and too often not at all equal as an exchange."

He repeated my last phrase slowly. "Too often—not equal?"

"Not by any means. We all have to prove that. Or most of us do. But that fact must not make too much difference with us; not work too much against our giving our best, even in receiving less than we wish. You may remember that a great French social philosopher has declared that when we love, we are happier in the emotion we feel than in that which we excite."

"That sounds like ... like that 'Maxims' gentleman—Rochefoucauld?"

"It was Rochefoucauld."[1]

My vis-à-vis again was mute. Presently he said sharply and with a disagreeable note of laughter. "That isn't true, my dear sir!—that nice little French sentiment! At least I don't believe it is! Perhaps I am not enough of a philosopher—yet. I haven't time to be, though I would be glad to learn how."

---

[1] La Rochefoucauld (1613–80) was famous for his *Maximes*, observations on human behavior expressed with the utmost brevity.

With that, he turned the topic. We said no more as to friends, friendship, or French philosophy. I was satisfied, however, that my new acquaintance was anything but a cynic, in spite of his dismissal, so cavalierly, of a subject on which he had entered with such abrupt confidentiality.

★   ★   ★   ★   ★

So had its course my breaking into an acquaintance—no, let me not use as burglarious and vehement a phrase, for we do not take the Kingdom of Friendship by violence even though we are assured that there is that sort of an entrance into the Kingdom of Heaven—so was my passing suddenly into the open door of my intimacy (as it turned out to be) with Lieutenant Imre von N. It was all as casual as my walking into the Erzsébet-tér Café. That is, if anything is casual. I have set down only a fragment of that first conversation; and I suspect that did I register much more, the personality of Imre would not be significantly sharpened to anyone, that is to say in regard to what was my impression of him then. In what I have jotted, lies one detail of some import; and there is shown enough of the swift confidence, the current of immediate mutuality which sped back and forth between us. "*Es gibt ein Zug, ein wunderliches Zug,*"[1] declares Grillparzer, most truthfully. Such an hour or so—for the evening was drawing on when we parted—was a kindly prophecy as to the future of the intimacy, the trust, the decreed progression toward them, even through our—reserves.

We met again, in the same place, at the same hour, a few days later; of course, this time by an appointment carefully and gladly kept. That second evening, I brought him back with me to supper, at the Hotel L.,[2] and it was not until a late hour (for one of the most early-to-bed capitals of Europe) that we bade each other good-night at the restaurant door. By the bye, not till that evening

---

[1]   "There is an attraction, a strange attraction" (German). EPS misquotes Medea's speech in Grillparzer's *Argonauts* (III): "Besteht ein Zug, ein geheimnisvoller Zug / Von Menschen zum Menschen, von Brust zu Brust" ["There exists an attraction, a mysterious attraction / From man to man, from breast to breast"].

[2]   Perhaps the no-longer-extant Hotel London, built in the 1870s, in today's Nyugati Square, on the Pest side of the Danube.

was rectified a minor neglect: complete ignorance of one another's names! The fourth or fifth day of our ripening partnership, we spent quite and entirely together; beginning it in the same coffeehouse at breakfast, making a long inspection of Imre's pleasant lodging, opposite my hotel, and of his music-library; and ending it with a bit of an excursion into one of Szent-Istvánhely's suburbs; and with what had already become a custom, our late supper, with a long aftertalk. The said suppers, by the bye, were always amusingly modest banquets. Imre was by no means a valiant trencher-man, though so strong-limbed and well-fleshed. So ran the quiet course of our first ten days, our first two weeks a term in which, no matter what necessary interruptions came, Lieutenant Imre von N. and I made it clear to one another, though without a dozen words to such effect, that we regarded the time we could pass together as by far the most agreeable, not to say important, matter of each day. We kept on continually adjusting every other concern of the twenty-four hours toward our rendezvous, instinctively. We seemed to have grown so vaguely concerned with the rest of the world, our interests that were not in common now abode in such a curious suppression, they seemed so colorless, that we really appeared to have entered another and a removed sphere inhabited by only ourselves, with each meeting. As it chanced, Imre was for the nonce free from any routine of duties of a regimental character. As for myself, I had come to Szent-Istvánhely with no set time-limit before me; the less because one of the objects of my stay was studying, under a local professor, that difficult and exquisite tongue which was Imre's native one, though, by the way, he was like so many other Magyars in slighting it by a perverse prefer-ence. (For a long time, we spoke only French or German when together.) So between my sense of duty to Magyar, and a sense, even more acute, of a great unwillingness to leave Szent-Istvánhely—it was growing fast to something like an eighth sense—I could abide my time, or the date when Imre must start for certain annual regimental maneuvers, down in Slavonia.[1] With

---

[1]   Many traditional military campsites were located in this part of southwest Hungary/ eastern Croatia, stemming from the Turkish battles of the fourteenth to eighteenth centuries.

reference to the idle curiosity of our acquaintances as to this so emphatic a state of dualism for Imre and myself—such an inseparable sort of partnership which might well suggest something

> ... too rash, too unadvised, too sudden,
> Too like the lightning which doth cease to be
> Ere one can say "It lightens ..."[1]

—why we were careful. Even in one of the countries of Continental Europe where sudden, romantic friendship is a good ·deal of a cult, it seems that there is neither wisdom nor pleasure in wearing one's heart on one's sleeve. Best not to placard sudden affinities; between soldiers and civilians, especially. It was Imre von N. himself who gave me this information, or hint; though not any clear explanation of its need. But he and I not only kept out of the most frequented haunts of social and military Szent-Istvánhely thenceforth, but spoke (on occasion) to others of my having come to the place especially to be with Imre again "for the first time in three years" since we had become "acquainted with each other down in Sarajevo one morning" during a visit to the famous Husruf-Beg Mosque there! This easy fabrication was sufficient. Nobody questioned it. As a fact, Imre and I when comparing notes one afternoon had found out that really we had been in Sarajevo at the exact date mentioned. "The lie that is half a truth" is ever the safest of lies, as well as the convenientest one.

Now of what did two men thus insistent on one another's companionship, one of them some twenty-five years of age, the other past thirty, neither of them vaporous with the vague enthusiasms of first manhood nor fluent with the mere sentimentalities of idealism, of what did we talk, hour in and hour out, that our company was so welcome to each other, even to the point of our being indifferent to all the rest of our friends round about, centering ourselves on the time *together* as the best thing in the world for us? Such a question repeats a common mistake, to begin with. For it presupposes that companionship is a sort of endless *conversazione*, a State-Council ever in session. Instead, the

---

[1] *Romeo and Juliet* II, 2.

silences in intimacy stand for the most perfect mutuality. And, besides, no man or woman has yet ciphered out the real secret of the finest quality, clearest sense, of human companionability— a thing that often grows up, flower and fruit, so swiftly as to be like the oriental juggler's magic mango-plant. We are likely to set ourselves to analyzing, over and over, the externals and accidence—the mere inflections of friendships, as it were. But the real secret evades us. It ever will evade. We are drawn together because we are drawn. We are content to abide together just because we are content. We feel that we have reached a certain harbor, after much or little drifting, just because it is for *that* haven, after all, that we have been moving on and on; with all the irresistible pilotry of the wide ocean-wash friendly to us. It is as foolish to make too much of the definite in friendship as it is in love, which is the highest expression of companionship. Friendship? Love? What are they if real on both sides, but the great Findings? Grillparzer (once more to cite that noble poet of so much that is profoundly psychic) puts all the negative and the positive of it into the appeal of his Jason:

> In my far home, a fair belief is found,
> That double, by the Gods, each human soul
> Created is; and, once so shaped, divided.
> So shall the other half its fellow seek
> O'er land, o'er sea, till when it once be found,
> The parted halves, long-sundered, blend and mix
> In one, at last! Feel'st thou this *half*-heart?
> Beats it with pain, divided, in thy breast?
> O ... come![1]

As a fact, my new friend and I had an interesting range of commonplace and practical topics, on which to exchange ideas. Sentimentalities were quite in abeyance. We were both interested in art, as well as in sundry of the less popular branches of litera-

---

[1] Jason speaks these lines in Act III of *The Argonauts*, the second play of Franz Grillparzer's dramatic trilogy *The Golden Fleece* (1818–20). In *The Intersexes* EPS applauds "the beautiful theory that the German Grillparzer has woven into verse: the creation of a protosex, a bisexual human type which has been divided" (256–57).

ture, and in what scientifically underlies practical life. Moreover, I had been longtime enthusiastic as to Hungary and the Hungarians, the land, the race, the magnificent military history, the complicated, troublous aspects of the present and the future of the Magyar Kingdom. And though I cannot deny that I have met with more ardent Magyar patriots than Imre von N. (for somehow he took a conservative view of his birth-land and fellow-citizens) still, he was always interested in clarifying my ideas. Again, contrariwise, Lieutenant Imre was zealous in informing himself on matters and things pertaining to my own country and to its system of social and military life, as well as concerning a great deal more; even to my native language, of which he could speak precisely seven words, four of them too forcible for use in general polite society. Never was there a quicker, a more aggressively intelligent mind than his; the intellect that seeks to take in a thing as swiftly yet as fully as possible—provided, as Imre confessed, with complete absence of shame, the topic "attracted" him. Fortunately, most interesting topics did so; and what he learned once, he learned for good and all. I smile now as I remember the range, far afield often, of our talks when we were in the mood for one. I think that in those first ten days of our intercourse we touched on, I should say, a hundred subjects— from Arpád the Great[1] to the Seventh Symphony,[2] from the prospects of the Ausgleich[3] to the theory of Bisexual Languages, from Washington to Kossuth,[4] from the novels of Jókai[5] to the best *gulyás*,[6] from harvesting-machines, drainage, income-taxes, and whether a woman ought to wear earrings or not, to the

---

[1] Tradition names Arpád the Great as the founder of Hungary, c. 895 A.D.

[2] Presumably of Beethoven.

[3] The Ausgleich or Compromise of 1867 between the Habsburgs and the Hungarians created the bipolar Austro-Hungarian Monarchy, already waning as this book was being written, and soon to fall with the advent of World War I.

[4] Lajos Kossuth (1802–94) was a national hero for Hungary's independence from the Habsburgs in the revolution of 1848–49. As the first governor of the country and afterwards an exile, Kossuth continued as a prominent symbol of Hungarian freedom.

[5] Mór Jókai (1825–1904) was the most famous Hungarian novelist of the nineteenth century. He was a fervent nationalist with an earthy and humorous style, often compared to Charles Dickens and Sir Walter Scott.

[6] Goulash (Hungarian).

Future State! No, one never was at a loss for a topic when with Imre, and one never tired of his talk about it, any more than one tired of Imre when mute as Memnon,[1] because of his own meditations, or when he was, apparently, like the Jolly Young Waterman, "rowing along, thinking of nothing at all."[2]

★ ★ ★ ★ ★

And besides more general matters, there was (for so is it in friendship as in love) ever that quiet undercurrent of inexhaustible curiosity about each other as an Ego, a psychic fact not yet mutually explained. Therewith comes in that kindly seeking to know better and better the Other, as a being not yet fully outlined, as one whom we would understand even from the farthest-away time when neither friend suspected the other's existence, when each was meeting the world *alone*—as one now looks back on those days, and was absorbed in so much else in life, before Time had been willing to say, "Now meet, you two! Have I not been preparing you for each other?" So met, the simple personal retrospect is an ever new affair of detail for them, with its queries, its confessions, its comparisons. "I thought that, but now I think this. Once on a time I believed that, but now I believe this. I did so and so, in those old days; but now, not so. I have desired, hoped, feared, purposed, such or such a matter then; now no longer. Such manner of man have I been, whereas nowadays my identity before myself is thus and so." Or, it is the presenting of what has been enduringly a part of ourselves, and is likely ever to abide as such? Ah, these are the moods and tenses of the heart and the soul in friendship, more and more willingly uttered and listened-to as intimacy and confidence thrive. Two natures are seeking to blend. Each is glad to be its own directory for the newcomer; to treat him as an expected and welcomed guest to the Castle of Self, while yet something of a stranger to it; opening to him any doors and windows that will throw light

---

[1] A colossal statue near Thebes in ancient Egypt said to produce a musical sound when the rays of the early morning sun struck it.

[2] A character in Charles Dickens's *Pickwick Papers*.

on the labyrinth of rooms and corridors, wishing to keep none shut ... perhaps not even some specially haunted, remote and even black-hung chamber. Guest? No, more than that, for is it not the tenant of all others, the Master, who at last has arrived!

Probably this is the best place in my narrative to record certain particularly personal aspects of Lieutenant Imre, though in giving them I must draw on details and impressions that I gained gradually—later. During even that earlier stage of our friendship, he insisted on my going with him to his father's house, to meet his parents. From them, as from two or three of his officer-friends with whom I occasionally foregathered, when Imre did not happen to be of the party of us, I derived facts—side-lights and perspectives—of use. But the most part of what I note came from Imre's tendency toward introspection; and from his own frank lips.

He had been a singularly sensitive, warmhearted boy, indeed too high-strung, too impressionable. He had been petted by even the merest strangers because of his engaging manners and his peculiarly striking boyish beauty. He had not been robust as a lad (though now superbly so) with the result that his schooling had been desultory and unsystematic.[1] "And I wanted to study art, I didn't care what art: music, painting, sculpture, perhaps music more than anything. I hated the army! But my father, his heart was set on my doing what the rest of us had done. I was the only son left. It had to be." And however little was Imre at heart a soldier, he had made himself into a most excellent officer. I soon heard that from all his comrades whom I met; and I have heard it often since those days in Szent-Istvánhely. His sense of his personal duty, his pride, his filial affection, his feeling toward his King, all contributed toward the outward semblance that was at least so desirable. He had already been highly commended; probably promotion would soon come. He had always won cordial words from his superiors. Loving not in the least the work, he played his unwelcome part well and manly, so that not more than half a dozen individuals could have been sure that Imre von N., *hadnagy*, would have doffed gladly, at any minute, the King's Coat

---

[1]   Cf. Teddy Roosevelt, then President of the United States and a chief proponent of the manly cult of the "strenuous life."

for a blouse.[1] Ambition failed him, alas! just because he was at heart indifferent to the reward. But he ran the race well. And for the matter of ambition the advancement in the Magyar service is as deliberate as in other armies in peace-times. Imre needed much stronger influence than what was at his request, to hurry him beyond a lieutenancy.

With only one such contest in his soul, no wonder that Imre led his life in Szent-Istvánhely so much to himself, however open to others it seemed to be. Yet whatever depressed him, he was determined not to be a man of moods to the cynical world's eyes. As a fact he was so happily a creature of buoyant temperament, that his popularity was not surprising, on the basis of comrade-intercourse and of the pleasantly superficial side of a regimental life. Every man was Imre's friend! Every woman was, such that I ever heard speaking of him, or spoken of along with his name. The paradox of living to oneself while living with everyone, the doors of an individuality both open and shut, could no farther go than in his instance.

How fully was I to realize that, in a little time!

As to physique, Imre had fulfilled in his maturity the promise of his boyhood. He was called "Handsome N.," right and left; and he deserved the sobriquet. Of middle height, he possessed a slender figure, faultless in proportions, a wonder of muscular development, of strength, lightness and elegance. His athletic powers were renowned in his regiment. He was among the crack gymnasts, vaulters and swimmers. I have seen him, often, make a standing-leap over an ordinary library table, to land, like a cat, on the other side. I have seen him, half-a-dozen times, spring out of a common barrel into another one placed beside it, without touching his hands to either. He could hold out a heavy garden-chair perfectly straight, with one hand; break a stout penholder or leadpencil between his second and third fingers; and bend a thick, brass curtain-rod by his leg-muscles. He frequently swam directly across the wide Duna, making nothing of its cross-currents at Szent-Istvánhely.[2] He was a consummate fencer, and

---

[1] I.e., civilian clothes.
[2] No small feat, considering the considerable width and strength of the Danube (Duna) as it flows through Budapest.

a prize-shot. He could jump on and off a running horse, like a *vaquero*.[1] Yet all this force, this muscular address, was concealed by the symmetry of his graceful, elastic frame. Not till he was nude, and one could trace the ripple of muscle and sinew under the fine, hairless skin, did one realize the machinery of such strength. I have never seen any other man—unless Magyar, Italian or Arab—walk with such elasticity and dignity. It was a pleasure simply to see Imre cross the street.

His head, a small, admirably shaped one, with its close-cut golden hair, carried out his Hellenic exterior. For it was really a small head to be set on such broad shoulders and on as well-grown a figure. As to his face (generally a detail of least relative importance in the male type), I do not intend to analyze retrospectively certainly one of the most engaging of manly countenances that I have ever looked upon. The actual features were delicate enough, but without womanishness. Imre was not a pretty man; but a beautiful man. And the mixture of maturity and of almost boyish youth, the outlook of his natural sincerity and warmth of nature, his self-unconsciousness and self-respect—these entered into the matter of his good looks, quite as much as his merely technical beauty. I did not wonder that not only the women in Szent-Istvánhely but the street-children, aye, the very dogs and cats it seemed to me, would look at him with friendly interest. Those lustrous hazel eyes, with the white so clear around the pupils, the indwelling laughter in them that nevertheless could be overcast with so penetrating a seriousness! It seems to me that now, as I write, I meet their look. I lay down my pen for an instant as my own eyes suddenly blur. Yet why? We should find tears rising for a living grief, not a living joy!

★ ★ ★ ★ ★

United with all this capital of a man's physical attractiveness was Imre's extraordinary modesty. He never seemed to think of his appearance for so much as two minutes together. He never glanced into a mirror when he happened to pass near that piece

---

[1] Cowboy or herdsman (Spanish).

52 EDWARD PRIME-STEVENSON

of furniture which seems to inflict a sort of nervous disease of the eyes—occasionally also of the imagination—on the average soldier of any rank and uniform, the world round. "Thanks, but I don't trouble myself much about looking-glasses, when I've once got my clothes on my back and am certain that my face isn't dirty!" was his reply to me one morning when I gave him an amused look because he had happened to plant his chair exactly in front of the biggest pier-glass in the K. Café. He never posed; never fussed as to his toilet, nor worried concerning the ultrafitting of his clothes, nor studied with anxiety details of his person. One day, another officer was lamenting the melancholy fact that baldness was gaining ground slyly, pitilessly, on the speaker's hyacinthine locks. He gave utterance to a sorrowful envy of Imre. "Pooh, pooh," returned Imre, *hadnagy*, scornfully, "It's in the family—and such a convenience in warm weather! I shall be bald as a cannon-shot by the time I am thirty!" He detested all jewelry in the way of masculine adornments, and wore none: and his civilian clothing was of the plainest.

★ ★ ★ ★ ★

The making-up of every man refers, or should do so, to a four-fold development: his physical, mental, moral and temperamental equipment, in which last-named class we can include the aesthetic individuality. The endowment of Imre von N. as to this series was decidedly less symmetrical than otherwise. In fact, he was a striking example of contradictions and inequations. He had studied hardest when in his school-courses just what came easiest—with the accustomed results of that sort of process. He was a bad, a perversely bad mathematician; an indifferent linguist, simply because he had found it "a hideous job to learn all those compli-cated verbs"; an excellent scholar in history; took delight in chemistry and in other physical sciences; and though so easily plagued by a simple sum in decimals, he had a passion for astron-omy, and he knew not a little about it, at least theoretically. Physical science appealed to him, curiously; his small library was two-thirds full of books on those topics. He loved to read popu-lar philosophy and biography and travel. For novels, as for poetry, he cared almost nothing. He would spare no pains to get to the bottom of some subject that interested him, a thing that "bit" him, as he called it; short of actually setting himself down to the calm and applicative study of it! Tactics did he somehow deliberately learn; grimly, angrily, but with success. They were indispensable to his professional credit. Such a result showed plainly enough that he lacked resolution, concentration as a duty, but did not lack capability. Many a sound lecture from myself, as from other friends, including particularly, as I found out, from the much-married Karvaly, did Imre receive respecting this defect. A course in training in the Officers' Military School (*Hadiskola*) was involved in the difficulty, or perversity, so in evidence. This *Hadiskola* course is an indispensable in such careers as Imre's sort should achieve, willing or unwilling. When a young officer is so obstinately cold to what lies toward good work in the *Hadiskola*, and in his inmost soul desires almost anything rather than becoming even a major, why, what can one say severe enough to him?

Yet, with reference to what might be called Imre's aesthetic self-expression, I wish to record one thing at variance with much which was negative in him. At least it was in contradiction to his showing such modest "literary impulses," and to his relative aversion to belles-lettres, and so on. When Imre was deeply stirred over something or other that "struck home," by some question to open the fountains of innermost feeling in him, it was remarkable with what exactitude—more than that, what genuine emotional eloquence of phrase—he could express himself! This even to losing that slight hesitancy of diction which was an ordinary characteristic. I was often surprised at the simple, direct beauty, sometimes downright poetic grace, in his language on such unexpected occasions. He seemed to become tinged with quite another personality, or to be following, in a kind of trance, the prompting of some voice audible to him only. I shall hardly so much as once attempt conveying this effect of sudden *ihletés*,[1] even in coming to the moments of our intercourse when it surged up. It must in most part be taken for granted; read between the lines now and then. But one must be mindful of its

---

[1] Inspiration (Hungarian).

natural explanation. For, after all, there was no miracle in it. Imre was a Magyar, one of a race in which sentimental eloquence is always lurking in the blood, even to a poetic passion in verbal utterance that is often out of all measure with the mere formal education of a man or a woman. He was a Hungarian: which means among other things that a cowherd who cannot write his name, and who does not know where London is, can be overheard making love to his sweetheart, or lamenting the loss of his mother, in language that is almost of Homeric beauty. It is the Oriental quality, ever in the Magyar, now to be admired by us, now disliked, according to the application of the traits. Imre had his full share of Magyarism of temperament, and of its impromptu eloquence, taking the place of much of a literal acquaintance with Dante, Shakespeare, Goethe, and all the rhetorical and literary Parnassus in general.

He detested politics, as might be divined. He "loved" his Apostolic King and his country much as do some children their nearest relatives; that is to say, on general principles, and to the sustaining of a correct attitude before himself and the world. On this matter also, he and I had many passages-at-arms. He had not much "religion." But he was a firm believer in God; in helping one's neighbor, even to most injudicious generosity; in avoiding debts "when one could possibly do so" (a reserve that I regretted to find out was not his case any more than it is usually the case with young Hungarian officers living in a capital city, with small home-subventions); in honor; in womanly virtue; in a true tongue and a clean one. His sense of fun was not limited to the kind that may pass between a rector of the Establishment and his daughters over afternoon tea. But Lieutenant Imre von N. had no relish for the stupid-smutty sallies and stock *raconteurs*[1] of the officers' mess and the barracks. Unless a "story" really possessed wit and humor, he had absolutely dull ears for it.

He wrote a shameful handwriting, with invariable hurry-scurry; he could not draw a pot-hook straight, and he took uncertain because untaught interest in painting. Sculpture and architecture appealed more to him, though also in an untaught

---

[1] Story-tellers (French).

way. But he was a most excellent practical musician, playing the pianoforte superbly well, as to general effect, with an amazingly bad technic of his own evolution, got together without any teaching, and not reading well and rapidly at sight. Indeed, his musical enthusiasm, his musical insight and memory, they were all of a piece, the rich and perilous endowment of the born son of Orpheus. His singing voice was a full baritone, smooth and sweet, like his irresistible speaking voice. He would play or sing for hours together, quite alone in his rooms, of an evening. He would go without his dinner (he often did) to pay for his concert ticket or standing-place in the Royal Opera. He did not care for the society of professional musicians, or of the theaterfolk in general. "They really are not worth while," he used to say. "Art is one thing to me and artists another—or nothing at all—off the stage." As for more general society, why, he said frankly that nowadays the N. family simply were too poor to go into it, and that he had no time for it. So he was to be met in only a few of the Szent-Istvánhely drawing rooms. Yet he was passionately fond of dancing, anything from a waltz to a *csárdás*.[1]

But, apropos of Imre's amusement, let me note here (for I daresay, the incredulity of persons who have stock ideas of what belongs to soldier life and soldier nature) that three usual pleasures were not his; for he abominated cards, indeed never played them; he did not smoke; and he seldom drank out his glass of wine or beer, having no taste for liquors of any sort. This in a champion athlete and an "all-round" active soldier—at least externally thoroughly such—in a smart regiment is not common. I should have mentioned above that he was oddly indifferent to the theater as the theater, declaring that he never could find "any great illusion" in it. He much liked billiards, and was invincible in them. His feeling for whatever was natural, simple, out-of-doors was great. He loved to walk, to walk alone, in the open country, in the woodlands and fields, to talk with peasants, who invariably "took to" him at once. He loved children, and was a born animal friend. In fact, between him and beasts little and big, there appeared to be a regular understanding. Never forthputting, he could delight, in a

---

[1] Typical Hungarian folk-based dance, performed at a ball.

quiet way, in the liveliest company. That buoyancy of his temperament, so in contrast with the other elements of his nature, was a vast blessing to him. He certainly had a supply of personal subjects sufficiently sobering for home consumption, some of which I soon knew; others not spoken till later. The gloom in his parents' house, the various might-have-beens in his own young life, the wearisome struggle to do his duty in a professional career whereto he had been called without its being chosen by him; weightier still the fact that he was in the hands of a couple of usurers on account of his generous share of the deficit in a foolish brother officer's finances, to the extent of some thousands of florins[1]—these were not trifles for Imre's private meditations. I could quite well understand his remarking "I have tried to cultivate cheerfulness on just about the same principle that when a man hasn't a *korona* in his pocket he does well to dress himself in his best clothes and swagger in the Officers' Casino as if he were a millionaire. For the time, he forgets that he isn't one, poor devil!"

But I am belated, I see, in alluding to two traits in our acquaintance, *ab initio*,[2] which are of significance in my outline of Imre's personality while new to me: and more than trifles in their weight. There were two subjects as to which remarkably little was said between us during the first ten days of my going about so much with him. Remarkably little, I say, because of Imre's own frank references to one matter, on our first meeting; and because we were both men, and neither of us octogenarians, nor troubled with super-sensitiveness in talking about all sorts of things. The first of these overpassed topics was the friendship between Imre and the absent Karvaly Miklos.[3] Since the afternoon on which we had met, Imre referred so little to Karvaly, he seemed so indifferent to his absence all at once— indeed he appeared to be shunning the topic—that I avoided it completely. It gradually was borne in upon me that he wished me to avoid it. So no more expansiveness on the perfections and gifts of the exile! Of Karvaly's young bride, on the other hand,

---

[1] The precursor of today's Hungarian unit of currency, the Forint.
[2] From the beginning; at the outset (Latin).
[3] Typical Hungarian name-inversion.

the fascinating Bohemian lady who sang Brahms' songs so beautifully, Imre was still distinctly eloquent, alluding often to one or another of her shining attributes, paragon that she may have been! I write "may have been" because to this day I know her, like Shakespeare's Olivia, "only by her good report."[1]

The other matter of our reticence was an instance of the difference between the general and the particular. Very early in my meeting with Imre's more immediate circle of soldier friends, I heard over and over again that to Imre, as one of the officers most distinguished in all the town for personal beauty, there attached a reputation of being an ever-campaigning and ever-victorious Don Juan, if withal one of most exceptional discretion. Right and left, he was referred to as a wholesale enemy to the peace of heart and to the virtue of dozens of the fair citizenesses of Szent-Istvánhely. Two of these romances, the heroine of one of them being an extremely beautiful and refined *déclassée* whose sudden suicide had been the gossip of the clubs, were heightened by the touch of the tragic. But along with them, and the more ordinary chatter about a young man's *bonnes fortunes*, or what were taken to be them, there were surmises and assertions of vague, aristocratic, deep, unconfessed ties and adventures. The Germans use the terms *Weiberfreund* and *Weiberfeind*[2] in rather a special sense sometimes. Now, I knew that Imre von N. was no woman-hater. He admired and had a circle of admiring women-friends enough to dismiss at once such an ungallant accusation. Never was there a sharper eye, not even in *Magyarország*,[3] for a harmonious female figure, a graceful carriage, a charming face. He was a *connoisseur de race!*

But when it came to his alluding, when we were by ourselves, to anything like really intimate sentimental—I would best plainly say amorous—relations with the other sex, Imre never opened his mouth for a word of the least real significance! He referred to himself, casually, now and then, and as it appeared to me in precisely the right key, as one to whom woman was a sufficiently definite

---

1   A character in Shakespeare's *Twelfth Night.*
2   I.e., woman-lover and woman-hater (German).
3   Hungary.

social and physical attraction—necessity—quite as essentially as is to be expected with a young soldier of normal health and robust constitution. When it suited his mixed society, he had as many "discreet stories" as Poins.[1] But when he and I were alone, no matter whatever else he spoke of—so unreservedly, so temperamentally!—he never did what is commonly called "talk women." He never so much as alluded to a light-o'-love, to an "affair," to any distinctly sexual interest in a ballerina or a princess! And when third parties were pleased to compliment him, or to question him, as to such a thing, Imre "smiling put the question by." His special reserve concerning these topics, so rare in men of his profession and age, was as emphatic as in the instance of the average English gentleman. I admired it, certainly not wishing it less. I often thought how well it became Imre's general refinement of disposition, manners and temperamental bias—most of all, suiting that surprising want of vanity as to his person, his character, his entire individuality.

★ ★ ★ ★ ★

In this connection came a bit of an incident that has its significance, as things came to pass later in our acquaintance. One evening, while I was dressing for dinner, with Imre making a random visit, I lapsed into hearty irritation as to a marvelously ill-fitting new garment that was to be worn for the first time. Imre was pleased to be facetious. "You ought to go into the tailoring line yourself," he observed, "then you can adorn yourself as perfectly as you would wish!" I threw out some sort of a return banter that his own carelessness as to his looks was "the pride that apes humility."

"One would really suppose," I remarked, "that you do not know why a pretty woman makes eyes at you! Are you under the impression that you are admired on account of the Three Christian Graces and the Four Theological Virtues, all on sight![2]

---

[1]   Shakespearian clown in *Henry IV*.
[2]   I.e., faith, hope, and charity (1 Corin. 13:13); prudence, justice, fortitude, and temperance.

Come now, my dear fellow, you really need not carry the pose so far!"

Imre opened his lips as if about to say something or other; and then made no remark. Once more he gave me the idea that he was minded to speak, but hesitated. So I suspended operations with my hairbrushes.

"You appear to be laboring with a remarkably difficult idea," said I.

He answered abruptly: "There are some things it is hard for a man to judge of, even in another fellow. At least people say so. See here, you! I wish ... I wish you would tell me something. You won't think me a conceited ass? Do you, for instance, do you ... find me *really* specially good-looking, when you look around the lot of other men one sees? In comparison with *plenty* of others, I mean?"

"Do you want an answer in chaff, or seriously?"

"Seriously."

"I most certainly think you 'specially' such, N."

"And you are of the opinion that most people—women, men, sculptors, for instance, or painters, a photographer if you like—ought to be of your opinion?"

"But yes, assuredly," I replied, laughing at what seemed the naïveté and uncalled-for earnestness in his tone. "You do not need to put me on oath, such a newcomer too into your society, to give you the conviction. Or stay, how would you like me to draft you a kind of technical schedule, my dear fellow, stating how and why you are—not repulsive? I could give it to you, if I thought it would be good for you, and if you would listen to it. For you are one of those lucky ones in the world whose good looks can be demonstrated, categorically, so to say—trait by trait—passport-style. Come, come, N.! Don't be so depressed because you are so beautiful! Cheer up! Probably there will always be somebody in the wide world who will not care to bestow even a half-eye on you! some being who remains, first and last, totally unimpressed, brutally unmoved, by all your manly charms! I daresay that if you consult *that* individual you will be assured that you are the most ordinary-looking creature in creation."

As I spoke, Imre who had been sitting, three-quarters turned from me, over at a window, whisked himself about quickly and gave me what I thought was a most inexplicable look. "Have I offended him?" I asked myself; ridiculous to me, even at so early a stage of our intimacy, as was the notion. But I saw that his look was not one of surprised irritation. It was not one of dissent. He continued looking at me—ah, his serious eyes!—whatever else he was seeing in his perturbed mind.

"Well," I continued, "isn't that probable? Have I made you angry by hinting at such a stupidity, such an aesthetic tragedy?"

"No, no," he returned hastily, "of course not!" And then with a laugh as curious as that look of his, for it was not his real, his cheerful and heart-glad laugh, but one that rang false even to being ill-humored, he added, "By God, you have spoken the truth! Yes, to the dot on the *I*!"

I did not pursue the subject. I saw that it was one, whatever else was part of it, that was better left for Imre himself to take up at some other time; or not at all. Apparently, I had stumbled on one little romance; possibly on a *grande passion*! In either case it was a matter not dead, if moribund it might be. Imre could open himself to me thereon, or not: I was not curious, nor a purveyor of reading-matter to fashionable London journals.

★ ★ ★ ★ ★

Two matters more in this diagnosis—shall I call it so?—of my friend. Let me rather say that it is a memorandum and guide-book of Imre's emotional topography.

Something has been said of the spontaneous warmth of his temperament, and of his enthusiasm for his closer friends. But his undemonstrativeness, also mentioned, seemed to me more and more curiously accentuated. Imre might have been an Englishman, if it came to outward signs of his innermost feelings. He neither embraced, kissed, caressed nor what else his friends; and, as I had surmised, when first being with him and them, he did not appear to like what in his part of the world are ordinary degrees of "demonstrativeness." He never invited nor returned (to speak as Brutus) "the shows of love in other men."[1] There was a certain captain in the A. Regiment, a man that Imre much liked and, what is more, had more than once admired in good set terms, when with me. ("He is as beautiful as a statue, I think!") This brother-soldier being suddenly returned to Szent-Istvánhely, after a couple of years of absence, hurried up to Imre and fairly threw his arms about him. Imre was cordiality itself. But after Captain R. had left him, Imre made a wry face at me, and said, "The best fellow in the world! and generally speaking, most rational! But I do wish he had forgotten to kiss men! It is so hideously womanish!" Another time we were talking of letters between intimate friends. "I hate, I absolutely hate to write letters, even to my nearest friends," he protested; "in fact, I never write unless there is no getting out of it! Five words on a post-card, once a month or so, two or three months, maybe, and lucky if they get that! How do I write? Something like this: 'I am here and well. How are you. We are very busy. I saw your cousin, Csodaszép Kisassony yesterday. No time today for more! Kindest regards. *Alá szolgája!*[2] N.' Now there you have my style to a dot. What more in the world is really called for? As for sentiment—sentiment! in letters to my friends!—well, I simply cannot squeeze *that* out, or in. Nobody need expect it from your most obedient servant! My correspondence is like telegrams."

"Thanks much," I returned, smiling. "Your remarks are most timely, considering that you and I have agreed to keep in touch with each other by post, after I leave here. Forewarned is fore-armed! Might I ask, by the bye, whether you are as laconic in

---

[1] In Shakespeare's *Julius Caesar* (I.ii. 39–47) Brutus says of himself:
   ...Vexed I am
   Of late with passions of some difference,
   Conceptions only proper to myself,
   Which give some soil, perhaps, to my behaviors;
   But let not therefore my good friends be grieved
   (Among which number, Cassius, be you one),
   Nor construe any further my neglect,
   Than that poor Brutus, with himself at war,
   Forgets the shows of love to other men.
   The considerable irony of the expression he quotes is not lost on EPS.

[2] Old Hungarian way of greeting someone of a higher position or rank.

writing, to—say, your friend Karvaly, over there in China? And if he is satisfied?"

"Karvaly? Certainly. He happens to like precisely that sort of communication particularly well. I never give him ten words where five will do." To which statement I retorted that it was a vast blessing that some persons were easily pleased, as well as so like-minded; and that perhaps it would be quite as wise under such conditions, not to write at all; except maybe on All Souls Day![1]

"Perhaps," assented Imre.

So much, then, of your outward individuality and environment, with somewhat of your inner self, my dear Imre, chiefly as I looked upon you and strove to sum you up during those first days. But was there not one thing more, one most special point of personal interest, of peculiar solicitude, one supreme undercurrent of query and wondering in my mind, as we were thus thrown together, and as I felt my thoughts more and more busied with what was our mutual liking and instinctive trust? Surely there was! I should find myself turning aside from the path of straightest truth which I would hold to in these pages, if I did not find *that* question written down early and frankly here, with the rest. It *must* be written; or be this record broken now and here!

Was Imre von N. what is called among psychiaters of our day a homosexual, a Urning[2] in his instincts and feelings and life, in his psychic and physical attitude toward women and men? Was he a Uranian?[3] Or was he sexually entirely normal and Dionian?[4] Or a blend of the two types, a Dionian-Uranian? Or what, or what not? For that something of a special sexual attitude, hidden, instinctive,

---

[1] Sarcasm seems intended here, as November 2nd was the day Hungarians remembered their dead.

[2] A contemporary term for homosexual.

[3] Another term for homosexual, derived from the idea that such sexual oddities must come from the planet Uranus, then considered the outermost member of the solar system.

[4] The terms Uranian and Dionian were in common usage among late 19th century psychologists. Karl Heinrich Ulrichs (1825–95) defines Dionian as "The thoroughly masculine [i.e., heterosexual] instinct, the man out of any sort of similisexual tendency" (qtd. in *The Intersexes*, 77). The expression comes from the Greek god Dionysos and the orgies held in his honor. Uranian, the homosexual instinct, is derived from Uranos.

was maintained by him, no matter what might be the outward conduct of his life. This I could not help believing, at least at times.

Uranian? Similisexual? Homosexual? Dionian?

Profound and often all too oppressive, even terrible, can be the significance of those cold psychic-sexual terms to the man who— "*knows*"! *To the man who "knows"!* Even more terrible to those who understand them not, may be the human natures of which they are but new and clumsy technical symbols, the mere labels of psychiatric study, within a few decades of medical explorers.

What, then, was my new friend?

★　★　★　★　★

I could not determine! The more I reflected, the less I perceived. It is so easy to be deceived by just such a mingling of psychic and physical and temperamental traits; easy to dismiss too readily the counterbalancing qualities. I had learned that much. Long before now, I had found it out as a practical psychiater, in my own interests and necessities, by painful experience. Precisely how suggestive, and yet how adverse (where quite vaguely? where with a fairly clear accent?) was inference in Imre's case to be drawn or thrown aside, those who are intelligent in the subtle problems of Uranianism or its absence can appreciate best. I had been a good deal struck with the passionate—as it seemed—note in Imre's friendship for the absentee, Karvaly Mihály. I noticed the dominance that men, simply as men, seemed to maintain in Imre's daily life and ideals. I studied his reserved relations toward the other sex; the general scope of his tastes, likes and dislikes, his emotional constitution. But all these suffice not to prove, to *prove* the deeply buried mystery of a heart's uranistic impulses, the mingling in the firm, manly nature of another inborn sexual essence which can be mercifully dormant; or can wax unquiet even to a whole life's unbroken anguish—!

And, after all, why should I—I—seek to drag out from him such a secret of his individuality? Was that for me? Hardly, even if I, probably, of all those who now stood near to Imre von N.— but there! I had *no* right! Even if I—but there! I swore to myself that I had *no* wish!

It was Imre himself who gave me a sort of determinative, just as—after the oaths at which Jove laughs—I was querying with myself what I might believe.

One evening, we were walking home, after an hour or so with his father and mother. As we turned the corner of a certain brilliantly lighted café, a man of perhaps forty years, with the unmistakable suggestion of a soldier about him, and of much distinction of person along with it, but in civilian's dress, came out and passed us. He looked at Imre as if almost startled. Then he bowed. Imre returned his salutation with so particular a coldness, an immediate change of expression, that I noticed it.

"Who is he?" I asked. "Somehow I fancy he is not in your best books."

"No, I can't say that he is," responded Imre. After a moment of silence he went on. "That gentleman used to be a captain in our regiment. He was asked to leave the service. So he left it—about three years ago."

"Why?"

"On account of"—here Imre's voice took on a most disagreeable sneer—"of a little love-affair."

"Really? Since when was a little love-affair a topic for the action of a regimental Ehrenrath?"[1]

"It happened to be his little love-affair with a ... cadet. You understand?"

"Ah, yes, now I understand. A great scandal, I presume?"

"Scarcely any at all. In fact, nobody, to this day, knows how far the intimacy really went. But gradually some sort of a story got about as to the discovery of 'relations'—perhaps really amounting to only a trifling incident. But the man's character was smirched. The regiment's Council didn't go into details, didn't even ask for the facts. He simply was requested privately to give up his charge. You know, or perhaps you do not know, how specially sensitive—indeed implacable—the Service is on *that* topic. Anything but a hint of *it*! There mustn't be a suspicion, a breath! One is simply ruined!"

---

[1]   Council; court-martial (German).

I stopped to pay our tolls for the long Suspension Bridge.[1] As we pursued our walk, Imre said:

"Do you have any such affairs in England?"

"Yes. Certainly."

"In military life?"

"In military and civil life. In every kind of life."

"Indeed. And how do *you* understand that sort of thing?"

"What sort of thing?"

"A ... a man's feeling *that* way for another man? What's the explanation, the excuse for it?"

"Oh, I don't pretend to understand it. There are things we would better not try to *understand*."

Ah, had I only finished that sentence—as I certainly meant to do in beginning it!—with some such words as "so much as often to pardon." But the sentence remained open; and I know that it sounded as if it was meant to end with some such phrase as "because they are so beyond any understanding, beyond any excuse!"

Imre walked on beside me, whistling softly. Just two or three notes, over and over, no tune. Then he remarked abruptly:

"Did you ever happen to meet with that sort a man ... *person* ... yourself, in your own circle of friends?"

Again the small detail, this time one of commission, not omission, on my part! Through it this narrative is, I suspect, twice as long as otherwise it would have been. "Did I ever know such a man ... a 'person' ... in my own circle of friends?" Irony could no farther go! I laughed, not in mirth, not in contempt, but in sheer bitterness of retrospect. There are instances when it may be said of other men than Cassius:

And when he smiles, he smiles in such a sort
As if he mocked himself....[2]

---

[1] The beautiful Chain Bridge, or Lánchíd, which figures so prominently in this novel, was built by the Englishman Adam Clark. Opened in 1849, it was the first permanent bridge over the Danube to link the two cities of Buda and Pest. A toll was exacted on travelers until well into the twentieth century. Destroyed in World War II, the Lánchíd has since been rebuilt, almost identically.

[2] Shakespeare, Julius Caesar (I.ii. 205–206):
   "Seldom he smiles, and smiles in such a sort/
   As if he mocked himself...."

Yes, I laughed. And unfortunately Imre von N. thought that I sneered; that I sneered at my fellow-men!

"Yes," I replied, "I knew such a man, such a 'person.' On the whole, pretty well. He had other rather acceptable qualities, you see; so I didn't allow myself to be too much stirred up by ... that remarkably queer one."

"Lately?" Imre asked.

"Oh, yes, very lately," I returned flippantly.

Imre spoke no word for several steps. Then, hesitatingly: "Perhaps you didn't know him quite as thoroughly as you supposed. Were you quite sure?"

"Quite sure." Then, sharply in another sentence that was uttered on impulse and with more of the equivocal in it which afterward I understood, I added, "I think we will not talk any more about him: I mean in that respect, Imre."

Again silence. One-two, one-two—on we went, step and step, over the resonant, deserted bridge. I had an impression that Imre turned his head, looking sharply at me in the fluttering gaslight, then glancing quickly away. I had other thoughts, far, far removed from him! I had well-nigh forgot where I was!—forgot him, forgot Szent-Istvánhely!

But now he laughed out, too, as if in angry derision.

"I say! I knew such a fellow too, two or three years ago. And I beg to tell you that he fell in love with me, no less! He was absolutely *bódult*[1] over your humble servant. Did you ever!"

"Really? What did you do? Slap his face, and give him the address of a doctor of nervous diseases?"

"Oh, Lord, no! I merely declined with thanks the ... honor of his farther acquaintance. I told him never to speak to me. He left town. I had rather liked him. But I heard he had been compromised already. I have no use for that particular brand of fool!"

Are there perverse demons, demons delighting to make mortal men blunderers in simplest word and action, that haunt the breezy Lánchíd in Szent-Istvánhely? If so, some of us would better cross that long bridge in haste and solitary silence after nightfall. For:

---

[1] Dazed, crazy, infatuated (Hungarian).

"You surprise me," I said lightly. I was thinking of one of his own jests as well of his unbelief in his personal attractions. "How inconsistent for *you*! Now *you* are just the very individual I should suspect! Yes, yes, I *am* surprised!"

To my astonishment, Imre stopped full in his steps, drew himself up, and faced me with instant formality.

"Will you be so good as to tell me *why* you are surprised?" asked he, in a tone that was—I will not write sharp, but which suggested to me immediately that I had spoken *mal-à-propos*[1] or misleadingly; the more so in view of what Imre had mentioned of his *ex professio*[2] and personal sensitiveness to the general topic. "Do you observe anything particularly womanish—abnormal— about me, if you please?"

Now, as it happened my remark, as I have said, was made in consequence of an impersonal and amusing incident, which I had supposed Imre would at once remember.

"Womanish? Abnormal? Certainly not, but you seem to forget what you yourself said to Captain Molton this afternoon in the billiard room about the menage-cooks—don't you remember?"

Imre burst into laughter. He remembered! (There is no need of my writing out here a piece of humor not transferable with the least *esprit* into English, though mighty funny in Magyar.) His mood changed at once. He took my arm, a rare attention from him, and we said no more till the Bridge was past, and the corner which divided our lodgings by a street's breadth was reached. We said, "Good night till tomorrow!" The *házmester*[3] opened his door. Imre waved his hand gaily and vanished.

★ ★ ★ ★ ★

I got to bed, concluding among other things that so far from Imre's being homosexual—as Uranian, or Dionian-Uranian, or Uranian-Dionian, or what else of that kind of juggling terminology in

---

[1] Inappropriately (French).
[2] Professional (Latin).
[3] Porter (Hungarian).

homosexual analysis—my friend was no sort of a Uranistic example at all. No! he was, instead, a thorough-going Dionian, whatever the fine fusions of his sensitive and complex nature! A complete Dionian, capable of warm friendship, yes—but a man to whom warm, even passionate, friendship with this or that other man never could transform itself into the bitter and burning mystery of Uranistic Love—the fittest names for which so often should be written Torment, Shame, and Despair!

Fortunate Imre! Yet, as I said so to myself, altruistically glad for his sake, I sighed, and surely that night I thought long, long thoughts till I finally slept.

I I

MASKS AND—A FACE

My whole life was a contest since the day
That gave me being, gave me that which marred
The gift ...

A silent suffering and intense ...
All that the proud can feel of pain,
The agony they do not show ...
Which speaks but in its loneliness.

—Byron[1]

A couple of miles out of Szent-Istvánhely, one finds the fine old seat, or what was such, of the Z. family, with its deserted chateau and neglected park. The family is a broken and dispersed one. The present owner of the premises lives in Paris. He visits them no oftener, and spends no more for their care than he cannot

---

[1] Lord Byron's bisexuality was well known to EPS.

help. The park itself is almost a forest, so large it is and so stately are the trees. Long, wide alleys wind through the acacias and chestnuts. You do not go far from the very house without hares running by you, and partridges and pheasant fluttering; so left to itself is the whole demesne. Like most old estates near Szent-Istvánhely, it has its legends, plentifully. One of these tales, going back to the days of the Turkish sieges of the city, tells how a certain Count Z., a young soldier of only twenty-six years, during the investment of 1565,[1] was sitting at dinner, in the citadel, when word was brought that a Turkish skirmishing-party had captured his cousin, to whom he was deeply attached; and had cruelly murdered the young man here, in the park of this same chateau, which during some days the lines of the enemy had approached. The officer sprang up from the table. He held up his sword, and swore by it, and Saint Stephen of Hungary, that he would not put the sword back into its sheath, nor sit down to a table, nor lie in a bed, till he had avenged his cousin's fate. He collected a little troop in an hour. Before another one had passed, he made a sortie, under a pretext, toward his invaded estate. He forced its defenses. He drove out the enemy's post. He found and buried his cousin's mutilated body. Then, before dawn, he himself was surprised by a fresh force of Turks. He was shot, standing by his friend's grave, in which he too eventually was buried. Their monument is there today, with the story on it, beginning: "To the Unforgettable Memory of Z. Lorand, and Z. Egon," after the customary Magyar name-inversion.[2]

The public was not admitted to this old bit of the Szent-Istvánhely suburbs. But persons known to the caretakers were welcome. Lieutenant Imre and I had been out there once before, with the more freedom because a certain family connection

---

[1] I.e., during the Turkish occupancy of Hungary.

[2] This location is fictional, although with every other place in the novel EPS strives for realistic accuracy. Dr. Géza Buzinkay, historian and senior curator at the Kiscelli Museum of the Budapest History Museum, argues that the name Egon is of nineteenth-century origin, derived from the Egmont Overture, by Beethoven, and so impossible as a sixteenth-century name. Derived as it was from German, the name would have been bourgeois, not aristocratic. Both the legend and the monument of the two Z. cousins, it seems, are symbolic inventions of the author.

existed between the Z.'s and the N.'s. So was it that about a week after the little incident closing the preceding portion of this narrative, we planned to go out to Z. for the end of the afternoon. A suburban electric tramway passed near the gates.

For two days, I had been superstitiously, absurdly, irresistibly oppressed with the idea that some disagreeable thing was coming my way. We all have such fits; sometimes justifiably, if often, thank Heaven! proving them quite groundless. I had laughed at mine, with Imre. I could think of no earthly reason for expecting ill to befall me. To myself, I accounted for the mood as a simple reaction of temperament, for I had been extremely happy lately; and now there was the ebb, not of the happiness, but of the hypersensitiveness of it all. The balance would presently be found, and I would be neither too glad nor too gloomy.

"But why, *why* have you found yourself so wonderfully happy lately?" had asked Imre, curiously. "You haven't inherited a million? Nor fallen in love?"

No—I had not inherited a million.

It was on my way to the tram, to meet Imre, that same afternoon, that I found from my letters from England why justly I should exclaim:

My soul hath felt a secret weight,
A warning of approaching fate....

I was wanted in London within four days! I must start within less than twenty-four hours! A near relative was in uncertainty and anxiety as to some special personal affairs. And not only was my entire programme for the next few weeks completely broken up; worse still, was a strong probability that I might be hindered from setting foot on the Continent for indefinite time. In any case, a return to Hungary under less than a full twelvemonth was not now to be thought of.

With this fall of the proverbial bolt out of a clear sky in the shape of that letter in my pocket from Onslow Square I hurried toward the tram and Imre. All my pleasure in the afternoon and in everything else was paralyzed. Astonishing was it how heavy-hearted I had become in course of glancing through that communication from Mrs. L., between the Ipar-Bank[1] and the street-corner.

Heavy-hearted? Yes, miserably heavy-hearted!

Why so? Was it because of the worriments of Mrs. L.? Because I could not loiter, as a traveling idler, in pleasant Szent-Istvánhely, could not go on studying Magyar there; and anon set out for the Herkules-Baths?[2] Hardly any of these were good and sufficient reasons for suddenly feeling as if life were not worth living! for feeling that a world where departures and partings along with them seemed to be the main reason for one's comings and meetings was a deceitful and joyless kind of planet.

Well then, was my gray humor just because I was under the need of shaking hands with Imre von N. and saying, "*A viszontlátásra!*"[3] or more sensibly, saying to him "Good-bye"? Was *that* the real weight in my breast? I, a man, strong-willed, firm of temper and character! Surely I had other friends, many and warm ones, old ones, in a long row of places between Constantinople and London; in France, Germany, Austria, England. O dear, yes! There were A., and B., and C. and so on very decently through a whole alphabet of amities. Why should I feel so fierce a hatred at this interrupting of a casual, pleasant but not extraordinary intimacy, quite one *de voyage*[4] on its face, between two men who, no matter how companionable, were of absolutely diverse races, unlike objects in life and wide-removed environments, who could not even understand each other's mother-tongues? Why did existence itself seem so ironical, so full of false notes, so capricious in its kindness, seem allowed us that we might *not* be glad in it as ... Elsewhere? The reply to each of these queries was close to another answer to another question (that one which Imre von N. had asked: "And why, pray, have you found yourself so wonderfully happy *lately*?") that I should find myself so wonderfully unhappy now? Perhaps so.

---

[1] A national trading bank in Bank Street, the industrial and financial center of Budapest, today near Freedom Square.

[2] These baths in Cerna in southeastern Hungary between the Serbia/Romania borders were a popular spa at the time. There was a contemporary waltz called the *Herkulesfürdö*.

[3] Hungarian for "Till we meet again"; or "Auf Wiedersehen!"

[4] Made during travel (French); i.e., casual.

Imre was at the tram, and in high spirits.

"We shall have a beautiful afternoon, my dear fellow, beautiful!" he began. Then: "What the mischief is the matter with you? You look as if you had lost your soul!"

In a few words I told him of my summons North.

"Nonsense!" he exclaimed. "You are making a bad joke!"

"Unfortunately I never have been less able to joke in my life! Tomorrow afternoon I must be off, as surely as Saint Stephen's Crown has the Crooked Cross."

Imre "looked right, looked left, looked straight before." For an instant his look was almost painfully serious. Then it changed to an amused bewilderment. "Well. Sudden things come by twos! You have got to start off for God knows where, tomorrow afternoon: I have got to be up at dawn, to rush my legs off! For, about noon I go out by a poky special-train, to the Summer-Camp at P. And I must stay there five, six, ten mortal days, drilling Slovaks, and other such cattle! No wonder we have had a fine time of it here together! Too beautiful to last! But, Lord, how I envy you! Won't you change places with me? You're such an obliging fellow, Oswald! You go to the Camp: let me go to London?"

At this moment, up came the tram. It was packed with an excursion-party. We were hustled and separated during our leisurely transit. Imre met some fair acquaintances, and made himself exceedingly lively company to them, till we reached the Z. crossroad. We stepped out alone.

I did not break the silence as the noisy tram vanished, and the country's quietness closed us in.

"Well?" said Imre, after fully five minutes, as we approached the Z. gateway.

"Well," I replied quite as laconically.

"Oh come, come," he began, "even if it is I routing out of bed by sunrise tomorrow, to start in for all that P. Camp drudgery, and you to go spinning along in the afternoon to England—why, what of it! We mustn't let the tragedy spoil our last afternoon. Eh? Philosophy, philosophy, my dear Oswald! I have grown so trained, as a soldier, to having every sort of personal plan and pleasure, great or small, simply blown to the winds on half-an-hour's notice, that I have ceased to get into bad humor over any such contretemps. What profits it? Life isn't at all a plaything for a good lot of us, more's the pity! We've got to suffer and be strong; or else learn not to suffer. That on the whole is decidedly preferable. Permit me to recommend it; a superior article for the trade, patent applied for, take only the genuine."

I was not in tune for being philosophic, in that moment. And, from the very first words and demeanor with which Imre had received the announcement that so cruelly preyed on my spirits, I was—shall I write piqued?—by what seemed to be his indifference; nay more, by his complete nonchalance. Whether Imre, as a soldier or through possessing a colder nature than I had inferred (at least, colder than some other natures), had indeed learned to sustain life's disagreeable surprises with equanimity was nothing now to me. Or, stay, it was a good deal that just then came cross-wise to my mood; so wholly *intransigeant*.[1] Angry irritation waxed hot in me all at once, along with increasing bitterness of heart. It is edifying to observe what successive and sheer stupidities a man will perpetrate under such circumstances—edifying and pitiable!

"I don't at all envy you your philosophy, my dear friend," I said sharply. "I believe a good deal in the old notion as to philosophic people being pretty often unfeeling people much too often. I think I'd rather not become a stoic. Stoic means a stock. I'm not so far along as you."

"Really? Oh, you try it and you'll like it, as the cannibals said to the priest who had to watch them eat up the bishop. It is far better to feel nothing than to feel unpleasant things too much—so much more comfortable and cheap in the end. *Ei*! you over there!" he called out to a brown-skinned *czigány*[2] lad, suddenly appearing out of a coppice, with something suspiciously like a snap-shot[3] in his hand. "Don't you let the *házmester* up at the house catch you with that thing about you, or you'll get yourself into trouble! Young poacher!" he added angrily. "Those snap-shots when a gypsy handles them are as bad as a fowling-piece. The devil take the little rascal! And the devil take everything else!"

---

1   Uncompromising, adamant (French).
2   Gypsy (Hungarian).
3   Slingshot.

We walked down an alley in silence. Neither of us had ever been in this sort of a mood till this afternoon. The atmosphere was a trifle electric! Imre drew his sword and began giving slashes at trees and weeds, an undesirable habit that he had, as we strolled onward. Thought I, "A pleasing couple of hours truly we are likely to pass!" I felt that I would better have stayed at home, to start my packing-up for London. Then I pulled myself together. I found myself all at once possessed of a decent stock of pride, if not "philosophy." I undertook to meet Imre's manner, if not to match his sentiments. I began to talk suavely of trifles, then of more serious topics of wholly general interest. I smiled much and laughed a little. I referred to my leaving Szent-Istvánhely and him, more to the former necessity, in precisely the neatest measure of tranquillity and even of humor. Imre's responsiveness to this delicate return for his own indifference at once showed me that I had taken the right course not to "spoil this last afternoon together"—probably the last such in our lives!

On one topic, most personal to Imre, I could speak with him at any time without danger of its being talk-worn between us; could argue with him about it even to forgetting any other matter in hand; if, alas! Imre was ever satirical, or placidly unresponsive toward it. That topic was his temperamental, obstinate indifference to making the most of himself in his profession; to "going-on" in it, with all natural energies or assumed ones. He was, as I have mentioned, a perfectly satisfactory officer. But there it ended. He seemed to think that he had done his duty, and must await such vague event as would carry him, *motu proprio*,[1] further toward efficiency and distinction. Or else, of all things foolish, not to say discreditable, he declared he still would "keep his eyes open for a chance to enter civil life," would give himself up to some more or less aesthetic calling, especially of a musical connection, become "free from this farce of *playing* soldier." He excused his plan by saying that his position now was "disgracefully insincere." Insincere, yes; but not disgraceful; and he was resting on his oars with the idea that he ought not to try to row on, just when such conduct was fatal. A man can remedy a good

---

[1] Of its own accord (Latin).

deal that he feels is an "insincere" attitude toward daily life. And what is more, any worthy, any elevating profession, and in the case of the soldier the sense of himself as a prop and moral element in the State, must not be insulted! The army-life even if chosen merely from duty, and led in times of peace, is a good deal like the marriage of respect. The man may never have loved the wife to whom he is bound, he may never be able to love her, he may find her presence lamentably *unsympathisch*. But mere self-respect and the outward duty to her, and duty to those who are concerned in her honor as in his, in her welfare as in his—there comes in the unavoidable and just demand! Honor and country are eloquent for a soldier, always. It was on the indispensable, unwelcome, ever-postponed *Hadiskola* course that, once more, this afternoon, I found myself voluble with Imre. If I could not well speak of myself, I could of him, in a parting appeal.

"You must go on! You have no right to falter now. For God's sake, N.! Put by all these miserable dreams of quitting the service. What in the world could you do out of it? You have plenty of time for entertaining yourself with strumming and singing, and what not. Everything is in your own hands. Oh, yes, I know perfectly well that special help is needed to push one along fast—friends at court. But you are not wholly without them. For your father's sake and yours—! You have shown already what you can do! If you will only work a bit harder! The War-School, Imre, the War-School! That must come. If you care for your own credit, success—stop, I forbid you to sneer—get into the School, hate it as much as you will!"

"I hate it! I hate it all, I tell you! I am sick of pretending to like it. Especially just lately. More so than ever!"

"Very possibly. But what of that? Is there anything else in the wide world that you feel you can do any better? Beginning such an experiment at twenty-five years of age, with no training for so much as digging a ditch? Do you wish to become a dance-music strummer in the Városliget?[1] Or a second-class acrobat in the Circus Wulff? Or will you throw off your uniform, to take flight

---

[1]   The famous City Park behind Heroes Square in Budapest, home then as now to circuses, funfairs, and a zoo.

to America, Australia, to be a riding-master or a waiter in a restaurant, or a vagabond, like some of the Habsburg arch-dukes? Imre, Imre! Instead be a man! A man in this, as in all else. You trifle with your certainty of a career. Be a man in this matter!"

He sighed. Then softly, with a strange despair of life in his tone: "Be a man? In this, as in *all*? God! how I wish I could be so."

"Wish you could be so! I don't know what you mean. A manlier fellow one need not be! Only this damnable neglect of your career! You surely wish to succeed in life?"

"I wish. But I cannot *will*. Do not talk any more about it just now. You can—*teremtette!*—you will write me quite enough about it. You are exactly like Karvaly, once that topic comes into your mind! Yes, like him to half-a-word. And I certainly am no match for either of you."

"I should think," returned I, coldly, "that if you possess any earnest, definite regard for such a zealous friend as Herr Karvaly, or for *any* true friend, you would prove it by just this very effort to make the most of yourself—for their sakes if not for your own."

I waited a second or so, as we stood there looking across an opening of the woodland. Then I added, "For his sake, if not for ... for such a newcomer's sake as mine. But I begin to believe that your heart does not so easily stir really, warmly, as ... as I supposed. At least, not for me. Possibly for nobody, my dear N.! Odd; for you have so many friends. I confess I don't see now just why. You are a strange fellow, Imre. Such a row of contradictions!"

One-two, one-two—again was Imre walking along in silence, exactly as on the evening when we came over the long Suspension Bridge in town together. And once more was he whistling softly, as if either wholly careless or buried in thought, those same two or three melancholy notes of what I had discovered was a little Bakony peasant-song, "O, jaj! az álom nelkül—!"[1]

So passed more than an hour. We spoke less and less. My moods of self-forgetfulness, of philosophy, passed with it. I could not recover either.

We had made a detour around the lonelier portion of the park. The sun was fairly setting as we came out before the open

---

[1] "Alas, I am sleepless, I fear to dream!" (Hungarian).

lawn, wide, and uncropped save by two cows and a couple of farm-horses. There were trees on either border. At farther range, was the long, low mansion, three stories high, with countless white-painted *croisées*, and lime-blanched chimneys; an odd Austro-Magyar-style dwelling, of a long-past fashion, standing up solid and sharp against that silver-saffron sky. Not a sign of life, save those slow-moving beasts, far off in the middle of the lawn. No smoke from the yet more removed old homestead. Not a sound, except a gentle wind, melancholy and fitful. We two might have been remote, near a village in the Siebenbürgen;[1] not within twenty minutes of a great commercial city.

Instead of going on toward the avenue which led to the exit (the hour being yet early) we sat down on a stone bench, much beaten by weather. A few steps away, rose the monument I have mentioned, "To the Unforgettable Memory" of Lorand and Egon Z.

Neither Imre nor I spoke immediately, each a trifle leg-weary. I once more was sad and angry. As we sat there, I read over for yet another time—the last time?—those carved words which reminded a reader, whether to his gladness of soul or dolor, that love, a *love* indeed strong as death, between two manly souls was no mere ideal; but instead, a possible crown of existence, a glory of life, a realizable unity that certain fortunate sons of men attained! A jewel that others must yearn for, in disappointment and folly, and with the taste of aloes, and the white of the egg, for the pomegranate and the honeycomb! I sighed.

"Oh, courage, courage, my well beloved friend!" exclaimed Imre, hearing the sigh and apparently quite misreading my innermost thoughts. "Don't be downhearted again as to leaving Szent-Istvánhely tomorrow; not to speak of being cheerful even if you must part from your most obedient servant. Such is life, unless we are born sultans and kaisers! And if we are that, we must die to slow music in the course of time."

I vouchsafed no comment. Could this be Imre von N.? Certainly I had made the acquaintance of a new and extremely uncongenial Imre, in exactly the least appropriate circumstances to lose sight of the sympathetic, gentler-natured friend whom I

---

[1] Area between the Netherlands and northwestern Germany.

had begun to consider as one well understood, and had found responsive to a word, a look. Did all his closer friends meet, sooner or later, with this underhalf of his temperament, this brusqueness which I had hitherto seen in his bearing with only his outside associates? Did they admire it, if caring for him? Bitterness came over me in a wave, it rose to my lips in a burst.

"It is just as well that one of us should show some feeling, a trifle, when our parting is so near."

A pause. Then Imre:

"The 'one of us,' that is to say the only one, who has any 'feeling' being yourself, my dear Oswald?"

"Apparently."

"Don't you think that perhaps you rather take things for granted? Or that, perhaps, you feel too much? That is, in supposing that I feel too little?"

My reply was quick and acid enough:

"Have you any sentiments in the matter worth calling by such a name, at all? I've not remarked them so far! Are friends that love you and value you only worth their day with you? Have they no real, lasting individuality for you? Your heart is not so difficult to please as mine; nor so difficult to occupy."

Again a brief interval. Imre was beating a tattoo on his braided cap, and examining the top of that article with much attention. The sky was less light now. The long, melancholy house had grown pallid against the foliage. Still the same fitful breeze. One of the cows lowed.

He looked up. He began speaking gravely, kindly, not so much as if seeking his words for their exactness, but rather as if he were fearful of committing himself outwardly to some innermost process of thought. Afraid, more than unwilling.

"Listen, my dear friend. We must not expect too much of one another in this world, must we? Do not be foolish. You know well that one of the last things that I regard as 'of a day' is *our* friendship, however suddenly grown. No matter what you think now, for just these few moments when something disturbs us both, *that* you know. Why, dear friend! Did I not believe it myself, had I not so soon after our meeting believed it, do you think I would have shown you so much of my real self, happy or unhappy, for better or worse? Sides of my nature unknown to others? Traits that you like, along with traits that I see you do not like? Why, Oswald, you understand *me*—the real *me*!—better than anybody else that I have ever met. Because I wished it: I hoped it. Because I—I could not help it. Just that. But you see the trouble is that, in spite of all, you do not *wholly* understand me. And ... and the worst of the reason is that I am the one most to blame for it! And I ... I cannot better it now."

"When do we understand one another in this life of half-truths, half-intimacies?"

"Yes, all too often half; whether it is with one's wife, one's mistress, one's friend! And I am not easy. Ah, how I have had to learn the way to keep myself so, to study it till it is a second nature to me! I am not easy to know! But, Oswald, Oswald, *ich kann nicht anders, nein, nein, ich kann nicht anders!*"[1] And then, in his own language, dull and doggedly he added to himself, "*Mit használ, mit használ az én nekem?*"[2]

He took my hand now, that was lying on the settle beside his own, and held it while he spoke; unconsciously clasping it tighter and tighter till it was in pain, or would have been so, had it not been, like his own, cold from sheer nervousness. He continued:

"One thing more. You seem to forget sometimes that I am a man, and that you too are a man. Not either of us a—woman. Forgive me: I speak frankly. We are both of us, you and I, a bit over-sensitive, *exalté* in type. Isn't that so? You often suggest a ... a regard so—what shall I call it?—so romantic, heroic, passionate—a *love* indeed (and here his voice was suddenly broken)—something that I cannot accept from anybody without warning him back, back! I mean back coming to me from any other *man*. Sometimes you have troubled me, frightened me. I cannot, will not try to tell you why this is so. But so it is. Our friendship must be friendship as the world of today accepts friendship! Yes, as the world of *our* day does. God! What else could it be today: friendship? What else—*today?*"

"Not the friendship which is love, the love which is friendship?" I said in a low voice; indeed, as I now remember more than half to myself.

---

[1] I can no other, no, no, I can no other! (German).
[2] "What use is it, what use is it for *me?*" I.e., it doesn't matter anymore (Hungarian).

Imre was looking at the darkened sky, the gray lawn, into the vague distance at whatsoever was visible save myself. Then his glance was caught by the ghostly marble of the monument to the young Z. heroes, at which I too was staring. A tone of appeal came as he continued:

"Once more, I beg, I implore you, not to make the mistake of ... of thinking me cold-natured. I, cold-natured? Ah, ah! If you knew me better, you'd not pack that notion into your trunks for London! Instead, believe that I value unspeakably all your friendship for me, dear Oswald. Time will prove that. I have had no friend like you, I believe. But though friendship can be a passion, can cast a spell over us that we cannot comprehend nor unbind" (here he withdrew his hand and pointed to the memorial stone set up for those two human hearts that after so ardently beating for each other were now but dust) "it must be only a spiritual, manlike regard! The world thought otherwise once. The world thinks *as* it thinks now. And the world, our today's world, must decide for us all! Friendship now—now—must stay as the *man* of our day understands it, Oswald. That is, if the man deserves the name, and is not to be not classed as some sort of an incomprehensible womanish outcast, counterfeit, a miserable puzzle—born to be every genuine man's contempt!"

We had come, once more, suddenly, fully, and because of me, on the topic which we had touched on, that night of our Lánchíd walk! But this time I faced it, in a sense of fatality and finality; in a rash, desperate desire to tear a secret out of myself, to breathe free, to be true to myself, to speak out the past and the present, so strangely united in these last few weeks, to reserve nothing, cost what it might! My hour had come!

"You have asked me to listen to you!" I cried. Even now I feel the despair, I think I hear the accent of it, with which I spoke. "I have heard you! Now I want you to listen to me! I wish to tell you a story. It is out of one man's deepest yet daily life. My own life. Most of what I wish to tell happened long before I knew you. It was far away, it was in what used to be my own country. After I tell it, you will be one of very few people in all the world who have known, even suspected, what happened to me. In telling you, I trust you with my social honor, with all that is outwardly and inwardly myself. And I shall probably pay a penalty, just because *you* hear the wretched history, Imre, *you*! For before it ends, it has to do with you; as well as with something that you have just spoken of—so fiercely! I mean how far a man, deserving to be called a man, refusing, as surely as God lives and has made him, to believe that he is (what did you call him?) 'a miserable womanish counterfeit, outcast,' even if he be incomprehensible to himself how such a being can suffer and be ruined in his innermost life and peace, by a soul-tragedy which he nevertheless can hide—*must* hide! I could have told you all on the night that we talked, as we crossed the Lánchíd. No, that is not true! I could not then. But I can now. For I may never see you again. You talk of our 'knowing' each other! I wish you to know me. And I could never write you this, never! Will you hear me, Imre?—patiently?"

"I will hear you patiently—yes, Oswald—if you think it best to tell me. Of *that* pray think, carefully."

"It is best! I am tired of thinking of it. It is time you knew."

"And I am really concerned in it?"

"You are immediately concerned. That is to say, before it ends. You will see how."

"Then you would better go on. Of course."

He consented thus, in the constrained but decided tone which I have indicated as so often recurring during the evening, adding, "I am ready, Oswald."

★ ★ ★ ★ ★

"From the time when I was a lad, Imre, a little child, I felt myself unlike other boys in one element of my nature. That one matter was my special sense, my passion, for the beauty, the dignity, the charm, the—what shall I say?—the loveableness of my own sex. I hid it, at least so far as, little by little, I came to realize its force. For, I soon perceived that most other lads had no such passional sentiment, in any important measure of their natures, even when they were fine-strung, impressionable youths. There was nothing unmanly about me; nothing really unlike the rest of my friends in school, or in town-life. Though I was not a strong-built, or rough-spirited lad, I had plenty of pluck and muscle, and was as lively on the playground, and fully as indefatigable, as my chums. I had a good many friends; close ones, who liked me well. But I felt sure, more and more, from one year to another even of that boyhood time, that no lad of them all ever could or would care for me as much *as* I could and did care for one or another of them! Two or three episodes made that clear to me. These incidents made me, too, shyer and shyer of showing how my whole young nature, soul and body together, Imre, could be stirred with a veritable adoration for some boy-friend that I elected, an adoration with a physical yearning in it. How intense was the appeal of bodily beauty, in a lad, or in a man of mature years.

"And yet, with that beauty, I looked for manliness, poise, will-power, dignity and strength in him. For somehow I demanded those traits, always and clearly, whatever else I sought along with them. I say 'sought.' I can say, too, won—won often to nearness. But this other, more romantic, emotion in me, so strongly physical, sexual, as well as spiritual, it met with a really like and equal and full response once only. Just as my school life was closing, with my sixteenth year (nearly my seventeenth) came a friendship with a newcomer into my classes, a lad of a year older than myself, of striking beauty of physique and uncommon strength of character. This early relation embodied the same precocious, absolutely vehement *passion* (I can call it nothing else) on both sides. I had found my ideal! I had realized for the first time, completely, a type; a type which had haunted me from first consciousness of my mortal existence, Imre; one that is to haunt me till my last moment of it. All my immature but intensely ardent regard was returned. And then, after a few months together, my schoolmate, all at once, became ill during an epidemic in the town, was taken to his home, and died. I never saw him after he left me.

"It was my first great misery, Imre. It was literally unspeakable! For I could not tell to anyone, I did not know how to explain even to myself the manner in which my nature had gone out to my young mate, nor how his being spontaneously so had blent itself with mine. I was not seventeen years old, as I said. But I knew clearly now what it was to *love* thus, so as to forget oneself in another's life and death! But also I knew better than to talk of such things. So I never spoke of my dead mate.

"I grew older, I entered my professional studies, and I was very diligent with them. I lived in a great capital,[1] I moved much in general society. I had a large and lively group of friends. But always, over and over, I realized that, in the kernel, at the very root and fiber of myself, there was the throb and glow, the ebb and the surge, the seeking as in a vain dream to realize again that passion of friendship which could so far transcend the cold modern idea of the tie: the Over-Friendship, the Love-Friendship of Hellas,[2] which meant that between man and man could exist the sexual-psychic love. That was still possible! I knew that now! I had read it in the verses or the prose of the Greek and Latin and Oriental authors who have written out every shade of its beauty or unloveliness, its worth or debasements—from Theokritos to Martial, or Abu-Nuwas,[3] to Platen, Michelangelo, Shakespeare. I had learned it from the statues of sculptors, with those lines so often vivid with a merely physical male beauty—works which beget, which sprang from, the sense of it in a race. I had half-divined it in the music of a Beethoven and a Tschaikovsky before knowing facts in the life-stories of either of them—or of a hundred other tone-autobiographists.

"And I had recognized what it all meant to most people today, from the disgust, scorn and laughter of my fellow-men when such an emotion was hinted at! I understood perfectly that a man must wear the Mask, if he—poor wretch!—could neither abide at the bound of ordinary warmth of feeling for some friend of friends that drew on his innermost nature, or if he were not content because the other stayed within that bound. Love between two men, however absorbing, however passional, must not be—so one was assured, solemnly or in disgusted incredulity—a sexual love, a physical impulse and bond. *That* was now as ever, a nameless horror—a thing against all civilization, sanity, sex, Nature, God!

---

[1] Oswald's tale eerily reflects the author's own life in many of its details. EPS lived in New York City at the beginning of his life, for example, before he began his nomadic career in Europe.

[2] Ancient Greece.

[3] A poet of Baghdad (died c. 85 A.D.) who celebrated the illicit joys of wine and boys.

Therefore, *I* was, of course—what then was I? Oh, I perceived it! I was that anachronism from old—that incomprehensible incident in God's human creation: the man-loving man! The man-loving man! whose whole heart can be given only to another man, and who when his spirit is passing into his beloved friend's keeping would demand, would surrender, the body with it. The man-loving man! He who seeks not merely a spiritual unity with him whom he loves, but seeks the embrace that joins two male human beings in a fusion that no woman's arms, no woman's kisses can ever realize. No woman's embrace? No, no! For instead of that, either he cares not a whit for it, is indifferent to it, is smilingly scornful of it: or else he tolerates it, even in the wife he has married (not to speak of any less honorable ties) as an artifice, a mere quietus to that undeceived sexual passion burning in his nature; wasting his really *unmated* individuality, years-long. Or else he surrenders himself to some woman who bears his name, loves him—to her who perhaps in innocence and ignorance believes that she dominates every instinct of his sex!—making her a wife that she may bear to him children; or thinking that marriage may screen him, or even (vain hope!) 'cure' him! But oftenest, he flies from any woman, as her sexual self; wholly shrinks from her as from nothing else created; avoids the very touch of a woman's hand in his own, any physical contact with woman, save in a calm cordiality, in a sexless and fraternal reserve, a passionless if yet warm friendship! Not seldom he shudders (he may not know why) in something akin to dread and to loathing, though he may succeed in hiding it from wife or mistress, at any near approach of his strong male body to a woman's trivial, weak, feminine one, however fair, however harmonious in lines! Yes, even were she Aphrodite herself!

"And yet, Imre, thousands, thousands, hundreds of thousands, of such human creatures as I am, have not in body, in mind, nor in all the sum of our virility, in all the detail of our outward selves, any openly womanish trait! Not one! It is only the ignoramus and the vulgar who nowadays think or talk of the homosexual as if he were a hermaphrodite! In every feature and line and sinew and muscle, in every movement and accent and capability, we walk the world's ways as men. We hew our ways through it as men, with vigor, success, honor, *one* master-instinct unsuspected by society for, it may be, our lives long! We plow the globe's roughest seas as men, we rule its States as men, we direct its finance and commerce as men, we forge its steel as men, we grapple with all its sciences, we triumph in all its arts as men, we fill its gravest professions as men, we fight in the bravest ranks of its armies as men, or we plan out its fiercest and most triumphant battles as men. In all this, in so much more, we are men! Why (in a bitter paradox), one can say that we always have been, we always are, always will be, too much *men*! So super-male, so utterly unreceptive of what is not manly, so aloof from any feminine essences, that we cannot tolerate woman at all as a sexual factor! Are we not the extreme of the male? its supreme phase, its outermost phalanx?—its climax of the aristocratic, the All-Man? And yet, if love is to be only what the narrow, modern, Jewish-Christian ethics of today declare it, if what they insist be the only *natural* and pure expression of 'the will to possess, the wish to surrender,' oh, then is the flouting world quite right! For then we are indeed *not* men! But if not so, what are we? Answer that, who can?

"The more perplexed I became in all this wretchedness (for it had grown to that by the time I had reached my majority), the more perplexed I became because so often in books, old ones or new, nay, in the very chronicles of the criminal courts, I came face to face with the fact that though tens of thousands of men in all epochs, of noblest natures, of most brilliant minds and gifts, of intensest energies, scores of pure spirits, deep philosophers, bravest soldiers, highest poets and artists, had been such as myself in this mystic sex-disorganization, that nevertheless of this same Race, the Race-Homosexual, had been also and apparently ever would be, countless ignoble, trivial, loathsome, feeble-souled and feeble-bodied creatures, the very weaklings and rubbish of humanity!

"Those, *those*, terrified me, Imre! To think of them shamed me; those types of man-loving-men who, by thousands, live incapable of any noble ideals or lives. Ah, those patently depraved, noxious, flaccid, gross, womanish beings, perverted and imperfect in moral nature and in even their bodily tissues! Those homosexual legions that are the straw-chaff of society; good for nothing except the fire that purges the world of garbage and rubbish! A Heliogabalus, a Gilles de Rais, a Henri Trois, a Marquis de Sade;[1] the painted male-prostitutes of the boulevards and twilight-glooming squares! The effeminate artists, the sugary and fiberless musicians! The Lady Nancyish, rich young men of higher or lower society twaddling aesthetic sophistries, stinking with perfume like cocottes! The second-rate poets and the neurasthenic, *précieux*[2] poetasters who rhyme forth their forged literary passports out of their mere human decadence; out of their marrowless shams of all that is a man's fancy, a man's heart, a man's love-life! The cynical debauchers of little boys; the pederastic perverters of clean-minded lads in their teens; the white-haired satyrs of clubs and latrines!

"What a contrast are these to great Oriental princes and to the heroes and heroic intellects of Greece and Rome! To a Themistocles, an Agesilaus, an Aristides and a Kleomenes; to Socrates and Plato, and Saint Augustine, to Servetus and Beza; to Alexander, Julius Caesar, Augustus, and Hadrian; to Prince Eugene of Savoy, to Sweden's Charles the Twelfth, to Frederic the Great, to indomitable Tilly, to the fiery Skobeleff, the austere Gordon, the ill-starred Macdonald; to the brightest lyrists and dramatists of old Hellas and Italia; to Shakespeare, (to Marlowe also, we can well believe,) Platen, Grillparzer, Hölderlin, Byron, Whitman; to an Isaac Newton, a Justus Liebig; to Michelangelo and Sodoma; to the masterly Jerome Duquesnoy, the classic-souled Winckelmann; to Mirabeau, Beethoven, Bavaria's unhappy King Ludwig; to an endless procession of exceptional men, from epoch

---

[1] In bravely touting such infamous homosexuals of history, EPS argues that gay people show the same spectrum of good and bad as heterosexuals. *The Intersexes* contains nearly identical lists (e.g., 77–78), where EPS distinguishes between those who were noble and those who were notorious. Antoninus Heliogabalus was a Roman emperor (fl. 218–222) who degraded the imperial office by the most shameful vices. Gilles de Rais (1404–40), a French general, lured over two hundred peasant boys into his castle where they were tortured and murdered. Henri III (1551–89) de Valois, king of Poland and France, was notorious for a liking for young men. The Marquis de Sade (1740–1814) was a French writer who forged a literacy career out of depravity; no sexual variation escaped his attention.

[2] Over-refined.

to epoch![1] Yet as to these and innumerable others, facts of their hidden, inner lives have proved without shadow of doubt (however rigidly suppressed as 'popular information') or inferences vivid enough to silence scornful denial, have pointed out that they belonged to Us.

"Nevertheless, did not the widest overlook of Uranianism, the average facts about one, suggest that the most part of homosexual humanity had always belonged, always would belong, to the worthless or the wicked? Was our Race gold or excrement? as rubies or as carrion? If *that* last were one's final idea, why then all those other men, the Normalists, aye, our severest judges, those others whether good or bad, whether vessels of honor or dishonor, who are not in their love-instincts as are we—the millions against our tens of thousands, even if some of us are to be respected—why, they do right to cast us out of society; for after all, we must be just a vitiated breed! We must be judged by our commoner mass.

"And yet, the rest of us! The Rest, over and over! men so high-minded, often of such deserved honor from all that world which has either known nothing of their sexual lives, or else has perceived

---

[1] Oswald's list of purported gay people continues with those who were contributors to humanity. Themistocles and Aristides were Greek generals in the Persian Wars who, according to Plutarch, were rivals for the love of the youth Stesilaos of Keos. Agesilaus, the "lame king" of Sparta (444–360 B.C.) had the reputation of being the greatest man in all of Greece. In *The Intersexes* EPS mentions "an account of Archidamos as the lover of a beautiful lad named Kleomenes, the same youth who presently died a glorious death in battle, and upon whose body another young man named Panteus committed suicide in his intense grief and love ..." (52). Socrates (469–399 B.C.) and Plato (428–347 B.C.) were Greek philosophers and teachers who espoused same-sex love in such works as *The Symposium*. St. Augustine (354–430), early Christian apologist, Michael Servetus (1511–53), Spanish physician and theologian opposed to John Calvin, and Théodore Beza (1519–1605), French theologian who supported Calvin, were all religious stalwarts; while Alexander the Great (356–323 B.C.) of Macedonia, Julius Caesar (100–44 B.C.), the great Roman statesman, Caesar Augustus (63 B.C.–14 A.D.), the first Roman emperor, and Hadrian (76–138), also Roman emperor (and famous for his love for the boy Antinous) were great world leaders. EPS takes pains to mention famous military fighters in his list of homosexuals: Prince Eugene of Savoy (1663–1736) laid the foundation of the Austro-Hungarian empire; Charles XII of Sweden (1682–1718) successfully fought Denmark, Russia, and Poland; Frederic the Great (1712–86), the powerful King of Prussia, and Armand-Louis de Gontaut, Duke of Tilly (1747–93) were famous military men, as were more recent choices: General Skobeleff of Russia who distinguished himself in the 1880s; General George Gordon (1833–85) who died at the great battle of Khartoum; and Sir Hector

vaguely, and with a tacit, a reluctant pardon! Could one really believe in God as making man to live at all, and to love at all, and yet at the same time believe that *this* love is not created, too, by God? is not of God's own divinest Nature, rightfully, eternally—in millions of hearts? Could one believe that the eternal human essence is in its texture today so different from itself of immemorial time before now, whether Greek, Latin, Persian, or English? Could one somehow find in his spirit no dread through *this*, none, at the idea of facing God, as his Judge, at any instant? Could one feel at moments such strength of confidence that what was in him *so* was righteousness? Oh, could all this be? And yet must a man shudder before himself as a monster, a solitary and pernicious being—diseased, leprous, gangrened—one that must stagger along on the road of life, ever justly shunned, ever justly bleeding and ever the more wearied, till Death would meet him, and say 'Come—enough! Be free of all! Be free of *thyself* most of all!'

I paused. Doing so, I heard from Imre, who had not spoken so much as a word—was it a sigh? Or a broken murmur of something coming to his lips in his own tongue? Was it—no, impossible! Was it a sort of sob, strangled in his throat? The evening had grown so

---

Archibald Macdonald (1853–1903), the British general who had recently committed suicide before facing court martial for sexual improprieties. William Shakespeare (1564–1616), makes the list in light of his famous sonnets to a young man, and Christopher Marlowe (1564–93) for his play *Edward II*, while nineteenth-century choices include favorite writers of EPS: the already-mentioned Platen and Grillparzer, German poet Friedrich Hölderlin (1770–1843), Lord Byron (1788–1824), the British Romantic poet known for his escapades with both sexes, and not surprisingly, Walt Whitman (1819–92), American author of the notorious Calamus poems whose name itself had become a marker for gay sensibility. Of scientists, there are Isaac Newton (1642–1727), the British astronomer and mathematician, and Justus Liebig (1803–73), the German chemist and sometime lover of von Platen (according to *Intersexes*, 564). Artists include Michelangelo (1475–1564), Sodoma (1477–1549), the aptly named High Renaissance painter, and Jerome Duquesnoy (d. 1654), the Flemish sculptor, who had been condemned to death for sodomy. Johann Joachim Winckelmann (1717–68) was a German scholar who in ushering in a new age of classicism had sanctioned homoeroticism in art, especially Greek. Honoré Gabriel Riquetti, comte de Mirabeau (1749–91), was a great French revolutionary and political leader. The bachelorhood of Ludwig van Beethoven (1770–1827), the unparalleled German composer, continually intrigued EPS the music critic, while King Ludwig II of Bavaria (1845–86) stood in recent memory as the great patron of Richard Wagner. Though the list of famous gay men is problematical to some present-day observers, to EPS their homosexuality was "without shadow of doubt."

dark that I could not have seen his face, even had I wished to look into it. However, absorbed now in my own tenebrous retrospect, almost forgetting that anyone was there at my side, I went on:

"You must not think that I had not had friendships of much depth, Imre, which were not, first and last, quite free from this *other* accent in them. Yes, I had had such; and I have many such now; comradeships with men younger, men of my own age, men older, for whom I feel warm affection and admiration, whose company was and is a true happiness for me. But somehow they were not and, no matter what they are they still are not, of *the* Type; of that eternal, mysteriously disturbing cruel Type, which so vibrates sexually against my hidden Self.

"How I dreaded, yet sought that Type! How soon was I relieved, or dull of heart, when I knew that this or that friend was not enough dear to me, however dear he was, to give me that hated sexual stir and sympathy, that inner, involuntary thrill! Yet I sought it ever, right and left, since none embodied it for me; while I always *feared* that someone might embody it! There were approaches to it. Then, then, I suffered or throbbed with a wordless pain or joy of life, at one and the same time! But fortunately these encounters failed of full realization. Or what might have been my fate passed me by on the other side. But I learned from them how I could feel toward the man who could be in his mind and body my ideal, my supremest Friend. Would I ever meet him, meet him *again*, I could say to myself, remembering that episode of my schooldays. Or would I never meet him! God forbid that! For to be all my life alone, year after year, striving to content myself with pleasant shadow instead of glowing verity! Ah, I could well exclaim in the cry of Platen:

O, weh Dir, der die Welt verachtet, allein zu sein
Und dessen ganze Seele schmachtet allein zu sein![1]

"One day a book came to my hand. It was a serious work, on abnormalisms in mankind: a book partly psychologic, partly

---

[1] "Woe to you whom all the world disdains just for being/
And whose entire soul yearns just to be."

medico-psychiatric, of the newest 'school.' It had much to say of homosexualism, of Uranianism. It considered and discussed especially researches by German physicians into it. It described myself, my secret, unrestful self, with an unsparing exactness! The writer was a famous specialistic physician in nervous diseases, abnormal conditions of the mind, and so on—an American. For the first time I understood that responsible physicians, great psychologists—profound students of humanities, high jurists, other men in the world besides obscene humorists of a clubroom, and judges and juries in police courts—knew of men like myself and took them as serious problems for study, far from wholly despicable. This doctor spoke of my kind as simply— diseased. 'Curable,' absolutely 'curable'; so long as the mind was manlike in all else, the body firm and normal. Certainly that was my case! Would I not therefore do well to take one step which was stated to be most wise and helpful toward correcting as perturbed a relation as mine had become to ordinary life? That step was—to marry. To marry immediately!

"The physician who had written that book happened to be in England at the time. I had never thought it possible that I could feel courage to go to any man (save that one vague sympathizer, my dream-friend, he who someday would understand all!) and confess myself, lay bare my mysterious nature. But if it were a mere disease, oh, that made a difference! So I visited the distinguished specialist at once. He helped me urbanely through my embarrassing story of my 'malady.' 'Oh, there was nothing extraordinary, not at all extraordinary in it, from the beginning to the end,' the doctor assured me, smiling. In fact, it was 'exceedingly common. All confidential specialists in nervous diseases knew of hundreds of just such cases. Nay, of much worse ones, and treated and cured them. A morbid state of certain sexual-sensory nerve-centers ...' and so on, in his glib professional diagnosis.

"'So I am to understand that I am curable?' 'Curable? Why, surely. Exactly as I have written in my work; as Doctor So-and-So, and the great psychiatric Professor Such-a-One, proved long ago. Your case, my dear sir, is the easier because you suffer in a sentimental and sexual way from what we call the obsession of a set, distinct Type, you see; instead of a general—h'm, how shall

I style it—morbidity of your inclinations. It is largely mere imagination! You say you have never really "realized" this haunting masculine Type which has given you such trouble? My dear sir, don't think any more about such nonsense! You never will "realize" it in any way to be—h'm—disturbed. Probably had you married and settled down pleasantly, years ago, you often would have laughed heartily at the whole story of such an illusion of your nature now. Too much *thought* of it all, my dear friend! Too much introspection, idealism, sedentary life, dear sir! Yes, yes, you must *marry*—God bless you!'

"I paid my distinguished specialist his fee and came away, with a far lighter heart than I had had in many a year.

"Marry! Well, that was easily to be done. I was popular enough with women of all sorts. I was no woman-hater. I had many true and charming and most affectionate friendships with women. For, you must know, Imre, that such men as I am are often most attractive to women, most beloved by them (I mean by good women) far more than through being their relatives and social friends. They do not understand the reason of our attraction for them, of their confidence, their strengthening sentiment. For we seldom betray to them our secret, and they seldom have knowledge, or instinct, to guess its mystery. But alas! it is the irony of *our* nature that we cannot return to any woman, except by a lie of the body and the spirit (often being unable to compass or to endure that wretched subterfuge), a warmer glow than affection's calmest pulsations. Several times, before my consulting Doctor D. I had had the opportunity of marrying 'happily and wisely'—if marriage with any woman could have meant only a friendship. Naught physical, no responsibility of sex toward the wife to whom one gives oneself. But 'the will to possess, the desire to surrender,' the negation of what is ourselves which comes with the arms of some one other human creature about us—ours about *him*—long before, had I understood that the like of this joy was not possible for me with wife or mistress. It had seemed to me hopeless of attempt. If marriage exact *that* effort, good God! then it means a growing wretchedness, riddle and mystery for two human beings, not for one. Stay! it means worse still, should they not be childless....

"But now I had my prescription, and I was to be cured. In ten days, Imre, I was betrothed. Do not be surprised. I had known a long while earlier that I was loved. My betrothed was the daughter of a valued family friend, living in a near town. She was beautiful, gifted, young, high-souled and gentle. I had always admired her warmly; we had been much thrown together. I had avoided her lately, however, because—unmistakably—I had become sure of a deeper sentiment on her part than I could exchange.

"But now, now, I persuaded myself that I did indeed return it; that I had not understood myself. And confidently, even ardently, I played my new role so well, Imre, that I was deceived myself. And she? She never felt the shade of suspicion. I fancied that I loved her. Besides, my betrothed was not exacting, Imre. In fact, as I now think over those few weeks of our deeper intimacy, I can discern how I was favored in my new relationship to her by her sensitive, maidenly shrinking from the physical nearness, even the touch, of the man who was dear to her; how troubling the sense of any man's advancing physical dominancy over her. Yet do not make the mistake of thinking that she was cold in her calm womanliness; or would have held herself aloof as a wife. It was simply virginal, instinctive reserve. She loved me; and she would have given herself wholly to me, as my bride.

"The date for our marriage was set. I tried to think of nothing but it and her; of how calmly, securely happy I should soon be, and of all the happiness that, God willing, I would bring into her young life. I say 'tried' to think of nothing else. I almost succeeded. But nevertheless, in moments....

"It was not to be, however, this deliverance, this salvation for me!

"One evening, I was asked by a friend to come to his lodgings to dine, to meet some strangers, his guests. I went. Among the men who came was one (I had never seen him before) newly arrived in my city, coming to pass the winter. From the instant that set me face to face with him, that let me hear his voice in only a greeting that put us to exchanging a few commonplace sentences, I thrilled with joy and trembled to my innermost soul with a sudden anguish. For, Imre, it was as if that dead schoolmate of mine—not merely as death had taken him, but matured, a man in his beauty and charm—it was as if every acquaintance that ever had quickened within me the same unspeakable sense of a mysterious bond of soul and of body—the Man-Type which owned me and ever must own me, soul and body together—had started forth in a perfect avatar. Out of the slumberous past, out of the kingdom of illusions, straying to me from the realm of banished hopes, it had come to me! The Man, the Type, that thing which meant for me the fires of passion not to be quenched, that subjection of my whole being to an ideal of my own sex, that fatal 'nervous illusion,' as the famous doctor's book so summarily ranged it for the world ... all had overtaken me again! My peace was gone—if ever I had had true peace. I was lost, with it!

"From that night, I forgot everything else except him. My former unchanged, unchangeable self in all its misery and mystery reverted. The temperament which I had thought to put to sleep, the invisible nature I had believed I could strangle—it had awakened with the lava-seethe of a volcano. It burned in my spirit and body, like a masked crater.

"Imre, I sought the friendship of this man, of my ideal who had recreated for me, simply by his existence, a world of feeling; one of suffering and yet of delight. And I won his friendship! Do not suppose that I dared to dream, then or ever, of more than a commonplace, social intimacy. Never, never! Merely to achieve his regard toward myself a little more than toward others; merely that he would care to give me more of his society, would show me more of his inner self than he inclined to open to others. Just to be accounted by him somewhat dearer, in such a man's vague often elusive degree, than the majority for whom he cared at all! Only to have more constant leave to delight my spirit in silence with his physical beauty while guarding from him in a sort of terror the psychic effects it wrought in me. My hopes went no further than these. And, as I say, I won them. As it kindly happened, our tastes, our interests in arts and letters, our temperaments, the fact that he came to my city with few acquaintances in it and was not a man who readily seeks them, the chance that he lived almost in the same house with me—such circumstances favored me immediately. But I did not deceive myself once, either as to what was the measure or the kind of my emotion for him, any more than about what (if stretched to its uttermost) would be his sentiment for me, for any man. He could not love a man *so*. He could love, passionately, and to the completing of his sexual nature, only a woman. He was the normal, I the abnormal. In that, alone, he failed to meet all that was I:

> O, the little more, and how much it is!
> And the little less, and what worlds away![1]

"Did I keep my secret perfectly from him? Perfectly, Imre! You will soon see that clearly. There were times when the storm came full over me, when I avoided him, when I would have fled from myself, in the fierce struggle. But I was vigilant. He was moved, now and then, at a certain inevitable tenderness that I would show him. He often spoke wonderingly of the degree of my 'absorbing friendship.' But he was a man of fine and romantic ideals, of a strong and warm temper. His life had been something solitary from his earliest youth, and he was no psychologist. Despite many a contest with our relationship, I never allowed myself to complain of him. I was too well aware how fortunate was my bond with him. The man esteemed me, trusted me, admired me ... all this thoroughly. I had more; for I possessed what in such a nature as his proves itself a manly affection. I was an essential element in his daily life all that winter; intimate to a depth that (as he told me, and I believe it was wholly true) he had never expected another man could attain. Was all *that* not enough for me? Oh, yes! and yet ... and yet....

"I will not speak to you more of that time which came to pass for me, Imre. It was for me, verily, a new existence! It was much such a daily life, Imre, as you and I might lead together, had fate allowed us the time for it to ripen. Perhaps we yet might lead it, God knows! I leave you tomorrow!

"But, you ask, what of my marriage-engagement?

"I broke it. I had broken it within a week after I met him, so far as shattering it to myself went. I knew that no marriage of any kind yet tolerated in our era would 'cure' me of my 'illusion,' my 'nervous disease,' could banish this 'mere psychic disturbance,' the result of 'too much introspection.' I had no disease! No. I was simply what

---

[1] Robert Browning (1812–89), "By the Fireside" (1855), stanza 39.

I was born!—a complete human being, of firm, perfect physical and mental health; outwardly in full key with all the man's world: but, in spite of that, a being who from birth was of a vague, special sex, a member of the sex *within* the most obvious sexes; or apart from them. I was created as a man perfectly male, save in the one thing which keeps such a 'man' back from possibility of ever becoming integrally male: his terrible, instinctive demand for a psychic and a physical union with a man—not with a woman.

"Presently, during that same winter, accident opened my eyes wider to myself. From then, I have needed no further knowledge from the Tree of my Good and Evil. I met with a mass of serious studies, German, Italian, French, English, from the chief European specialists and theorists on the similisexual topic: many of them with quite other views than those of my well-meaning but far too conclusive Yankee doctor. I learned of the much-discussed theories of 'secondary sexes' and 'intersexes.' I learned of the theories and facts of homosexualism, of the Uranian Love, of the Uranian Race, of 'the Sex within a Sex.' I could, at last, inform myself fully of its mystery, and of the logical, inevitable and necessary place in sexualism, of the similisexual man, and of the similisexual woman.

"I came to know their enormous distribution all over the world today; and of the grave attention that European scientists and jurists have been devoting to problems concerned with homosexualism. I could pursue intelligently the growing efforts to set right the public mind as to so ineradicable and misunderstood a phase of humanity. I realized that I had always been a member of that hidden brotherhood and Sub-Sex, or Super-Sex. In wonder too I informed myself of its deep, instinctive freemasonries—even to organized ones—in every social class, every land, every civilization: of the signs and symbols and safeguards of concealment. I could guess that my father, my grandfather and God knows how many earlier forerunners of my unhappy Ego, had been of it! 'Cure?' By marriage? By marriage, when my blood ran cold at the thought! The idea was madness, in a double sense. Better a pistol-shot to my heart! So first, I found pretexts to excuse meetings with my bride-not-to-be, avoiding thus a comedy which now was odious as a lie and insupportable as a nervous demand. Next, I pleaded business worries. So the marriage was postponed for three months further. Then I discovered a new obstacle to bring forward. With that, the date of the wedding was made indefinite. Then came some idle gossip, unjust reflections on my betrothed and on myself. I knew well where blame enough should fall, but not that sort of blame. An end had to be! I wrote my betrothed, begging my freedom, giving no reason. She released me, telling me that she would never marry any other man. She keeps her word today. I drew my breath in shame at my deliverance. 'Any other *man!*'

"So seldom had I referred to my betrothal in talking with my new friend that he asked me no questions when I told him it was ended. He mistook my reserve; and respected it rigidly.

"During that winter, I was able to prove myself a friend in deed and need to him. Twice, by strange fatality, a dark cloud came over his head. I might not dare to show him that he was dearer than myself; but I could protect and aid him. For, do not think that he had no faults. He had more than a few; he was no hero, no Galahad. He was careless, he was foolishly obstinate, he made missteps; and punishment came. But not further than near. For I stood between! At another time his over-confidence in himself, his unsuspiciousness, almost brought him to ruin, with a shameful scandal! I saved him, stopping the mouths of the dogs that were ready to howl, as well as to tear. I did so at the cost of impairing my own material welfare; worse still, alas! with a question of duty to others. Then, once again, as that year passed, he became involved in a difference, in which certain of my own relatives, along with some near friends of my family were concerned, directors in a financial establishment in our city. I took his part. By that step, I sacrificed the good-will and the longtime intimacy of the others. What did I care? 'The world well lost!' thought I.

"Then, from that calm sky, thickened and fell on me the storm; and for my goodly vineyard I had Desolation!

"One holiday, he happened to visit some friends in the town where was living my betrothed that had been. He heard there, in a club's smoking-room, a tale 'explaining,' positively and circumstantially, why my engagement had been broken. The story was a silly falsehood; but it reflected on my honor. He defended me instantly and warmly. That I heard. But his host, after the sharp passing altercation was over, the evening ended, took him aside to tell him privately that, while friendship for me made it a credit to stand out for me, the tale was 'absolutely true.' He returned to me late that night. He was thoroughly annoyed and excited. He asked me, as I valued my good name and his public defense of it, to give him, then and there, the real, the decisive reason for my withdrawing from my engagement. He would not speak of it to anyone; but he would be glad to know, now, on what ground he rested. I admitted that my betrothed had not wished the withdrawing.

"That was the first thing counter to what he had insisted at the club. He frowned in perplexity. Ah, so the matter was wholly from myself? I assented. Would I further explain, so that at least he could get rid of one certain local statement ... of that other one? An argument rose between us that grew to a sharp altercation. It was our first one, as well as our last. We became thoroughly angry, I the more so, because of what I felt was a manifest injustice to myself. Finally there was no other thing left than for me to meet his appeal—his demand. 'No matter what was the root of the mystery, no matter what any attitude toward me because of it, he must *know*.' Still I hung back. Then, solemnly, he pledged me his word that whatever I might disclose, he 'would forgive it'; it should 'never be mentioned between us two again,' only provided that it bore out his defense of my relation to a faithful and pure woman.

"So—I yielded! Lately, the maddening wish to tell him all at any risks, the pressure of passion and its concealment ... they had never so fiercely attacked me! In a kind of exalted shame, but in absolute sincerity, I told him all! I asked nothing from him, except his sympathy, his belief in whatever was my higher and manlier nature as the world judges any man, and the toleration of our friendship on the lines of its past. Nothing more: not a handclasp, not a look, not a thought more; the mere continued sufferance of my regard. Never again need pass between us so much as a syllable or a glance to remind him of this pitiable confession from me, to betray again the mysterious fire that burned in me underneath our intimacy. He had not suspected anything of it before. It could be forgotten by him from now, onward.

"Did I ask too much? By the God that made mankind, Imre, that made it not only male or female but also as We are, I do not think I did!

"But he, *he* thought otherwise! He heard my confession through with ever more hostile eyes, with an astonished unsympathy, disgust curling his lips. Then, he spoke, slowly, pitilessly: 'I have heard that such creatures as you describe yourself are to be found among mankind. I do not know, nor do I care to know, whether they are a sex by themselves, a justified, because helpless, play of Nature; or even a kind of *logically* essential link, a between-step, as you seem to have persuaded yourself. Let all that be as it may be. I am not a man of science nor keen to such new notions! From this moment, you and I are strangers! I took you for my friend because I believed you to be a ... man. You chose me for your friend because you believed me—stay, I will not say *that*!—because you wished me to be ... a something else, a something more or less like to yourself, whatever you *are*! I loathe you! I loathe you! When I think that I have touched your hand, have sat in the same room with you, have respected you—! Farewell! If I served you as a man should serve such beings as you, this town should know your story tomorrow! Society needs more policemen than it has, to protect itself from such lepers as you! I will keep your hideous secret. Only remember never to speak to me, never to look my way again! Never! From henceforward I have never known you and never will think of you—if I can forget anything so monstrous in this world!'

"So passed he out of my life, Imre. Forever! Over the rupture of our friendship not much was said, nevertheless. For he was called to London a few days after that last interview; and he was obliged to remain in the capital for months. Meantime I had changed my life to meet its new conditions, to avoid gossip. I had removed my lodgings to a suburb. I had taken up a new course in professional work. It needed all my time. Then, a few months later, I started quietly on a long travel-route on the Continent, under excuse of ill-health. I was far from being a stranger to life in at least half a dozen countries of Europe, east or west. But now, now, I knew that it was to be a refuge, an exile!

"For so began those interminable, those mysterious, restless pilgrimages, with no set goals for me; those roamings alone, of which even the wider world, not to say this or that circle of friends, has spoken with curiosity and regret. My unexplained and perpetual exile from all that earlier meant home, sphere, career, life! My wandering and wandering, ever striving to forget, ever struggling to be beguiled intellectually at least; to be diverted from so profound a sense of loss. Or to attain a sort of emotional *assoupissement*,[1] to feel myself identified with new scenes, to achieve a new identity. Little by little, my birth-land, my people, became strange to me. I grew wholly indifferent to them. I turned my back fuller on them, evermore. The social elements, the grades of humanity really mine, the concerns of letters, of arts—from these I divorced myself utterly. They knew me no more. In some of them already I had won a certain repute; but I threw away its culture as one casts aside some plant that does not seem to him worth watering and tending.

"And indeed the zest of these things, their reason for being mine, seemed dead, asphyxiated! For they had grown to be so much a part of what had been the very tissue of intimacy, of life, with *him*! I fled them all. Never now did my foot cross the threshold of a picture-gallery, never did I look twice at the placard of a theater, never would I enter a concert-room or an opera-house, never did I care to read a romance, a poem, or to speak with any living creature of aesthetics that had once so appealed to me! Above all did my aversion to music (for so many years a peculiar interest for me) become now a dull hatred, a detestation, a contempt, a horror, super-neurotic, quintessentially sexual, perniciously homosexual art—mystery—that music is! For me, no more symphonies, no more sonatas, no more songs! No more exultations, elegies, questions to Fate of any orchestra! Nevermore!

"And yet, involuntarily, subconsciously, I was always hoping, seeking *something*. Hoping, seeking ... what? Another such man as I? Sometimes I cried out as to *that*, 'God forbid it!' For I dreaded such a chance now; realizing the more what it would most likely *not* offer me. And really, unless a miracle of miracles were to be wrought just for me, unless I should light upon another human creature who in sympathies, idealisms, noble impulses, manliness,

---

[1] Numbness; stupor (French).

and a virile life could fill, and could wish to fill, the desolate soli-
tudes of mine, could confirm all that was deepest fixed in my soul
as the concept of true similisexual masculinity ... oh, far better
meet none! For such a miracle of miracles I should not hope.
Even traversing all the devious ways of life may not bring us face
to face with such a friend. Yet I was hoping—seeking—I say: even
if there was no vigor of expectancy, but rather in my mind the
melancholy lines of the poet:

> And are there found two souls, that each the other
> Wholly shall understand? Long must man search
> In that deep riddle—seek that Other soul
> Until he dies! Seeking, despairing—dies![1]

"Or, how easy to meet such a man, he also 'seeking, despairing' and not to recognize him, anymore than he recognizes us!
The Mask—the eternal social Mask for the homosexual!—worn
before our nearest and dearest, or we are ruined and cast out! I
resolved to be content with tranquillity, pleasant friendships.
Something like a kindly apathy often possessed me.

"And nevertheless, the Type that still so stirred my nature? The
man that is, inevitably, to be *loved*, not merely liked; to be feared
while yet sought; the friend from whom I can expect nothing,
from whom never again will I expect anything, more than calm
regard, his sympathy, his mere leave for my calling him 'barátom'[2]—
my brother-friend? He, by whom I should at least be respected as
an upright fellow-creature from the workshop of God, not from
the hand of the Devil; be taken into companionship because of
what in me is worthily companionable? The fellow-man who will
accept what of good in me is like the rest of men, nor draw away
from me, as from a leper? Have I really ceased to dream of this
grace for me, this vision—as years have passed?

"Never, alas! I have been haunted by it, however suppressed in
my heart. And something like its embodiment has crossed my
way, really nearly granted me again, more than once. There was a

---

[1] August von Platen, "Ode VIII (Lebensstimmung)" ["Morale of Life"].
[2] Friend (Hungarian).

young English officer, with whom I was thrown for many weeks, in a remote Northern city. We became friends; and the confidence between us was so great that I trusted him with the knowledge of what I am. And therewith had I in turn, a confession from him of a like misfortune, the story of his passion for a brother-officer in a foreign service, that made him one of the most wretched men on the face of the world—while everyone in his circle of home-intimates and regimental friends fancied that he had not a trouble in life! There was, too, one summer in Bosnia, a meeting with a young Austrian architect, a fellow of noble beauty and of high, rich nature. There was a Polish friend, a physician, now far off in Galizien. There was an Italian painter in Rome. But such incidents were not full in the key. Hence, they moved me only so far and no farther. Other passings and meetings came. Warm friendship often grew out of them; tranquil, lasting, sustaining friendship!—that soul-bond not over-common with *us*, but, when really welded, so beautiful, so true, so enduring!

"But one thing I had sworn, Imre; and I have kept my word! That so surely as ever again I may find myself even halfway drawn to a man by the inner passion of a Uranian love—not by the mere friendship of a colder psychic complexion—if that man really shows me that he cares for me with respect, with intimate affection, with trust, then he shall know absolutely what manner of man I am! He shall be shown frankly with what deeper than common regard he has become a part of my soul and life! He shall be put to a test, with no shrinkings on my part. Better break apart early than later, if he say that we break! Never again, if unquiet with such a passion, would I attempt to wear to the end the mask, to fight out the lie, the struggle! I must be taken as I am, pardoned for what I am; or neither pardoned nor taken. I have learned my lesson once and well. But the need of my maintaining such painful honesty has come seldom. I have been growing into expecting no more of life, no realizing whatever of the Type that had been my undoing, that must mean always my peace or my deepest unrest, till I met you, Imre! Till I met you!

"Met you! Yes, and a strange matter in my immediately passionate interest in you—another one of the coincidences in our interest for each other—is the racial blood that runs in your

veins. You are a Magyar. You have not now to be told of the
unexplainable, the mysterious affinity between myself and your
race and nation; of my sensitiveness, ever since I was a child, to
the chord which Magyarország and the Magyar sound in my
heart. Years have only added to it, till thy land, thy people, Imre,
are they not almost my land, my people? Now I have met thee.
Thou wert *to be*; somewhat, at least, to be for me! That thou wast
ordained to come into the world that I should love thee, no
matter what thy race, that I believe! But, see! Fate also has willed
that thou shouldst be Magyar, one of the Children of Emesa,[1]
one of the Folk of Arpád!

"I cannot tell thee, Imre—oh, I have no need now to try!—
what *thou* hast become for me. My Search ended when thou and
I met. Never has my dream given me what is this reality of
thyself. I love this world now only because thou art in it. I respect
thee wholly—I respect myself—certain, too, of that coming time,
however far away now, when no man shall ever meet any intelligent civilization's disrespect simply *because* he is similisexual,
Uranian! But—oh, Imre, Imre!—I *love* thee, as can love only the
Uranian, once more helpless, and therewith hopeless! But this
time no longer silent, before the Friendship which is Love, the
Love which is Friendship.

"Speak my sentence. I make no plea. I have kept my pledge to
confess myself tonight, but I would have fulfilled it only a little
later, were I not going away from thee tomorrow. I ask nothing,
except what I asked long ago of that other, of whom I have told
thee. Endure my memory, as thy friend! Friend? That at least! For
I would say farewell, believing that I shall still have the right to
call thee 'friend' even—O God!—when I remember tonight. But
whether that right is to be mine, or not, is for thee to say. Tell me!"

I stopped.

Full darkness was now about us. Stillness had so deepened that
the ceasing of my own low voice made it the more suspenseful.
The sweep of the night-wind rose among the acacias. The birds
of shadow flitted about us. The gloom seemed to have entered
my soul—as Death into Life. Would Imre ever speak?

---

[1]   Traditional folktale character; the ancient mother of the Hungarian tribe.

His voice came at last. Never had I heard it so moved, so melancholy. A profound tenderness was in every syllable.

"If I could—my God! if I only could!—say to thee what I cannot. Perhaps ... some time. Forgive me, but thou breakest my heart! Not because I care less for thee as my friend, no, above all else, not that reason! We stay together, Oswald! We shall always be what we have become to each other. Oh, *we* cannot change, not through all our lives! Not in death, not in anything! Oh, Oswald! that thou couldst think, for an instant, that I—I—would dream of turning away from thee, suffer a break for us two, because thou art made in thy nature as God makes mankind, as each and all, or not as each and all! We are what we are! This terrible life of ours, this existence that men insist on believing is almost *all* to be understood nowadays, probed through and through, decided, but that ever was and will be just mystery, *all*! Friendship between us? Oh, whether we are near or far! Forever! Forever, Oswald! Here, take my hand. As long as I live, and beyond *then*. Yes, by God above us, by God in us! Only, only, for the sake of the bond between us from this night, promise me that thou wilt never speak again of what thou hast told me of thyself—never, unless I break the silence. Nevermore a word of ... of thy ... thy feeling for me. There are other things for us to talk of, my dear brother? Thou wilt promise?"

With his hand in mine, my heart so lightened that I was as a new creature, forgetting even the separation before me, I promised. Gladly, too. For, instead of loss, with this parting, what gain was mine. Imre knew me now as myself! He really knew me: and yet was now rather the more my friend than less, so I could believe, after this tale of mine had been told him. His sympathy, his respect, his confidence, his affection, his continued and deeper share in my strange and lonely life even if lands and seas should divide us two— ah, in those instants of my reaction and relief, it seemed to me that I had everything that my heart had ever sought of him, or would seek. I made the promise too, gladly with all my soul. Why should he or I ever speak of any stranger emotions again?

Abruptly, after another long pressure of my hand, my friend started up.

"Oswald, we must go home!" he exclaimed. "It's nearly nine

o'clock, surely. I have a regimental report to look at before ten, this affair of mine tomorrow."

Nearly the whole of our return-ride we were silent. The tram was full as before with noisy pleasure-trippers. Even after quitting the vehicle, neither of us said more than a few sentences: the beauty of the night, the charm of the old Z. park, and so on. But again Imre kept his arm in mine, all the way we walked. It was, I knew, not accident. It was the slight sign of earnest thoughts, that he did not care to utter in so many words.

We came toward my hotel.

"I shall not say farewell tonight, Oswald," said Imre. "You know how I hate farewells at any time, hate them as much as you. There is more than enough of such a business. Much better to be sensible, to add as few as one can to the list. I will look in on you tomorrow, about ten o'clock. I don't start till past midday."

I assented. I was no longer disturbed by any mortal concerns, not even by the sense of the coming sundering. Distrust, loneliness—the one was past, even if the other were to come!

The hotel porter handed me a telegram, as we halted in the light of the doorway.

"Wait till I read this," I said.

The dispatch ran: "Situation changed. Your coming unnecessary. Await my letter. Am starting for Scotland."

I gave an exclamation of pleasure, and translated the words to Imre.

"What! Then you need not leave Szent-Istvánhely?" he asked quickly, in the tone of heartiest pleasure that a friend could wish to hear. "*Teremtette*! I am as happy as you! What a good thing, too, that we were so sensible as not to allow ourselves to make a dumpish, dismal afternoon of it, over there at the Z. You see, I am right, my dear fellow, I am always right! Philosophy, divine philosophy! Nothing like it! It makes all the world go round."

With which Imre touched his *csákó*,[1] laughed his jolliest laugh, and hurried away to the Commando of the regiment.

I went upstairs, not aware of there being stairs to climb, unless they might be steps to the stars. In fact the stars, it seemed to me,

---

[1] Military hat, similar to Napoleon's (Hungarian).

could not only shine their clearest in Szent-Istvánhely; but, after all, could take clement as well as unfriendly courses, in mortal destiny.

III

FACES—HEARTS—SOULS

> Think'st thou that I could bear to part
> With thee?—and learn to halve my heart?
>
> No more reproach, no more despair!
>
> —Byron

> ... Et deduxit eos in portam voluntatis eorum.[1]
>
> —Psalm CVI, 30

Next morning, before I was dressed, came this note:

"I have just received word that I must take my company out to the camp at once. Please excuse my not coming. It does not make so much difference, now that you are to stay. Will write you from the Camp. Only a few days' absence. I shall think of you. Imre.
P.S. Please write me."

I was amused, as well as pleased, at this characteristic missive.

My day passed rather busily. I had not time to send even a card to Imre; I had no reason to do so. To my surprise, the omission was

---

[1] ...And he brought them unto the haven where they longed to be.

noticed. For, on the following morning I was in receipt of a lively military *Ansichtskarte*[1] with a few words scratched on it; and at evening came the ensuing communication; which, by the bye, was neither begun with the "address of courtesy," as the "Complete Letter-Book" calls it, nor ended with the "salute of ceremony," recommended by the same useful volume; they being both of them details which Imre had particularly told me he omitted with his intimate "friends who were not prigs." He wrote:

"Well, how goes it with you? With me it is dull and fatiguing enough out here. You know how I hate all this business, even if you and Karvaly insist on my trying to like it. I have a great deal to say to you this evening that I really cannot write. Today was hot and it rained hard. Dear Oswald, you do not know how I value your friendship. Yesterday I saw the very largest frog that ever was created. He looked the very image of our big vis-à-vis in the Casino, Hofkapellan Számbor. Why in God's name do you not write? The whole city is full of *tiz-fillérs*[2] picture-postcards! Buy one, charge it to my account, write me on it.—Imre.
P.S. I think of you often, Oswald."

This communication, like its predecessor, was written in a tenth-century kind of hand, with a blunt lead-pencil! I sent its author a few lines, of quite as laconical a tone as he had given me to understand he so much preferred.

The next day, yet another communication from the P. Camp! Three billets in as many days, from a person who "hated to write letters," and "never wrote them when he could get out of it!" Clearly, Imre in camp was not Imre in Szent-Istvánhely!

"Thank you, dear Oswald, for your note. *Azon régi bolondság*[3] about not writing letters. *It depends.* I send this in a spare

---

[1] Picture-postcard (German).
[2] Ten fillers, the smallest unit of Hungarian money, quite worthless; i.e., the cheapest postcards.
[3] Do not think too much of that old nonsense (Hungarian).

moment. But I have nothing whatever to say. Weather here warm and rainy. Oswald, you are a great deal in my thoughts. I hope I am often in yours. I shall not return tomorrow, but I intend to be with you on Sunday. Life is wearisome. But so long as one has a friend, one can get on with much that is part of the burden; or possibly with *all* of it.—Yours ever—
Imre."

I have neglected to mention that the second person of intimate Magyar address, the "thou" and "thee," was used in these epistles of Imre, in my answers, with the same instinctiveness that had brought it to our lips on that evening in the Z. park. I shall not try to translate it systematically, however; anymore than I shall note with system its disused English equivalents in the dialogue that occurs in the remainder of this record. More than once before the evening named, Imre and I had exchanged this familiarity, half in fun. But now it had come to stay. Thenceforth we adhered to it; a kind of serious symbolism as well as intimate sweetness in it.

I looked at that note with attention: first, because it was so opposed in tenor to the Imre von N. "model." Second, because there appeared to have been a stroke under the commonplace words "Yours ever." That stroke had been smirched out, or erased. Was it like Imre to be sentimental, for an instant, in a letter, even in the most ordinary accent? Well, *if* he had given way to it, to try to conceal such a sign of the failing, particularly without re-writing the letter, why, that was characteristic enough! In sending him a newspaper-clipping, along with a word or so, I referred to the unnecessary briskness of our correspondence: "Pray do not trouble yourself, my dear N., to change your habits on my account. Do not write, now or ever, only because a word from you is a pleasure to me. Besides I am not yet on my homeward-journey. Save your postal artillery."

To the foregoing from me, Imre's response was this:

"It is three o'clock in the morning, and everybody in this camp must be sound asleep, except your most humble servant. You know that I sometimes do not sleep well, Lord knows why. So I

sit here, and scrawl this to thee, dear Oswald, all the more willingly because I am *awfully* out of sorts with my self. I have nothing special to write thee; and nevertheless how much I would *now* be glad to *say* to thee, were we together. See, dearest friend, thou hast walked from that other world of thine into my life, and I have taken my place in thine, because for thee and for me there shall be, I believe, a happiness henceforth that not otherwise could come to us. I have known what it is to suffer, just because there has been no man to whom I could speak or write as to thee. Dear friend, we are much to one another, and we shall be more and more. No, I would not write if it were not a pleasure to me to do it. I promise thee so. We had a great regimental athletic contest this afternoon, and I took two prizes. I will try to sleep now, for I must be on my feet very early. Good night, or rather good morning, and remember ...
Thine own
Imre."

This letter gave me many reflections. There was no need for its closing injunction. To tell the truth, Imre von N. was beginning to bewilder me, this Imre of the P. Camp and of the mailbag, so unlike the Imre of our daily conversations and moods when vis-à-vis! There was certainly a curious, a growing psychic difference. The naïveté, the sincerity of the speaking and of the acting Imre was written into his lines spontaneously enough. But there was that odd new touch of an equally spontaneous something, a suppressed emotion that I could not define. My own letters to Imre certainly did not ring to the like key. On the contrary (I may as well mention that it was not of mere accident, but in view of a resolution carefully considered, and held to) the few lines which I sent him during those days were wholly lacking in any such personal utterances as his. If Imre chose to be inconsistent, I would be steadfast.

All such cogitations as to Imre's letters were however soon unnecessary, inasmuch as on the tenth day of his Camp-service, he wrote:

"Expect me tomorrow. I am well. I have *much* to tell thee. After all, a camp is not a bad place for reflections. It is a tiresome, rainy day here. I took the second prize for shooting at long range today.

Imre."

Now, I did not suppose that Imre's pent-up communicativeness was likely to burst out on the topic of the Hungarian local weather, much less with reference to his feats with a rifle, or in lifting heavy weights. I certainly could not fancy just what meditations promoted that remark about the Camp! So far as I knew anything of such localities, camps were not favorable to much consecutive thinking except about the day's work.

★　★　.★　★　★

I did not expect him till the afternoon should close. I was busy with my English letters. It was a warm August noon, and even when coat and waistcoat had been thrown aside, I was oppressed. My high-ceilinged, spacious room was certainly amongst the cooler corners of Szent-Istvánhely; but the typical ardor of any Central-Hungary midsummer is almost Italian. Outside, in the hotel-court, the fountain trickled sleepily. Even the river steamers seemed too torpid to signal loudly. But suddenly there came a most wide-awake sort of knock; and Imre, with an exclamation of delight—Imre, erect, bronzed, flushed, with eyes flashing—with that smile of his which was almost as flashing as his eyes—Imre, more beautiful than ever, came to me, with both hands outstretched.

"At last ... and really!" I exclaimed as he hurried over the wide room, fairly beaming, as with contentment at being once more out of camp-routine. "And back five hours ahead of time!"

"Five hours ahead of time indeed!" he echoed, laughing. "Thou art glad? I know I am!"

"Dear Imre, I am immeasurably happy," I replied.

He leaned forward, and lightly kissed my cheek.

What! He, Imre von N., who so had questioned the warm-hearted greetings of his friend Captain M.! An odd lapse indeed!

"I am in a state of regular shipwreck," he exclaimed, standing up particularly straight again, after a demonstration that so confounded me as to leave me wordless! "I have had no break- fast, no luncheon, nothing to eat since five o'clock. I am tired as a dog, and hungry, *oh, mint egy vén Kárpáti medve!*[1] I stopped to have a bath at the Officers' Baths—you should see the dust between here and the Camp—and to change, and write a note to my father. So, if you don't mind, the sooner I have something to eat and perhaps a nap, why the better. I am done up!"

In a few moments we were at table. Imre manifestly was not too fagged to talk and laugh a great deal, with a truly Homeric exhibition of his appetite. The budget of experiences at the Camp was immediately drawn upon, with much vivacity. But as lunch- eon ended, my guest admitted that the fatigues of the hot morn- ing-march with his troop from P. (during which several sunstrokes had occurred, those too-ordinary incidents of Hungarian army movements in summer) were reacting on him. So I went to the Bank, as usual, for letters; transacted some other business on the way; and left Imre to himself. When I returned to my room an hour or so later, he was stretched out, sound asleep, on the long green sofa. His sword and his close-fitting fatigue-blouse were thrown on a chair. The collarless, unstarched shirt (that is so much an improvement on our civilian garment) was unbuttoned at the throat; the sleeves rolled up to his shoulders, in unconscious emphasizing of the deepened suntan of his fine skin. The long brown eyelashes lying motionless against his cheek, his physical abandonment, his deep, regular, soundless breathing—all beto- kened how the day had spent itself on his young strength. Once left alone, he had fallen asleep where he had sat down.

A great and profoundly human poet, in one famous scene, speaks of those emotions that come to us when we are watching, in his sleep, a human being that we love. Such moments are indeed likely to be subduing to many a sensitive man and woman. They bring before our eyes the effect of a living statue; of a beauty self-uncon- scious, almost abstract, if the being that we love be beautiful. Strongly, suddenly, comes also the hint at helplessness; the suggestion of

---

[1]   as an old Carpathian bear (Hungarian).

protection from *us*, however less robust. Or the idea of the momentary but actual absence of that other soul from out of the body before us, a vanishing of that spirit to whom we ourselves cling. We feel a subconscious sense of the inevitable separation forever, when there shall occur the Silence of "the Breaker of Bonds, the Sunderer of Companionships, the Destroyer of Fellowships, the Divider of Hearts," as (like a knell of everything earthly and intimate!) the old Arabian phrases lament the merciless divorce of death!

I stood and watched Imre a moment, these things in my mind. Then, moving softly about the room, lest he should be aroused, I began changing my clothes for the afternoon. But more than once the spell of my sleeping guest drew me to his side. At last, scarce half dressed, I sat down before him, to continue to look at him. Yes, his face had the same expression now, as he slumbered there, that I had often remarked in his most silent moments of waking. There were not only the calm regular beauty, the manly uprightness, his winning naïveté of character written all through such outward charm for me; but along with that came again the appealing hint of an inward sadness; the shadow of some enrooted, hidden sorrow that would not pass, however proudly concealed.

"God bless thee, Imre!" my heart exclaimed in benediction. "God bless thee, and make thee happy, happier than I! Thou hast given me thy friendship. I shall never ask of God, of Fate, anything more—save that the gift endure till we two endure not!"

The wish was like an echo from the Z. park. Or, rather, it was an echo from a time far earlier in my life. Once again, with a mystic certainty, I realized that *those* days of Solitude were now no longer of any special tyranny upon my moods. That was at an end for me, verily! O, my God! *That* was at an end!

Imre opened his eyes.

"Great Arpád!" he exclaimed, smiling sleepily, "is it so late? You are dressing for the evening!"

"It is five o'clock," I answered. "But what difference does that make? Don't budge. Go to sleep again, if you choose. You need not think of getting supper at home. We will go to the F. Restaurant."

"So be it. And perhaps I shall ask you to keep me till morning, my dear fellow! I am no longer sleepy, but somehow or other I do feel most frightfully knocked-out! Those country roads are misery, and I am a poor sleeper often—that it is, in a way. I get to worrying, to wondering over all sorts of things that there's no good in studying about. In daylight or dark."

"You never told me till lately, in one of your letters, that you were so much of an insomniac, Imre. Is it new?"

"Not in the least new. I have not wished to say anything about it to anybody. What's the use? Oh, there are many things that I haven't had time to tell you—things I have not spoken about with anyone—just as is the case with most men of sense in this world, eh? But do you know," he went on, sitting up and continuing with a manner more and more reposeful, thoughtful, strikingly unlike his ordinary nervous self, "but do you know that I have come back from the Camp to you, my dear Oswald, certain that I shall never be so restless and troubled a creature again. Thanks to you. For you see, so much that I have shut into myself I know now that I can trust to your heart. But give me a little time. To have a friend to trust myself to *wholly*—that is new to me."

I was deeply touched. I felt certain again that a change of some sort—mysterious, profound—had come over Imre, during those few days at the Camp. Something had happened. I recognized the mood of his letters. But what had evolved or disclosed it?

"Yes, my dear von N.," I returned, "your letters have said that, in a way, to me. How shall I thank you for your confidence, as well as for your affection?"

"Ah, my letters! Bother my letters! They said nothing much! You know I cannot write letters at all. What is more, you have been believing that I wrote you as ... as a sort of duty. That whatever I said—or a lot of it—well, there were things which you fancied were not really I. I understood why you could think it."

"I never said that, Imre," I replied, sitting down beside him on the sofa.

"Not in so many words. But my guilty conscience prompted me. I mean that word 'conscience,' Oswald. For—I have not been fair to you, not honest. The only excuse is that I have not been honest with myself. You have thought me cold, reserved, abrupt—a fantastic sort of friend to you. One who valued you, and yet could hardly speak out his esteem—a careless fellow into whose life you have taken only surface-root. That isn't all. You have believed that I ... that I never could comprehend things, feelings, which you have lived through to the full, have suffered from with every beat of your heart. But you are mistaken."

"I have no complaint against you, dear Imre." No, no! God knows that!

"No? But I have much against myself. That evening in the Z. park—you remember, when you were telling me—"

I interrupted him sharply: "Imre!"

He continued. "That evening in the Z. park when you were telling me—"

"Imre, Imre! You forget our promise!"

"No, I do *not* forget! It was a one-sided bargain; *I* am free to break it for a moment, *nem igaz*?[1] Well then, I break it! There! Dear friend, if you have ever doubted that I have a heart, that I would trust you utterly, that I would have you know me as I am, then from this afternoon forget to doubt! I have hid myself from you, because I have been too proud to confess myself *not enough for myself*! I have sworn a thousand times that I could and would bear anything alone—alone—yes, till I should die. Oswald—for God's sake—for our friendship's sake—do not care less for me because I am weary of struggling on thus alone! I shall not try to play hero, even to myself, not any longer. Oswald, listen; you told me your story. Well, I have a story to tell you. Then you will understand. Wait, wait one moment! I must think how, where, to begin. My story is short compared with yours, and not so bitter; yet it is no pleasant one."

As he uttered the last few words, seated there beside me, whatever sympathy I could ever feel for any human creature went out to him, unspeakably. For now, now, the trouble flashed into my mind! Of course it was to be the old, sad tale. He loved, loved unhappily—a woman!

The singer! The singer of Prague! That wife of his friend Karvaly. The woman whose fair and magnetic personality had wrought unwittingly or wittingly her inevitable spell upon him! One of those potent and hopeless passions, in which love, and probably loyalty to Karvaly, burdened this upright spirit with an irremediable misfortune!

---

[1] Is it not true? (Hungarian).

"Well," I said very gently, "tell me all that you can, if there be one touch of comfort and relief for you in speaking, Imre. I am wholly yours, you know, for every word."

Instead of answering me at once, as he sat there so close beside me, supporting his bowed head on one hand, and with his free arm across my shoulder, he let the arm fall more heavily about me. Turning his troubled eyes once—so appealingly, so briefly!—on mine, he laid his face upon my breast. And then, I heard him murmur, as if not to me only, but also to himself:

"O, thou dear friend! Who bringest me, as none have brought it before thee ... *rest!*"

Rest? Not rest for me! A few seconds of that pathetic, trusting nearness which another man could have sustained so calmly, a few instants of that unspeakable joy in realizing how much more I was in his life than I had dared to conceive possible, just those few throbs upon my heart of that weary spirit of my friend—and then the Sex-Demon brought his storm upon my traitorous nature, in fire and lava! I struggled in shame and despair to keep down the hateful physical passion which was making nothing of all my psychic loyalty, asserting itself against my angriest will. In vain! The defeat must come; and, worse, it must be understood by Imre. I started up. I thrust Imre from me, falling away from him, escaping from his side, knowing that just in his surprise at my abruptness, I must meet his detection of my miserable weakness. No words can express my self-disgust. Once on my feet, I staggered to the opposite side of the round table between us. I dropped into a chair. I could not raise my eyes to Imre. I could not speak. Everything was vanishing about me. Of only one thing could I be certain; that now all was over between us! ·Oh, this cursed outbreak and revelation of my sensual weakness! this inevitable physical appeal of Imre to me! This damned and inextricable ingredient in the chemistry of what ought to be wholly a spiritual drawing toward him, but which meant that I desired my friend for his gracious, virile beauty—as well as loved him for his fair soul! Oh, the shame of it all, the uselessness of my newest resolve to be more as the normal man, not utterly the Uranian! Oh, the folly of my oaths to love Imre *without* that thrill of the plain sexual Desire, that would be a sickening horror to him! All was over! He knew me for what I was. He would have none of me. The flight of my dreams, departing in a torn cloud together, would come with the first sound of his voice!

But Imre did not speak. I looked up. He had not stirred. His hand was still lying on the table, with its open palm to me! And oh, there was that in his face, in the look so calmly bent upon me that was—good God above us!—so kind!

"Forgive me," I said. "Forgive me! Perhaps you can do that. Only that. You see, you know now. I have tried to change myself, to care for you only with my soul. But I cannot change. I will go from you. I will go to the other end of the world. Only do not believe that what I feel for you is wholly base, that were you not outwardly what you are, had I less of my terrible sensitiveness to your mere beauty, Imre, I would care less for your friendship. God knows that I love you and respect you as a man loves and respects his friend. Yes, yes, a thousand times! But ... but nevertheless—oh, what shall I say. You could never understand! So no use! Only I beg you not to despise me too deeply for my weakness; and when you remember me, pardon me for the sake of the friendship bound up in the love, even if you shudder at the love which curses the friendship."

Imre smiled. There was both bitterness as well as sweetness in his face now. But the bitterness was not for me. His voice broke the short silence in so intense a sympathy, in a note of such perfect accord, such unchanged regard, that I could scarcely master my eyes in hearing him. He clasped my hand.

"Dear Oswald! Brother indeed of my soul and body! Why dost thou ask me to forgive thee? Why should *I* 'forgive'? For—oh, Oswald, Oswald!—I am just as art thou. I am just as art thou!"

"Thou! Just as *I* am? I do not understand!"

"But that will be very soon, Oswald. I tell thee again that *I am as thou art*, wholly, wholly! Canst thou really not grasp the truth, dear friend? Oh, I wish with all my heart that I had not so long held back my secret from thee! It is I who must ask forgiveness. But at least I can tell thee today that I came back to thee to give thee confidence for confidence, heart for heart, Oswald, before this day should end! With no loss of respect—no weakening of our friendship. No, no! Instead of that, only with more; with ... with *all*!"

"Imre. Imre! I do not understand. I do not dare ... to understand."

"Look into thyself, Oswald! It is all *there*. I am a Uranian, as thou art. From my birth I have been one. Wholly, wholly homosexual, Oswald! The same fire, the same, that smoulders or flashes in thee! It was put into *my* soul and body too, along with whatever else is in them that could make me wish to win the sympathy of *just* such a friend as thee, or make thee wish to seek mine. My youth was like thine; and to become older, to grow up to be a man in years, a man in every sinew and limb of my body, there was no changing of my nature in *that*. There were only the bewilderments, concealments, tortures that come to us. There is nothing, nothing, that any man can teach me of what is one's life with it all. How well I know it! That inborn mysterious, frightful sensitiveness to whatever is the *man*—that eternal vague yearning and seeking for the unity that can never come save by a love that is held to be a crime and a shame! The instinct that makes us cold toward the woman, even to hating her, when one thinks of her as a sex. And the mask, the eternal mask! to be worn before our fellowmen for fear that they should spit in our faces in their loathing of us! Oh God, I have known it all—I have understood it all!"

It was indeed my turn to be silent now. I found myself yet looking at him in incredulity—wordless.

"But that is not the whole of my likeness to thee, Oswald. For I have endured that cruelest of torments for us—which fell also to thy lot. I believe it to be over now, or soon wholly so to be. But the remembrance of it will not soon pass, even with thy affection to heal my heart. For I too have loved a man, loved him—hiding my passion from him under the coldness of a common friendship. I too have lived side by side, day by day, with him; in terror, lest he should see *what* he was to me, and so drive me from him. Ah, I have been unhappier, too, than thou, Oswald. For I must needs to watch his heart, as something not merely impossible for me to possess (I would have cast away my soul to possess it!)—but given over to a woman, laid at her feet, with daily less and less of thought for what was his life with me. Oh, Oswald! The wretchedness of it is over now, God be thanked! and not a little so because I have found thee, and thou hast found me. But only to think of it again—"

He paused as if the memory were indeed wormwood. I understood now! And oh, what mattered it that I could not yet understand or excuse the part that he had played before me for so long, his secrecy almost inexplicable if he had had so much as a guess at my story, my feelings for him! As in a dream, believing, disbelieving, fearing, rejoicing, trembling, rapt, I began to understand Fate!

Yet, mastering my own exultant heart, I wished in those moments to think only of him. I asked gently:

"You mean your friend Karvaly?"

"Even so. Karvaly."

"O, my poor, poor Imre! My brother indeed! Tell me all. Begin at the beginning."

* * * * *

I shall not detail all of Imre's tale. There was little in it for the matter of that, which could be set forth here as outwardly dramatic. Whoever has been able, by nature or accident, to know, in a fairly intimate degree, the workings of the similisexual and uranistic heart; whoever has marveled at them, either in sympathy or antipathy, even if merely turning over the pages of psychiatric treatises dealing with them—he would find nothing specially unfamiliar in such biography. I will mention here, as one of the least of the sudden discoveries of that afternoon, the fact that Imre had some knowledge of such literature, whether to his comfort or greater melancholy, according to his author. Also he had formally consulted one eminent Viennese specialist[1] who certainly was much wiser, far less positive, and not less calming than my American theorist.

The great Viennese psychiater had not recommended marriage to Imre: recognizing in Imre's case that inborn homosexualism that will not be dissipated by wedlock, but perhaps only intensifies, and so is surer to darken irretrievably the nuptial future of husband and wife, and to visit itself on their children after them. But the Austrian doctor had not a little comforted and strengthened Imre morally; warning him away from despising himself: from thinking himself alone, and a sexual pariah; from over-morbid sufferings; from that bitterness and despair which year by year all over the world can explain, in hundreds

---

[1] Perhaps EPS here thinks of Richard von Krafft-Ebing, the dedicatee of *The Intersexes*, at whose prompting, EPS claims, that work was undertaken.

of cases, the depressed lives, the lonely existences, the careers mysteriously interrupted—broken. What Asmodeus[1] could look into the real causes (so impenetrably veiled!) of sudden and long social exiles; of sundered ties of friendship or family; of divorces that do not disclose their true ground? Longer still would be the chronicle of ruined peace of mind, tranquil lives maddened, fortunes shattered—by some merciless blackmailer who trades on his victim's secret! Darker yet the "mysterious disappearances," the sudden suicides "wholly inexplicable," the strange, fierce crimes that are part of the daily history of hidden uranianism, of the battle between the homosexual man and social canons—or of the battle with just himself! Ah, these dramas of the Venus Urania, played out into death in silent but terribly-troubled natures among all sorts and conditions of men!

C'est Venus, tout entière à sa proie attachée....[2]

Imre's youth had been, indeed, one long and lamentable obsession of precocious, inborn homosexuality. Imre (just as in many instances) had never been a weakling, an effeminate lad, nor cared for the society of the girls about him on the playground or in the house. On the contrary, his sexual and social indifference or aversion to them had been always thoroughly consistent with the virile emotions of that sort. But there had been the boy-friendships that were passions; the sense of his being out of key with his little world in them; the deepening certitude that there was a mystery in himself that "nobody would understand"; some element rooted in him that was mocked by the whole boy-world, by the whole man-world. A part of himself to be crushed out, if it could be crushed, because base and vile. Or that, at any rate, was to be forever hid ... hid ... hid ... for his life's sake hid! So Imre had early put on the Mask; the Mask that millions never lay by till death—and many not even then![3]

---

[1]   An evil spirit, in Jewish demonology.

[2]   "It is Venus, so entirely battened on her prey ..." From Racine's *Phèdre* (I.3. 306). See also *Intersexes*, 572.

[3]   The mask of concealment as a trope has a literary popularity all its own. See "We Wear the Mask" (1896) by Paul Laurence Dunbar; "The Minister's Black Veil" (1836) by Nathaniel Hawthorne; *The Great God Brown* (1926) by Eugene O'Neill; *Confessions of a Mask* (1949) by Yukio Mishima; as well as others.

And in Imre's case there had come no self-justification till late in his sorrowful young manhood. Not until quite newly, when he had discovered how the uranistic nature is regarded by men who are wiser and wider-minded than our forefathers were, had Imre accepted himself as an excusable bit of creation.

Fortunately, Imre had not been born and brought up in an Anglo-Saxon civilization; where is still met, at every side, so dense a blending of popular ignorances; of century-old and century-blind religious and ethical misconceptions, of unscientific professional conservatism in psychiatric circles, and of juristic barbarisms; all, of course, accompanied with the full measure of British or Yankee social hypocrisy toward the daily actualities of homosexualism. By comparison, indeed, any other lands and races—even those yet hesitant in their social toleration or legal protection of the Uranian—seem educative and kindly; not to distinguish peoples whose attitude is distinctively one of national common-sense and humanity. But in this sort of knowledge, as in many another, the world is feeling its way forward (should one say *back*?) to intelligence, to justice and to sympathy, so spirally, so unwillingly! It is not yet in the common air.

Twice Imre had been on the point of suicide. And though there had been experiences in the Military Academy, and certain much later ones to teach him that he was not unique in Austria-Hungary, in Europe, or the world, still unluckily, Imre had got from them (as is too often the hap of the Uranian) chiefly the sense of how widely despised, mocked, and loathed is the Uranian Race. Also how sordid and debasing are the average associations of the homosexual kind, how likely to be wanting in idealism, in the exclusiveness, in those pure and manly influences which ought to be bound up in them and to radiate from them! He had grown to have a horror of similisexual types, of all contacts with them. And yet, until lately, they could not be torn entirely out of his life. Most Uranists know why!

Still, they had been so expelled, finally. The turning-point had come with Karvaly. It meant the story of the development of a swift, admiring friendship from the younger soldier toward the older. But alas! this had gradually become a fierce, despairing homosexual love. This, at its height, had been as destructive of Imre's peace as it was hopeless. Of course, it was impossible of confession to its object. Karvaly was no narrow intellect; his affection for Imre was warm. But he would never have understood, not even as some sort of a diseased illusion, this sentiment in Imre. Much less would he have tolerated it for an instant. The inevitable rupture of their whole intimacy would have come with Imre's betrayal of his passion. So he had done wisely to hide every throb from Karvaly. How sharply Karvaly had on one occasion expressed himself on masculine homosexuality, Imre cited to me, with other remembrances. At the time of the vague scandal about the ex-officer Clement, whom Imre and I had met, Imre had asked Karvaly, with a fine carelessness, "whether he believed that there was any scientific excuse for such a sentiment"? Karvaly answered, with the true conviction of the dionistic temperament that has never so much as paused to think of the matter as a question in psychology, "If I found that you cared for another man that way, youngster, I should give you my best revolver, and tell you to put a bullet through your brains within an hour! Why, if I found that you thought of me so, I should brand you in the Officers Casino tonight, and shoot you myself at ten paces tomorrow morning. Men are not to live when they turn beasts. Oh, damn your doctors and scientists! A man's a man, and a woman's a woman! You can't mix up their emotions like *that*."

The dread of Karvaly's detection, the struggle with himself to subdue passion, not merely to hide it, and along with these nerve-wearing solicitudes, the sense of what the suspicion of the rest of the world about him would inevitably bring on his head, had put Imre, little by little, into a sort of panic. He maintained an exaggerated attitude of safety, that had wrought on him unluckily, in many a valuable social relation. He wore his mask each and every instant; resolving to make it his natural face before himself! Having discovered through intimacy with Karvaly how a warm friendship on the part of the homosexual temperament, over and over takes to itself the complexion of homosexual love—the one emotion constantly likely to rise in the other and to blend itself inextricably into its alchemy—Imre had simply sworn to make no intimate friendship again! This, without showing himself in the least unfriendly; indeed, with his being more hail-fellow-well-met with his comrades than otherwise.

But there Imre stopped! He bound his warm heart in a chain, he vowed indifference to the whole world, he assisted no advances of warm, particular regard from any comrade. He became that friend of everybody in general who is the friend of nobody in particular! He lived in a state of perpetual defense in his regiment, and in whatever else was social to him in Szent-Istvánhely. So surely as he admired another man—would gladly have won his generous and virile affection—Imre turned away from that man! He covered this morbid state of self-inclusion, this solitary life (such it was, apart from the relatively short intimacy with Karvaly) with laughter and a most artistic semblance of brusqueness; of manly preoccupation with private affairs. Above all, with the skillful cultivation of his repute as a Lothario who was nothing if not sentimental and absorbed in—woman! This is possibly the most common device, as it is the securest, on the part of a Uranian. Circumstances favored Imre in it; and he gave it its full show of honorable mystery. The cruel irony of it was often almost humorous to Imre.

"They have given me the credit of being the most confirmed rake in high life. Think of that! I, and in high life to be found in town. The less they could trace as ground for it, why, so much the stronger rumors! You know how that sort of a label sticks fast to one, once pinned on. Especially if a man *is* really a gentleman and holds his tongue, ever and always, about his intimacies with women. Why, Oswald, I have never felt that I could endure to be alone five minutes with any woman—I mean in *that* way! Not even with a woman most dear to me, as many, many women are. Not even with a wife that loved me. I have never had any intimacies—not one—of *that* sort, merely semblances of such! Queer experiences I've tumbled into with *them*, too! You know."

Oh, yes ... I knew!

Part of Imre's exaggerated, artificial bearing toward the outer world was the nervous shrinking from commonplace social demonstrativeness on the part of his friends. To that mannerism I have already referred. It had become a really important accent, I do not doubt, in Imre's acting-out of a friendly, cheerful, yet keep-your-distance sort of personality. But there was more than that in it. It was a detail in the effort toward his self-transformation; a minor article in his compact with himself never to give up the struggle to "cure" himself. He was convinced that this was the most impossible of achievements. But he kept on fighting for it. And since one degree of sentiment led so treacherously to another, why, away with all!

"But Imre, I do not yet see why you have not trusted me sooner. There have been at least two moments in our friendship when you could have done so; and one of them was when you *should*!"

"Yes, you are right. I have been unkind. But then, I have been as unkind to myself. The two times you speak of, Oswald—you mean, for one of them, that night that we met Clement, and spoke about such matters for a moment while we were crossing the Lánchíd? And the other chance was after you had told me your own story, over there in the Z. park?"

"Yes. Of course, the fault is partly mine—once. I mean that time on the Bridge. I fenced you off from me—I misled you—didn't help you—I didn't help myself. But even so, you kept me at sword's length, Imre! You wore your mask so closely—gave me no inch of ground to come nearer to you, to understand you, to expect anything except scorn—our parting! Oh, Imre! I have been blind, yes! But you have been dumb."

"You wonder and you blame me," he replied, after busying himself a few seconds with his own perplexing thoughts. "Again, I say 'Forgive me.' But you must remember that we played at cross-purposes too much (as I now look back on what we said that first time) for me to trust myself to you. I misunderstood you. I was stupid—nervous. It seemed to me certain, at first, that you had me in your mind—that I was the friend you spoke of—laughed at, in a way. But after I saw that I was mistaken? Oh, well, it appeared to me that, after all, you must be one of the Despisers. Gentler-hearted than the most; broader minded, in a way; but one who, quite likely, thought and felt as the rest of the world. I was afraid to go a word farther! I was afraid to lose you. I shivered afterward, when I remembered that I had spoken then of what I did. Especially about that man who cared for me once upon a time in that way. And so suddenly to meet Clement! I didn't know he was in Szent-Istvánhely; the meeting took me by surprise. I heard next morning that his mother had been very ill."

"But afterwards, Imre? You surely had no fear of what you call 'losing' me then? How could you possibly meet my story—in that hour of such bitter confidence from me!—as you did? Could you come no further toward me? When you were certain that to find you my Brother in the Solitude would make you the nearer-beloved and dearer-prized!"

"That's harder for me to answer. For one reason, it was part of that long battle with myself. It was something against the policy of my whole life as I had sworn to live it for all the rest of it, before myself or the world. I had broken that pledge already in our friendship, such as even then it was! Broken it suddenly, completely, before realizing what I did. The feeling that I was weak, that I cared for you, that I was glad that you sought my friendship ... ah, the very sense of nearness and companionship in that. But I fought with all *that*, I tell you! Pride, Oswald, a fool's pride! My determination to go on alone, alone, to make myself sufficient for myself, to make my punishment my tyrant, to be martyred under it! Can you not understand something of that? You broke down my pride that night, dear Oswald. Oh, *then* I knew that I had found the one friend in the world, out of a million-million men not for me! And nevertheless I hung back! The thought of your going from me had been like a knife-stroke in my heart all the evening long. But *yet* I could not speak out.[1] All the while I understood how our parting was a pain to you— I could have echoed every thought that was in your soul about it! But I would not let myself speak one syllable to you that could show you that I cared! No! *Then* I would have let you go away in ignorance of everything that was most myself, rather than have opened that life-secret, or my heart, as we sat there. Oh, it was as if I was under a spell, a cursed enchantment that would mean a new unhappiness, a deeper silence for the rest of my life! But the wretched charm was perfect. Good God, what a night I passed! The mood and the moment had been so fit, yet both thrown away! My heart so shaken, my tongue so paralyzed! But before morning came, Oswald, that fool's hesitation was over. I was clear and resolved, the devil of arrogance had left me. I was amazed at

---

[1] This inability to speak when faced with an overwhelming truth finds a curious and not inappropriate parallel in Roderick Usher's similar declaration at the end of Edgar Allan Poe's "The Fall of the House of Usher" (1839) when he realizes he has buried his sister alive: "I dared not speak!"

myself. You would have heard everything from me that day. But the call to the Camp came. I had not a moment. I could not write what I wished. There was nothing to do but to wait."

"The waiting has done no harm, Imre."

"And there is another reason, Oswald, why I found it hard to be frank with you. At least, I think so. It is—what shall I call it?— the psychic trace of the woman in me. Yes, after all, the woman! The counter-impulse, the struggle of the weakness that is womanishness itself, when one has to face any sharp decision ... to throw one's whole being into the scale! Oh, I know it, I have found it in me before now! I am not as you, the Uranian who is too much man! I am more feminine in impulse—of weaker stuff. I feel it with shame. You know how the woman says 'no' when she means 'yes' with all her soul! How she draws back from the arms of the man that she loves when she dreams every night of throwing herself into them? How she finds herself doing, over and over, just that which is *against* her thought, her will, her duty! I tell you, there is something of *that* in me, Oswald! I must make it less. You must help me. It must be one of the good works of your friendship, of your love, for me. Oh, Oswald, Oswald! You are not only to console me for all that I have suffered, for anything in my past that has gone wrong. For, you are to help me to make myself over, indeed, in all that *is* possible, whatever cannot be so."

"We must help each other, Imre. But do not speak so of woman, my brother! Sexually, we may not value her. We may not need her, as do those Others. But think of the joy that they find in her to which we are cold; the ideals from which we are shut out! Think of your mother, Imre; as I think of mine! Think of the queens and peasants who have been the light and the glory of races and peoples. Think of the gentle, noble sisters and wives, the serene, patient rulers of myriad homes. Think of the watching nurses in the hospitals, of the spirits of mercy who walk the streets of plague and foulness! Think of the nun on her knees for the world!"

The shadows in the room were almost at their deepest. We were still sitting face to face, almost without having stirred since that moment when I had quitted his side so suddenly—to divine how much closer I was to be drawn to him henceforth. Life! Life and Death! Life—Love—Death! The sense of eternal kinship in their mystery: somehow it haunted one then, as it is likely to do when not our unhappiness but a kind of over-joy swiftly oppresses us; making us to feel that in some other sphere, and if less grossly "set within this muddy vesture of decay," we might understand all three, might find all three to be one! Life—Love—Death!

"Oswald, you will never go away from me!"

"Imre, I will never go away from thee. Thy people shall be mine.[1] Thy King shall be mine. Thy country shall be mine, thy city mine! My feet are fixed! We belong together. We have found what we had despaired of finding, 'the friendship which is love, the love which is friendship.' Those who cannot give it—accept it—let them live without it. It can be 'well, and very well' with them. Go they their ways without it! But for Us, who for our happiness or unhappiness cannot think life worth living if lacking it—for Us, through the world's ages born to seek it in pain or joy, it is the highest, holiest Good in the world. And for one of us to turn his back upon it, were to find he would better never have been born!"

★ ★ ★ ★ ★

It was eleven o'clock. Imre and I had supped and taken a stroll in the yellow moonlight, along the quais, overlooking the shimmering Duna; and on through the little Erzsébet-tér where we had met, a few weeks ago—it seemed so long ago! I had heard more of Imre's life and individuality as a boy, full of the fine and unhappy emotions of the uranistic youth. We had laughed over his stock of experiences in the Camp. We had talked of things grave and gay.

Then we had sauntered back. It was chance; but lo! we were on the Lánchíd, once more! The Duna rippled and swirled below. The black barges slumbered against the stone *rakpartok*.[2] The glittering belts of the city-lights flashed in long perspectives along the wide river's sweeping course and twinkled from square to square, from terrace to terrace. Across from us, at a garden-café, a *cigány* orchestra was pulsating; crying out, weeping, asking,

---

[1] Cf. The Book of Ruth.
[2] Riverbanks (Hungarian).

refusing, wooing, mocking, inebriating, despairing, triumphant! All the warm Magyar night about us was dominated by those melting chromatics, poignant cadences—those harmonies eternally oriental, minor-keyed, insidious, nerve-thrilling. The arabesques of the violins, the vehement rhythms of the clangorous *czimbalom*! Ah, this time on the Lánchíd, neither for Imre nor me was it the somber Bakony song, "*O jaj! az álom nelkül,*" but instead the free, impassioned leap and acclaim, "*Huszár legény vagyok!—Huszár legény vagyok!*"[1]

We were back in the quiet room, lighted now only by the moon. Far up, on the distant Pálota heights, the clear bell of Szent-Mátyás[2] struck the three-quarters. The slow notes filled the still night like a benediction, keyed to that haunting, divine, prophetic triad, Life—Love—Death! Benediction threefold and supreme to the world!

"Oh, my brother! Oh, my friend!" exclaimed Imre softly, putting his arm about me and holding me to his heart. "Listen to me. Perhaps ... perhaps even yet, canst thou err in one, only one thought. I would have thee sure that when I am with thee here, now, I *miss* nothing and no one—I seek nothing and no one! My quest, like thine, is over! I wish no one save thee, dear Oswald, no one else, even as I feel thou wishest none save me, henceforth. I would have thee believe that I am glad *just* as thou art glad. Alike have we two been sad because of our lonely hearts, our long restlessness of soul and body, our vain dreams, our worship of this or that hope—vision—which has been kept far from us—it may be, overvalued by us! We have suffered so much, thou and I, because of what never could be! We shall be all the happier now for what is real for us. I love thee, as thou lovest me. I have found, as thou hast found, 'the friendship which is love, the love which is friendship.' Come then, O friend! O brother, to our rest! Thy heart on mine, thy soul with mine! For us two it surely is ... Rest!"

---

[1] "I am a Hussar!—I am a Hussar!" Hussars, those dashing, moustached military horsemen, had become something of cult figures in Hungary and elsewhere.

[2] The beautiful spires of Saint Matthew Church dominate the hills of Buda, along with the noble lines of the Palace (Pálota).

Truth? What is truth? Two human hearts
Wounded by men, by fortune tried,
Outwearied with their lonely parts,
Vow to beat henceforth side by side.

—Matthew Arnold

THE END

Introduction to the Appendices

The goal of the documentary material that follows is trifold. First, to provide a sense of the cultural milieu from which *Imre* appeared and give a sense of the medical establishment's dominance over the formation of the turn-of-the-century homosexual. Second, to illuminate at least one type of life a contemporary homosexual man who was cautious yet self-assured might have led; it also brings more insight, knowledge, and clarity to an author whose life has remained largely unknown. Third and finally, to suggest the necessarily strong and overbearing relationship between life and fiction as gay authors like Stevenson at this time were compelled to see it.

Appendix A provides all three at a glance. Paul Elmer More (1864–1937) had served as literary editor for *The Independent* (1901–1903), the periodical where Edward Prime-Stevenson had been music critic until 1900. From 1903 until 1909 More served in the same capacity for the *New York Evening Post*, where his traditional critical standards and classical restraint appealed to Stevenson. In writing him to praise More's latest volume of essays, Stevenson surprisingly (More not being known as homosexual himself) takes the opportunity to reveal in some detail the "other" type of writing he was doing once he had left the New York publishing world and settled in Europe after the turn of the century. In discussing the origins of *Imre* and *The Intersexes*, he makes clear the trouble that an author might then expect in trying to get gay-inflected works into print, and the necessity of his using the pseudonym of Xavier Mayne.

Appendix B shows several examples of the type of case histories that served to define the homosexual by the late nineteenth century. Though intended solely for doctors and psychiatrists (its "lurid" sections were written in Latin), such works as R. von Kraff-Ebing's pioneering *Psychopathia Sexualis* (1886) from the outset found a far wider readership and significantly influenced how contemporary homosexual people defined themselves. Though Krafft-Ebing regarded homosexuality as a pathological and degenerate condition, we know that it was at his suggestion that Stevenson's own enormous defense of homosexuality, *The Intersexes* (1908), was undertaken, contemporaneous with *Imre*, which in many ways reflects—and disputes—that work.

In the early 1890s heterosexual Havelock Ellis and homosexual John Addington Symonds agreed to co-author what was to become the first book of Ellis's projected multi-volume examination of sexuality. When Symonds died in 1893, Ellis continued alone, and published *Sexual Inversion* in 1897. It is clear that Stevenson knew that work well; indeed, it would be worthwhile to study that volume alongside *Imre* in its entirety. Appendix C contains two short excerpts that tell us exactly how dominant the Krafft-Ebing case-study model had become in just a few short years (despite its negativity, homosexuals were clearly using it as a way to define and express themselves), as well as the interesting connection that had already been "observed" between homosexuals and art and music—something that music-critic Stevenson corroborates emphatically in his writing.

Appendix D provides two case studies that Stevenson included in *The Intersexes*. They not only demonstrate a more sensitive and sympathetic rendering of the harsher psychiatric models, but interestingly suggest where Stevenson got the idea for *Imre*'s opening scene.

Appendix E shows us a "literary" rather than a scientific case study. Much of Stevenson's gay writing, it can be shown, seems based upon his own experience and people that he knew. Here in his own words we witness an incident regarding the person who was perhaps the great love of his life, Harry Harkness Flagler. Flagler was the rich scion of the wealthy oil and railroad tycoon Henry Flagler. A handsome and prepossessing man who loved music far more than business (much to his father's chagrin), young Flagler met Stevenson during his college years at Columbia and the two found an instant rapport. After a long and close "friendship," Flagler cooled in his affections for Stevenson and went on to marry, much to Stevenson's sorrow. The letters in Appendix E, published here for the first time, were written to Carl Woodberry, who had been Flagler's literature professor at Columbia and who eventually acted as a confidant for the troubled Stevenson. The correspondence shows how circumspect a homosexual man in that period had to be in expressing his sexuality, and how grateful Stevenson is to find an outlet for his feelings. Sometime after his breakup with Flagler, Stevenson sublimated the experience into a powerful and typically tragic short story, "Once—But Not Twice," here reprinted for the first time. Not only may we here observe a further projection of his feelings in the affair, but more significantly we enjoy a firsthand view how Stevenson transmogrifies a personal situation into fiction. The imagination of the homosexual author at this point in time seemed very much grounded in his own experience.

The Appendix F gives us a rare glimpse of Edward Prime-Stevenson as he was seen by a young man who was to become an acolyte of sorts, Leonard Bacon (1887–1954). Only 20 when he met Stevenson at a hotel in Switzerland, Bacon was at once entranced and enamored of him. Though they saw each other rarely, a lively correspondence ensued, until Bacon became disenchanted and they eventually became estranged. Though he went on to marry and become a Pulitzer Prize-winning poet, he never forgot Stevenson. In 1939 when writing his memoirs, Bacon was loath to reveal Stevenson's identity if not his influence—probably for several reasons, but we may suspect that it was chiefly because he wanted to forget that he had ever been "in love" with the older man, and put this homosexually-tainted memory into a more acceptable perspective. The excerpt from Bacon's autobiography is paired with a surviving letter of Stevenson's, one of many that Bacon was unable to throw away and that now rest in his papers at Princeton University. Here we see yet another view of Stevenson in his own words, this time as the Socratic yet unashamedly saturnine figure he clearly represented to Bacon. We also get a final glimpse of the wandering and lonely life-style into which Stevenson would continue until his death in 1942. Just as Stevenson says to More in the letter in Appendix A regarding John Addington Symonds, Stevenson's own "less obvious biography" is perhaps more "pathologically interesting" than many of his writings, which is why so many of his letters have been included in this set of appendices.

Last, a rare contemporary review of *Imre* is presented (Appendix G).

Appendix A: On the Origin of Imre

[Letter from Edward Prime-Stevenson to Paul Elmer More. More Collection, Manuscripts Division, Department of Rare Books and Special Collections, Princeton University Library. Published with permission of the Library.]

Naples,
March 10, 1906.
Dear Mr. More:-

So kind of you to write anything in the shape of a letter to me. Your courtesy and your hand must be rivals of Flute's "truest horse that never yet"[1] etc. (By the by, I hope that before I finish this my writing-machine, which has been out of repair, will return to me— lest you curse my worst Primer hand—or Neapolitan one.) If I should analyze to you all, or even a decimal fraction, of the pleasure that your Third Series in the S— Essays[2] has given me, & say what *I* think of it, you would have a hideously long communication that would read like a réchauffé[3] of most of the gracious appreciations of your reviewers. It is *so* true that the essayist is born not made! There must be such a clear pleasure in feeling sure that you can do, and are doing, something, that in a specially subtle, refined, yet edged and penetrant way—and never with the reader's thinking of the means as compared with his absorption in the end—not anyone else at hand can do, on the whole, about as well. That is, of course, provided the game to be played-at interests the player. It has pleased me somewhat specially—I say 'somewhat,' pray believe me, because your whole group of topics is here so attractive—so harmonious as a general, limpid low-color scheme—it has pleased me somewhat specially I say, your having discussed Cowper's[4] Correspondence—the Christina Rossetti[5] study—and your estimate of our amiable friend

---

[1]   *A Midsummer Night's Dream* III, I, 98.
[2]   *The Shelburne Essays*, 11 vol. (1904–21), are More's best known work. The volume EPS refers to came out in 1906.
[3]   Reheating; rehash (French).
[4]   William Cowper (1731–1800), English poet.
[5]   Christina Rossetti (1830–94), English poet. Her 1862 poem "Goblin Market" carries sexual undertones.

Algernon Charles[1]—the last-named, likely because you have expressed with materially more address than I could have utilized two or three sensations that have always annoyed me; and have seemed to me simply indisputable as defects or mannerisms, that even his more conservative critics haven't spoken-out. (The "Post" I should say gave you as good a 'working-medium' for all this sort of thing, that any except one other New York journal could afford you—perhaps not that one. I wish I could say to you, how perfectly I echo any laudations as to your style: its balance, its reserves, its economy of diction—and its sensitiveness to your idea. Best of all, that one never thinks about it at all, unless he stops to think—as an Irishman might put it. But America is *so* full of elaborate, painstaking, *verbal* self-consciousness. For that reason, as one among others, I seldom read any American books, however be-praised; and never, for any general matters, an American journal. The Gallic and Latin & other temperaments give tremendous leeway toward self-consciousness—or even give themselves quite up to it—so differently from the Anglo-Saxon. I ought to say here, too, that a thorough sincerity and elegance of literary manner, together have a strong charm for me. For you might know that my literary influences have been peculiarly Latin & Gallic, and of those derivations, like my blood; and the tendency toward rhetoric is a thorn in my flesh. Fortunately, it need not be considered very deeply now; for I have no mind to trouble the public, in general; unless I should at this latish stage of my Road to Damascus,[2] meet with a specially impressive (and flattering) vision and "call." But no—even so, I would say that an automobile or a cinematograph was at the bottom of it. Ápropos, you are very kind to suggest that I could offer the "Post" anything. But I can only say "truly, la, I thank you, as much as if I did." The thing is gone from me. Others can do it vastly better; and above all do it with conviction that it is important, or interesting, to be done—and to be done by *them* ... the Gods be with them! Besides—during that relatively short, but so busy run of winters in New York, I put into print such a hideous, hideous lot of matters & things—on all which, or with so painfully few exceptions, I look back with such a

---

[1] British poet Algernon Charles Swinburne (1837–1909) scandalized Victorian readers. His works display an interest in bisexuality, lesbianism, and flagellation, often as forms of social and cultural rebellion.

[2] On a journey to Damascus to persecute Christians, the Roman citizen Saul had a vision of Christ and was converted into St. Paul, one of Christendon's early pillars.

feeling of apology to myself & to anybody who can read ... nothing season by season, month by month, week by week of the heterogeneous output that I now ever wish to remember for itself, or wish to have anybody else remember—why, it seems to me that my abstinence would be only decently expiatory, were it not fluxed by indifference to amending the record,—by quite diverted & graver interests in some part—by a happy life without one scintilla of enthusiasms for so many things that once appeared engaging, by— well, I fear I must not forget that it may be, too, by years that bring the "&s."[1] (Did I happen earlier to mention in a letter to you that the great-nephew of the authour[2] cited lived in Capri, in a charming villa? and is, without exception, one of the most boresome, dull-mannered, dull-voiced—(O, God, *what* a voice!) *adagiosissimo*[3] old English gentlemen that ever 'seasoned his discourse with personal talk.' (For he is the abstract of kindly gossipry.) Also, he rides a small donkey, thus; being tall and timid of sun [here appears a caricature of a rear-view of a man with a great umbrella straddling a horse too small for him]—and generally is in full key with your ideas (and, surely, mine!) of the agony that ideas produce in modern Britons.) — But my letter is degenerating to the vulgar—to "making game of the Patriarchs" indeed!—such of "The [fore-mentioned] Excursive" itself.

Let me be serious: and apparently—but only for a few instants, as you will see—inconsistent too: when I say that I am going to send you, by next post, or so, a little book. And a little book by myself. But you will observe that the circumstances that have effected such a curious circumstance *as* my writing it, or any book, are wholly apart from those of merely literary purport or inclination—wholly. I shall wait till tomorrow to narrate them in type-writing: which, if judiciously done, extenuates a good deal.

March 11th.

The facts in the case are these: and I must excuse myself for entering on so long a history. During my many longer or shorter stays, of the

---

1 Etceteras.
2 Prime-Stevenson's manifest disdain for the American literary establishment had the side-effect of his adoption of this idiosyncratic spelling. As he throughout his life rigorously used the designation "authour" in both private and public writing, it is retained here.
3 Extremely slow (Italian).

back-and-forth kind, in Continental Europe, especially before I discontinued regular personal or literary interests in the States, and fixed myself for good over here, I kept pretty assiduously at work on a peculiarly serious project, quite out of the demesne of belles-lettres; which had gradually assumed larger and definite aspects. That project was the writing of a very full, carefully systematized, minutely *complete* History of Homosexualism, and study of the homosexual instinct—reviewing it in every social phase, every relationship to human civilization, and analyzing, or presenting, clinically and typically each projection so to say of this mysterious impulse—temperamental, social, ethical and what not. In short, as far as possible, a completely *informing* review of the topic. There is nothing of the sort in English—in spite of numerous contributions toward this or that aspect, by English-writing psychiaters of more or less weight. For, such larger things as those by Havelock Ellis and John Addington Symonds, or the late Dr. Hammond[1] are far from adequate; deal with pathologic conditions, with only limited 'typic' aspects, and are too much from and for exclusively a professional-psychiatric standpoint. Even in German, French, Italian, Russian, etc., where the literature of homosexual study is enormous nowadays, there is no work covering the scope of my book—not even Dr. Moll's big volumes, nor those by Krafft-Ebing and Raffalovitch, *et al.* I made my scheme of chapters one that depicts everything typical or exceptional—classic or modern, barbarous or civilized, oriental or occidental, vicious and debased, aesthetic or practical, ennobling and ethic—and as to instances for study, why all—from the male-prostitute of the boulevard to a Winckelmann or Charles XII of Sweden. In short, a full panorama and discussion; and the matter one that is more and more demanding such Anglo-Saxon study in the same proportion that it has won it in other circles of European science, even that more or less 'popular.' The bibliography of my book merely as one appendix-detail, includes over six hundred works.[2] Those of authority or other

---

[1] Probably the American William Alexander Hammond (1828–1900) who was Surgeon General of the U.S. and became a specialist in neuropathology. See Henry Hay, "The Hammond Report [1885]" in *One Institute Quarterly* 6 (1963): 1–21, 65–67.

[2] Regrettably, this important appendix was never included in *The Intersexes*. EPS felt that it was out of date by the time the book was printed (1908), noting in the Introduction that he was never able to "advance it beyond the year 1901." Its absence is a major loss, as it would have been an invaluable indication which books had been "coded lavender" at the turn of the century.

pertinence, have been more or less consulted, digested and, when advisable, cited. I have however had much direct and particular aid and interest in this plan of mine from many of the most eminent psychiatric specialists in homosexualism in the world. Worth mentioning here in that connection may be the fact that the late Dr. Richard von Krafft-Ebing (that noble pioneer in the modern theories of, and examination of the homosexual instinct) himself urged *me* to write this book: went (years ago) over every detail of its plan with me, chapter by chapter; and gave what he saw of it before his sudden death in Vienna, his fullest approval. (It is dedicated to his memory.) But greatly to the *individuality* of my book is the amount of original and personal observations, clinical portraitures of types, and confidential communications coming into my hands, illustrating the various topical chapters. Some of the latter are long as many monographs—for example, such chapters as "The Homosexual Type in Arts and Letters," "The Homosexual Instinct in the Military Temperament: and Military Prostitution" and "The Homosexual as Degenerate, Criminal or Victim" are extremely full of new matter. Knocking around Continental Europe as I have so long done, speaking half-a-dozen languages, and certainly at ease in dozens of mighty diverse grades of social class—and incorrigibly inclined to adventure—it would be odd if I hadn't picked up a wrinkle or so for my own score, in such a book, that can give it anything but simply a derivative quality—or an adust [*sic*] complexion in personal statements. This book will make a volume of about 800 pages of fair size. Now this thing I cannot bring out at once, though it is practically every word done. What is more, I may have to bring it out myself. For, while a sincere, and scientific work, it has popular aspects (as it has some popular good to do, I want it to have them)—and that means that to "place" it will be not too easy. In part, it is a book for a firm that specializes [in] scientific-medical literature—psychiatrics, and so on. In part, it would restrict its utility to be brought out by such a house. I must try to find some publisher who combines something of *appropriate* popular science matters in his catalogues. The amazing and indiscriminating ideas as to what books are "fit to" put before "the public," in any case, and what not, over in England and America might invite attacks on it and its promoters, just in proportion to its popularity—relative popularity—judging from past incidents in New York and London—though in all my book there is not one line that ought to shock the sense of literary or ethical propriety in any educated and decent man or woman who wishes to study a mighty important social topic *au-fond*.[1] I *can* have it brought out in Germany or in France or Italy—but that is not a good start for a work in English, and for English-reading students of psychologics, and it would be a long and troublesome matter to give it headway. I have already accepted an offer for a German translation of it: but I will not allow that till after the English issue.[2] So there for that! Such a work must start well, or *not* start, I think. I will add, that after a good deal of consideration and consulting I have determined that the book is not to be brought out under my name. It would suggest a dilettante study of so grave and deep a human topic—and it might make it lightly regarded by the ever-jealous professional psychiater. Even the late John Addington Symonds had to associate himself with Havelock Ellis to excuse his intrusion into the field.[3] (By the by I wonder if *you* have ever heard the less obvious biography of Mr. Symonds? It is interesting, pathologically.) So I shall use the pseudonym "Xavier Mayne."

Now during my laboring at the oar of this book (and, mind you, not five of my personal acquaintance in America ever have been informed of its going-on, nor should be so, for time yet indefinite— indeed the matter is so far clandestine, except in directions immediate to its developments) I have been urged to write "something or other" in the way of merely belles-lettres on this same topic—a rather startling idea to the average reader! In German and French, etc. there is a considerable catalogue of more or less openly and absolutely homosexual fictions—several are by authours of national distinction, sometimes under their names, sometimes not. In English, the field has nothing—it is virgin to the audacious!—: except so far as a vague suggestion hangs around episodes in Wilde's melodramatic "Dorian Gray,"[4] or the portraitures and satiric *double entendres* in Hitchens' [*sic*] "Green Carnation"[5]—also a feeble and crude story,

---

[1] In depth.

[2] Though *Imre* was apparently translated into German ca. 1910 by "D.G." [see Wolfram Setz's 1997 excellent reprint of the German edition], there is no record that *The Intersexes* ever was.

[3] There were grounds for EPS's fear. The collaboration between Ellis and Symonds— with the subsequent erasure of the latter in later editions—is fully explored in Wayne Koestenbaum's *Double Talk: The Erotics of Male Literary Collaboration* (New York: Routledge, 1989), pages 43–67.

[4] *The Picture of Dorian Gray* (1891) is a novel by Oscar Wilde.

[5] *The Green Carnation* (1894) by Robert Hichens satirized Oscar Wilde.

with a vulgar title, "A Marriage Below Zero" by one "Alan Dale,"[1] a journalist in New York: and a strikingly pathetic, graceful and delicately-written study of boyish homosexualism—"Tim," (the anonymous and in the "Tauchnitz" Edition, of all vehicles![2]) to authourship of which a remarkable name in British belles-lettres is linked.[3] They do not compare well with the large developments of the catalogue in Germany and France—I dare say you know some of the most notable matters. Well, I said over and over again, that I did not see the expediency of any such thing from myself. But after a particular conversation about it, a few years ago, with an English authour of world-recognized repute (the more recondite biography of whom would be far more interesting than his best history in print)—I said I would write a tale: and I kept my word. It is a perfectly sincere, simple straightforward story, of only about two-hundred pages; put on paper with care. It has gone about not a little in manuscript-form. The impression of it now from this side, now that, has been such that I decided recently to print it privately: under the pseudonym mentioned, in a small edition. I did so here in Naples: the task not so simple as might seem, for Italians are perhaps *the* most ignorant and careless of printers of any language except Italian—and this firm here in Naples has not *one* type-setter or proof-reader who knows how one English word is spelled or divided; except (possibly) "London." Still, the little book has not too many disfigurements. It is in merely brochure-form. And so—I send you a copy. Kindly read it through at your leisure. I shall not pretend to its being what a better man in craft might have made it: but it will, I think, make the impression of at least "a strange sincerity." I may add that as it will probably make its way, in its present limited edition, to a certain distinctly literary element of English readers, there is likely to be some amiable curiosity as to "who the devil has written it." One most amusing and positive, but wholly wrong disposal of its authourship, a year ago,

---

1   Pseudonym of Alfred J. Cohen (1861–1928). This 1889 novel is reprinted in *Pages Passed from Hand to Hand*, edited by Mark Mitchell and David Leavitt (1997).

2   Christian Bernhard Tauchnitz (1816–95) was only twenty-five years old when he began to publish—in Leipzig, Germany—the series of literary works in English known as the *Collection of British and American Authors*.

3   Like his friend and fellow expatriate Henry James, Howard Overing Sturgis (1855–1920) was fascinated by the British aristocracy and their foibles. He published *Tim: A Story of Eton* anonymously in 1891; his third novel *Belchamber* (1905) creates the definitive yet satirical portrait of the "domestic" homosexual (see my study *Dayneford's Library*).

considerably astonished and flattered Mr. Mayne, and perhaps sometime I shall make you laugh by telling you the affair. When I speak
of any of this sub-current of literary interest in it, you mustn't fancy
I am praising my own teeth; as our Calabrese peasants say: I merely
mean that it inevitably will be attributed to a writer of a certain
assured literary "quality," and of a romantic divergence in his wandering life from Anglo-Saxondom, in every sense: and the question will
be *who* has been free enough from literary harness and yet experi-
enced enough in literary art—and also enough interested in aspects
of the topic to treat it so individually. I am not sure but what ultimately I can induce Mr. Heinemann,[1] or somebody of that ilk, to
"take up" the story more publicly, if—*if*—that shall seem desired. I
need not say there is not a word in it that ought to offend anyone.
When I think of the all-but pornographic filth, of themes and
suggestions, in heterosexual literature, accepted, printed and read
without comment of disapproval everywhere—and then of the
idealism and in fact ethical dignity of this little tale—h'm—it is to
make another mental comment on our so-called "ethical civilization." I will note that in Part Three, there is a didactic element—
though it springs directly from the situation, and is in the way of a
dramatic narrative. This, however, gives the little book some informative purport that was specially urged on me; and seemed neither an
excrescence, nor amiss otherwise.

And so enough of so long a preface for so little a forwarding! But
I have wished you to get the book by its right end at the start; and
I wish to know if it pleases you as a literary performance or not.
Pray tell me. Especially what you don't like in its manner. I have
now so few critics "to warn, to comfort and command."

March 12.
The type-writing machine, as you may have inferred, began to show
strong signs of rachitis as the foregoing page closed, and today will
not budge. Still this desultory letter would not be longer, even with
its insinuating speed. Having come to its end, I beg you *alla
Irlandese*[2] "to read it at your leisure only." Do not hasten to read the

---

[1] Butterworth/Heinemann Publishing, still in existence, was known for its professional
and especially medical texts. As we know, EPS never had *Imre* or *The Intersexes* profes-
sionally published, preferring instead a private press.

[2] As the Irish say (Italian).

little book the account of which has so drawn my epistle out. I need not add that absolutely nobody save yourself should know of it—and in fact few might take its pages save as a curiosity. I ought not to forget to remark that I want whatever line of animadversion you may have future time to give me, simply to be your trouble in regard to the literary aspects of the tale: as in that regard I know I can give you the pains to express yourself—just as you would toward any book big or little. The theme & the atmosphere of which might be utterly as uninteresting and distasteful to you as oysters and sugar.—

Down comes the *scirocco*[1] like one of Ezechiel's beasts,—and this letter must go forthright.

Ever sincerely & cordially,
E. I. P. St.

p.s. Did you ever ask yourself, or any acquaintance who admires & knows his Shorthouse how "John Inglesant"[2] is *pronounced*? Nineteen persons in twenty speak it ....

---

[1] A hot dusty humid southeast wind in southern Europe that begins in the Sahara and picks up moisture as it crosses the Mediterranean.

[2] Joseph Henry Shorthouse (1834–1903) wrote the philosophical romance *John Inglesant*, published in 1881. An essay on Shorthouse had been included in the volume of *The Shelburne Essays* EPS had just read.

Appendix B: The Medical Establishment and Homosexuality—A Sample Case Study

[From *Psychopathia Sexualis; with Especial Reference to the Antipathic Sexual Instinct: A Medico-Forensic Study* by Richard von Krafft-Ebing (English trans. F.J. Rebman; Twelfth German Edition, originally published 1886; 1929.]

Case 148. C., age twenty-eight, gentleman of leisure; father neuropathic; mother very nervous. One brother suffered from paranoia, another was psychically degenerated. Three younger members of the family were normal.

C. was neuropathically tainted; slight convulsive tic. As long as he can remember he felt drawn to male persons, at first only to his schoolmates. When puberty set in he fell in love with male teachers, who used to visit at the house of his parents. He felt himself in the female *rôle*. His dreams, with pollutions, were always about men. He was gifted in music and poetry and loved the theatre. For science, especially mathematics, he had no talents and passed his final examinations only with difficulty. Psychically, he declared, he was a woman. Loved to play with dolls and concerned himself by preference with woman's affairs, disdaining all the pursuits of men. He liked best the society of young girls, because they were sympathetic and had an affinity of soul. When in the company of men he was shy and confused like a maiden. He never smoked, and disliked alcoholic drinks. He feign would have liked to spend his time in cooking, knitting and embroidering. He had no libido. Sexual intercourse with men only a few times, although his ideal was to play the *rôle* of the woman on such occasions. Coitus cum muliere[1] he abhorred. After reading "Psychopathia Sexualis," he became alarmed, was afraid of coming in conflict with the police and avoided sexual relations with men. But pollutions became very frequent, and neurasthenia supervened. He came for medical advice.

C. had an abundant beard, and was of a decidedly masculine type, excepting soft features and a remarkably fine skin. Genitals normal, except a deficient *descensus* of one of the testicles. In his behavior,

---

[1]   Sex with a woman (Latin).

gait, and appearance nothing unusual, though he had the illusion that everybody noticed his abnormal sexual proclivity. He shunned society for that reason. Lascivious talk made him blush like a maiden. Once when someone turned the topic of conversation on antipathic sexual instinct, he fainted. Music brought on a heavy perspiration all over his body. Upon closer acquaintance he showed psychical femininity; he was as timid as a girl, and without a vestige of independence. Nervous restlessness, convulsive tic, numerous neurasthenic complications put on him the stamp of a constitutionally tainted neuropathic individual.

Case 128. Sch., aged thirty, physician, one day told me the story of his life and malady, asking for explanation and advice concerning certain anomalies for his *vita sexualis*. The following description gives, for the most part verbatim, the details of the autobiography; only in some portions it is shortened:—

"My parents were healthy. As a child I was sickly; but with good care I thrived, and got on well in school. When eleven years old, I was taught to masturbate by my playmates, and gave myself up to it passionately. Until I was fifteen, I learned easily. On account of frequent pollutions, I became less capable, and did not get on well in school, and was uncertain and embarrassed when called on by the teacher. Frightened by my loss of capability, and recognizing that the loss of semen was responsible for it, I gave up masturbation; but the pollutions became even more frequent, so that I often had two or three in a night. In despair, I now consulted one physician after another. None were able to help me.

"Since I grew weaker and weaker, by reason of the loss of semen, with the sexual appetite growing more and more powerful, I sought houses of prostitution. But I was there unable to find satisfaction; for, even though the sight of a naked female pleased me, neither orgasm nor erection occurred; and even manustupration by the *puella*[1] was not capable of inducing erection. Scarcely would I leave the house, when the impulse would seize me again, and I would have violent erections. I grew ashamed before the girls, and ceased to visit such houses. Thus a couple of years passed. My sexual life consisted of pollutions. My inclination toward the opposite sex grew less and less. At nineteen I went to the university. The theatre had

---

[1]   Manipulation of the genitals by the girl.

more attractions for me: I wished to become an actor. My parents were not willing. At the metropolis I was compelled now and then to visit girls with my comrades. I feared such a situation; because I knew that coitus was impossible for me, and because my friends might discover my impotence. Therefore, I avoided, as far as possible, the danger of becoming the butt of their jokes and ridicule.

"One evening, in the opera-house, an old gentleman sat near me. He courted me. I laughed heartily at the foolish old man, and entered into his joke. Exinopinato genitalia mea prehendit, quo facto statim penis meus se erexit.[1] Frightened, I demanded of him what he meant. He said that he was in love with me. Having heard of hermaphrodites in the clinics, I thought I had one before me, and became curious to see his genitals. The old man was very willing, and went with me to the water closet. Sicuti penem maximum ejus erectum adspexi, perterritus effugi.[2]

"This man followed me, and made strange proposals which I did not understand, and repelled. He did not give me any rest. I learned the secrets of male love for males, and felt that my sexuality was excited by it. But I resisted the shameful passion (as I then regarded it) and, for the next three years, I remained free from it. During this time I repeatedly attempted coitus with girls in vain. My attempts to free myself of my impotence by means of medical treatment were also in vain. Once, when my *libido sexualis* was troubling me again, I recalled what the old man had told me: that male-loving men were accustomed to meet on the E. Promenade.

"After a hard struggle, and with beating heart, I went there, made the acquaintance of a blonde man, and allowed myself to be seduced. The first step was taken. This kind of sexual love was satisfactory to me. I always preferred to be in the arms of a strong man. The satisfaction consisted of mutual manustupration; occasionally in *osculum ad penem alterius*.[3] I was then twenty-three years old. Sitting, together with my comrades, on the beds of patients in the clinic during the lectures, excited me so intensely that I could scarcely listen to the lectures. In the same year I entered into a formal love-relation with a merchant of thirty-four. We lived as man and wife. X. played the man, and fell more and more in love. I gave up to him, but now and

---

[1] Out of the blue he seized my genitals, which at once gave me an erection (Latin).
[2] When I saw that his penis had reached full erection, I fled, terrified (Latin).
[3] Oral sex (Latin).

then I had to play the man. After a time I grew tired of him, became unfaithful and he grew jealous. There were terrible scenes, which led to temporary separation, and finally to actual rupture. (The merchant afterwards became insane, and died by suicide.)

"I made many acquaintances, and loved the most ordinary people. I preferred those having a full beard, who were tall and of middle age, and able to play the active *rôle* well. I developed a *proctitis*. The professor thought it was the result of sitting too much while preparing for examinations. I developed a fistula, and had to undergo an operation; but this did not cure me of my desire to let myself be used passively. I became a physician and went to a provincial town, where I had to live like a nun. I developed a desire to move in ladies' society, and was gladly welcomed there; because it was found that I was not so one-sided as most men, and was interested in toilettes and such feminine things. However, I felt very unhappy and lonesome. Fortunately, in this town, I made the acquaintance of a man, a 'sister,' who felt like me. For some time I was taken care of by him. When he had to leave I had an attack of despair, with depression, which was accompanied by thoughts of suicide.

"When it became impossible for me to longer endure the town, I became a military surgeon in the capital. There I began to live again, and often made two or three acquaintances in one day. I had never loved boys or young people; only fully developed men. The thought of falling into the hands of the police was frightful. Thus far I have escaped the clutches of the blackmailer. At the same time, I could not keep myself from the gratification of my impulse. After some months I fell in love with an official of forty. I remained true to him for a year, and we lived like a pair of lovers. I was the wife and was formally courted by the lover. One day I was transferred to a small town. We were in despair. The last night was spent in continually kissing and caressing one another.

"In T. I was unspeakably unhappy, in spite of some 'sisters' whom I found. I could not forget my lover. In order to satisfy my sexual desire, which cried for satisfaction, I chose soldiers. Money obtained men; but they remained cold, and I had no enjoyment with them. I was successful in being retransferred to the capital, where there was a new love relation, but much jealousy; because my lover liked to go into the society of 'sisters,' and was proud and coquettish. There was a rupture. I was very unhappy and very glad to be transferred from the capital. I now stayed in C., alone and in despair. Two infantry privates were brought into service, but with the same unsatisfactory results. When shall I ever find true love again?

"I am over medium height, well developed, and look somewhat aged; and, therefore, when I wish to make conquests I use the arts of the toilet. My manner, movements and face are masculine. Physically I feel as youthful as a boy of twenty. I love the theatre, and especially art. My interest in the stage is in the actresses, whose every movement and gesture I notice and criticize.

"In the society of gentlemen I am silent and embarrassed, while in the society of those like myself I am free, witty, and as fawning as a cat if a man is sympathetic. If I am without love, I become deeply melancholic; but the favors of the first handsome man dispel my depression. In other ways I am frivolous and very ambitious. My profession is nothing to me. Masculine pursuits do not interest me. I prefer novels and going to the theatre. I am effeminate, sensitive, easily moved, easily injured and nervous. A sudden noise makes my whole body tremble, and I have to collect myself in order to keep from crying out."

Remarks: The foregoing case is certainly one of acquired antipathic sexual instinct, since the sexual instinct and impulse were originally directed toward the female sex. Sch. became neurasthenic through masturbation.

As an accompanying manifestation of the neurasthenic neurosis, lessened impressionability of the erection-center and consequent relative impotence developed. As a result of this, sexual sensibility toward the opposite sex decreased, with simultaneous persistence of *libido sexualis.* The acquired antipathic sexual instinct must be abnormal, since the first touch by a person of the same sex is an adequate stimulus for the erection-center. The perverse sexual feeling becomes complete.—At first Sch. felt like a man in the sexual act; but more and more, as the change progressed, the feeling and desire of satisfaction changed to the form which, as a rule, characterizes the (congenital) urning.

This eviration induces a desire for the passive *rôle,* and, further, for (passive) pederasty. It makes a deeper impress on the character. The character becomes feminine, inasmuch as Sch. now prefers to move in the society of actual females, has an increasing desire for feminine occupations, and indeed makes use of the arts of the toilet in order to improve his fading charms and make "conquests."

Appendix C: Homosexuality and the Artistic Temperament

[Excerpts from *Sexual Inversion* by Havelock Ellis and John Addington Symonds, 1897. These are two footnotes by Ellis.]

Symonds's attention had long been struck by the frequency of inversion among actors and actresses. He knew an inverted actor who told him he adopted the profession because it would enable him to indulge his proclivity; but on the whole he regarded this tendency as due to "hitherto unconsidered imaginative flexibilities and curiosities in the individual. The actor, *ex hypothesi*, is one who works himself by sympathy (intellectual and emotional) into states of psychological being that are not his own. He learns to comprehend—nay, to live himself into—relations which were originally alien to his nature. The capacity for doing this—what makes a born actor—implies a faculty for extending his artistically acquired experience into life. In the process of his trade, therefore, he becomes at all points sensitive to human emotions, and, sexuality being the most intellectually undetermined of the appetites after hunger, the actor might discover in himself a sort of sexual indifference, out of which a sexual aberration could easily arise. A man devoid of this imaginative flexibility could not be a successful actor. The man who possesses it would be exposed to divagations of the sexual instinct under aesthetical or merely wanton influences.

"Something of the same kind is applicable to musicians and artists, in whom sexual inversion prevails beyond the average. They are conditioned by their aesthetical faculty, and encouraged by the circumstances of their life to feel and express the whole gamut of emotional experience. Thus they get an environment which (unless they are sharply otherwise differentiated) leads easily to experiments in passion. All this joins on to what you call the 'Variational diathesis' of men of genius. But I should seek the explanation of the phenomenon less in the original sexual constitution than in the exercise of sympathetic, assimilative emotional qualities, powerfully stimulated and acted on by the conditions of the individual's life. The artist, the singer, the actor, the painter, are more exposed to the influences out of which sexual differentiation in an abnormal direction may arise. Some persons are certainly made abnormal by nature, others, of this sympathetic artistic temperament, may become so through their sympathies plus their conditions of life." It is possible there may be some element of truth in this view, which Symonds acknowledged to be purely hypothetical.

★　★　★　★　★

It cannot be said of my cases, as it has been said of some—though without any definite evidence being brought forward—that their views of themselves have been modeled on Krafft-Ebing's *Psychopathia Sexualis* and similar works. Apart from the fact that such books were until quite lately unknown in England, if, indeed, they can yet be said to be known, the attitude of the individuals whose cases I have brought forward has very little in common with the self-pitying attitude of inverts who are anxious for medical treatment. It is, on the whole, better expressed by the stanzas written by one of my subjects—a man of social and literary distinction, temperate, moderate, and self-respecting, who treats his perversion in the same way as well-bred people treat their normal propensities—after a friend had striven to interest him in the scientific aspects of this subject:—

UNISEXUALIS CUJUSDAM RESPONSIO.[1]
I love my friend, and he loves me:
A better pair could never be;
And yet you say that I am mad,
Or else you swear that I am bad;
And all because I am not you!
Krafft-Ebing, or Tarnowsky,[2] or Tardieu![3]

Were you like me, I think you'd find
How sound, how sane, how good, how kind

---

[1] The Unisexual Reply of a Certain Someone.
[2] Benjamin Tarnowsky (1839–1906) was a Russian sexologist who claimed that homosexuality was sometimes acquired by a degenerate environment or sometimes inborn due to parents' damaged genes.
[3] Ambroise Tardieu, (1818–79) an influential French pathologist, in his text on forensic medicine of 1857, *Etude médico-légale sur les Attentats aux Moeurs*, portrayed homosexuals as degraded monsters, not only morally but physically different from other human beings.

This love of man for man may be,
In spite of all your theory;
But since you're not, I'd not be you!
Krafft-Ebing, or Tarnowsky, or Tardieu!

And yet I hope some kindly Moll[1]
Will solve your problem once for all,
And prove me neither mad nor bad;
Only, sometimes, exceeding glad
To be what is condemned by you,
Krafft-Ebing, or Tarnowsky, or Tardieu!

---

[1]   Albert Moll (1862–1939), a German sexologist, considered homosexuality an inborn
     illness yet treated the subject with more compassion than the majority of his contem-
     poraries.

Appendix D: Excerpts from The Intersexes (1908)

In the late Otto de Joux's study of uranianism entitled "Die Enterbten des Liebesglücks,"[1] a book which despite its tendency to a romantic accentuation and even to ill-placed levity contains useful matters for lay-reading, the authour gives the following sketch of an Uranian's "love at sight." The narrator is spoken of as a young scion of a noble family of the Continent: and the object of his passion is a German or Austrian army-officer.

"I have absolutely nothing feminine in me as to my looks; my bearing indeed is noted for its genuine masculinity. But, for all that, I have a soul like a woman's. I am a man: but I love another man, burningly, passionately, to death itself. I know too it is a mad hopeless struggle that I have kept up against my all too-tender nature, since my boyhood's years. So I have given up struggling against my fate.

"I was young, free, rich but not happy ... I fell in love with a man whose name I did not know. It came over me like a flash of lightning when I saw him for the first time. It was in a café: my eye caught sight of a dignified officer. He had an illustrated paper before him, but his glance was far from it: visibly he was sunk in deep thought. My first idea was of what preoccupied him ... the noble profile with lines so strong and definite; everything about him suggested intellect and will-power ... Finally he got up and went away; and I followed him, compelled by an irresistible force. How is it possible that one human creature can exert such a violent influence over another of like sex? I had never had any experience like this. The fresh air brought me to my senses: 'You are a fool!' I said to myself, and went home." (pp. 109–111)

Before the close of the thirties, in the nineteenth century, occurred, in Vienna, a chain of episodes in army-life, based almost wholly on uranistic facts. How much so was known to few persons outside of a trio directly involved. Among the Magyar Imperial Life-Guards in Vienna, was a certain young Count U., a member of an excellent family as well as of an aristocratic circle. Count U. was of a physical

---

[1] Trans. *The Disinherited of Love* (1893).

beauty which made him the object of feminine admiration in half the drawing-rooms of Vienna. Complaisant proposals were lavished on this Apollo of one of the most picturesque regiments in Europe. He was a Don Juan as to the women. Nevertheless, Count U. was a Dionian-Uranian. He maintained a sexual relation with a young brother-officer in Budapest, a famous swordsman and rider, of notable attractiveness. Between the two young men came a difference. The *fidus Achates* of Count U. was a declared woman-hater, entirely homosexual. But in course of time, Count U., apparently reverting to the normal, fell in love with a young and beautiful girl. It became a question of his marriage. The Count offered his hand and name. Fraulein X. accepted him. Unhappily one obstacle to the marriage existed. The young lady was of Jewish stock, the daughter of a wealthy financier. At that time the local prejudice against such marriages, on the part of aristocratic Vienna, was more sharp than it is today. The engagement might however have been acceptable to the U. family, but for a direct intervention, made by the friend of Count U. He had been willing to tolerate Count U.'s passing flames, but the idea of the marriage was unendurable. Whatever he could do to strengthen the opposition of the family of Count U. he did. But he maneuvered this so adroitly that Count U. had no idea of any such intrigue. The jealous soldier played his role with the finesse of an actor. He could not succeed in bringing the parents of Count U. to a definite refusal to receive the young lady into their intimacy, should the marriage occur, until about a week prior to its date. Some of the members of the U. family had declared their willingness to be present, but others had not. The night before the date set for the marriage, Count U. visited his parents, having every reason to suppose that displeasure as any obstruction was past. He found the situation changed. His father nor mother would neither be present at the ceremony, nor under any circumstances would receive the bride socially. A violent scene ensued. There was no mistaking the obstinacy of the family. Count U. went to his rooms, and shot himself dead. The young officer who had been the real agency of the resolution of the U. family was overwhelmed at a result which he had not foreseen. In remorse and grief he followed his friend to the grave, by putting a bullet through his own heart on the evening after the funeral of Count U. He left a note to a well-known officer, in which he confessed the sexual history. The young lady, by the bye, survived the tragedy, and presently married—into her own faith. The U. family, it is of interest to note, included more than one abnormal member. Another member, Countess U., was always believed to be an Uraniad, so masculine was her individuality, in spite of the fact that she married and had children. Her separation from her husband was supposed to refer to this element. She also, when in middle life, without any obvious reason, committed suicide suddenly in a foreign land where, as a sort of interesting amazon, she long had resided. (pp. 198–200)

Appendix E: From Life to Fiction

[The following six letters by Edward Prime-Stevenson to George E. Woodberry outline the real-life troubled love-affair between Stevenson and Harry Harkness Flagler; they are followed by the short story where Stevenson converts the same material into fiction.]

1. Letter from Edward Prime-Stevenson to George E. Woodberry. [All letters reprinted by permission of the Houghton Library, Harvard University.]

The Independent
New York
Oct. 27, 1892

Prof. George E. Woodberry,
My dear Sir:-

I presume you are quite at the end of your special labors connected with your forthcoming volumes of Shelley, and consequently the question that I meant to put to you some months ago has merely the interest of curiosity in it.

Have you ever, in the course of your examination of matter relating to Shelley and to literary types which may be associated with him, met with any study, biographical and critical, of Friedrich Hölderlin, a German poet, neo-Hellenist, pantheist, and much beside?[1] It seems to me that the life and attitude toward poetical thought and toward nature maintained by Hölderlin during all his brief and sad career, sustains a very curious relationship to Shelley; at least it does so sufficiently to strike the English student and biographer of Shelley who has leisure to gather together many side considerations of Shelley and of Shelleyism. I do not know whether you have happened to have

---

[1]   EPS would later identify Friedrich Hölderlin (1770–1843) as "wholly homosexual" in *The Interesexes*, where he quotes extensively from "Hyperion" as a text displaying "hellenic similisexuality" (297). A footnote there records that "A considerable study of Hölderlin, published some years ago, by the present writer, deals somewhat minutely with Hölderlin's Hellenism." Mention of Hellenism or the ancient Greeks at this time was often a coded reference to homosexuality. It may well be that at this point in their friendship, before they actually met, EPS is trying to determine Woodberry's sexual orientation. The letters which follow suggest that by then homosexual sympathies are clearly understood between them.

your attention drawn to this chapter before, as of course it is rather an esoteric one in German literature. I am not aware that any translation of anything of Hölderlin's except a very few fragments exist. The remarkable Hellenism and pantheism and everything else of his there, seems to be buried in German, and his prose masterpiece "Hyperion," I think has never been put into English any more than the rest.

I presume my friend, Mr. Harry Flagler, will have already mentioned to you that we had the mutual pleasure of spending the entire summer together, in the course of which (I need not say at the sacrifice of a good deal of time from my own private literary work) we went over no small ground together in English literature, which would have some reference with his course in it with you.

I hope some time I may have the pleasure of meeting you even if not until we get to a world where we do not both of us lead such excessively busy lives.

Some years ago we had a servant in our family, a Negress, who was an inveterate whistler. The other domestics complained of it. My sister made an inquiry and elicited the following excuse: "The fact is Miss Mareea (my sister's name is Marie) I'se so busy in this house that I hain't got time to say no prayers! I'se 'bleeged to whistle. When I hain't got time to say 'Our Father,' in the morning I whistles 'Dixey'." It has often seemed to me a pity that other exercises than those of piety cannot be accomplished equally stenographically.

Very truly yours,
E. Irenaeus Stevenson
p.s. I can't dictate dialect very well.

2. Letter from Edward Prime-Stevenson to George Woodberry.

143 E. 55th St.
Friday
March 24 [18]93

My dear Mr. Woodberry,
    This note is not merely to say to you—thanking you for yours—that I shall hope to find you at home some evening, presently, and not too tired nor too occupied to receive—what is the phrase?—a "visit of digestion."

I have been wondering whether you will think I impose on your tact and your good-nature, in telling you as fully as I can the story of how has come about the unhappy state of affairs between my friend and myself—and asking you to "censure me in your wisdom" from other than general principles only. I am as "perplexed extremely" as ever was Othello. I am not sure that any counselor in friendship can make the future of matters kindlier to my expecting, any more than the lawyer can improve on an ill case in more tangible chancery. But—I do know that the affair is making me, week by week, less pleased with life, more indifferent to things that might well be its interests—and worse harm to me.

I ask myself sufficiently often whether I am a fool—or a *lusus naturae*[1] of other sort; a relic of some early stratum of emotional geology, unluckily quickened. Can I not—no, I must—shake myself out of myself, as man does when—Phyllida flouts him, and he makes up his lover's mind to whistle his feeling down the wind. I say all manner of things to myself, as one become the very creature I hate—the sentimentalist, and the sentimentalist in friendship. I accept as logic and common-sense and manliness the remembrance that a man's life apart from love in it ought to be so much, and the love compared with the rest of his life as small. I work, I go about, I do my best to fight away anything like the emotional balanced morbid deflection. And then—all at once—I find myself undone, and saying that if Harry and I are as we have become, the rest of life is stale and stupid and hateful; and that what has been the beginning & middle and end of my content with it for so long is as inexplicably arbitrary as ever for my interest in it now; and that whether I understand it or not, or try to throw it away from me or not, estrangement in him from me means some sort of mischief in all my chemistry that is as magical as it is hideous to me—and so do I become either in my best estate of judgment, or foolishest.

It is less and less clear to me, I must say, how ever in this mortal world I could touch on this intensely personal chapter & speak of it so openly as I somehow came to doing that evening I was your guest. I say this with every allowance of your tact and kindly feeling. I have a tolerably large group of acquaintances, of my own sex, more or less approaching the degree of friends, and pretty amply varied, I think, in temperaments & ages & experiences. It is the last of topics that I could

---

[1] Play or freak of nature (Latin).

broach with any of them. The whole experience of my taking Harry into my life—or rather of his entrance into it so many years ago—belongs to another phase of regard, perhaps of the world, that I have felt would not be in touch with the heart of the most thoroughly perceptive man I've known. If I couldn't understand it myself—how should he?—at least by anything I could say to him. And then—there *was* nothing to think of or speak of, with oneself, except a perfectly tranquil happiness. But you—well, I do not know how far I abuse your friendliness & your patience (I met you in a Player's Club, you know) or anything else: but I fancy that you may understand—and so doing tell me where I have made a mistake, or where the fault has not been mine, and give me some further word of what seems to you to bear on the situation. I think, too, you can decide me as to whether my whole chapter of life with Henry has been my mistake, first & last. I do not know if I be more unhappy than bewildered.

What Olympian or saint or philosopher has brought me to think of you as I do, I don't know. I feel intrusive enough, pray believe me. But I think as I do—and my writing so frankly here carries out the thought. You will forgive me?

I have been waiting for some time to try and fix an evening when I can have the pleasure of getting you to find your way up here to dinner or a Sunday night tea or something more than merely the finding me at home & in my own rooms; but some persistent half-illnesses in our little family trio[1] have not departed, & our usual quiet hospitality has been interrupted in many matters. And, further, I ought to be the visitor—without reference to any special matter that as one I'might want to discuss. In any case, if, say, within the fortnight coming you are quite free as to any evening, and really can sacrifice your freedom to me, kindly let me know. (There is no haste.) And it will be, if you will let me, for nothing so much as to ask you to tell a man who loves another man with all his heart how what is to him a supreme loss—seems in your eyes & ought to seem in his—& what his course.

I had no idea that this would become a letter, much less so long a one, when I began it tonight.

Very gratefully & sincerely,
Edward I. St.—

---

[1] Doubtless his elderly mother and sister Marie.

3. Letter from Edward Prime-Stevenson to George Woodberry.

[March 28, 1893]
143 E. 55th St.
Tuesday night.

My dear Mr. Woodberry,

You are very obliging. I shall get to No 5, early, on Saturday night, between half-after-eight and nine.

I am afraid, in spite of what I am able to believe as a corrective that you will fault me a sentimentalist that a little dangerous and rash kindness incontinently proves a bore. Please do not.

The sense of the "good" of saying to you what I will try to, as briefly and plainly as I can, is not strong—in fact it has rather gone by the board since I have been thinking, lately. Nor do I believe that anyone can find a remedy, or a standpoint from which to attempt one. But I have not felt that I wished you to be in my confidence in the matter because of the possibility of your direct help in it. I have already good reason to understand that service you have done me, quite wide of that.

I happened to be remembering an odd thing—if anything in life be odd—the other evening. I bethought me of you—and of the fact that for many months prior to the month-just-past, I now & then looked forward with interest to 'meeting' you some day in passing—and to having therewith some sort of a slight and pleasant acquaintance with you, as a friend of friends of mine & yours—and, that likewise, I kept on rather—well—'fighting shy' of meeting you in spite of some opportunities that came on—a tendency not new to me. And then—I did meet you; and somehow was so very glad to have you meet *me*—with a courage that I can't unriddle—. For there is nothing deeper in a man, or I think oughtn't be, than his heart, & I couldn't keep mine shut to what is the deepest and I know the best thing in it.

I am quite certain that it is not merely as a strangely interested visitor, who walks curiously & sympathetically through a suite of rooms, with shut-up things in them—and so out again—that I think of you as having been so good as to make your entrance. If I did, I shouldn't consider myself so lacking as I do now, because I can't phrase just the sort of benediction that might please you best, and be as potent as the wish of any friend would ever be.

Always sincerely & gratefully,
Edward I. St.

4. Letter from Edward Prime-Stevenson to George E. Woodberry.

432 Madison Ave.
June 28th 1893

My dear Mr. Woodberry:

I am sorry that I could not get to see you before you left the city
for the coming months, and that I must wish you, by letter, what
restfulness and leisure can be part of them. I fancy that you are likely
to be as busy as the law allows, and I hope that what you have in
hand as the summer's main task may be a pleasure and one readily
rounded out to your mind.

I have seen nothing of my friend for many weeks now; nor have
I heard anything. The world seems a strangely different place. What
view I shall be able to bring myself to taste of it is yet a question. I
am extremely busy, as it happens; but the object, the point, the use,
the pleasure of—anything—is not. And—forgive me, for saying so—
I have now excellent reason to conclude that whatever was the
weight of one possible error on my part—my believing that the
time had come when I must not act the most aggressive part in a
curious drama, with my friend, in plain words & understanding with
him—whatever, was the mischief done thereby, it was of little
purport in the strange and unhappy situation now mine. Deeper
than that, are causes and emotions and influences, which I shall
never very definitely know, perhaps; quite putting it to one side.

I shall take this summer to think less of the past than of the
future, so far as I can carry out the choice of two evils. The grief
does not lessen. It only grows bitterer and more potent. All that
meant the interest and happiness of life to me was, is, part of that
strange & supreme love which has been so set at fault by events. I
wonder whether matters will ever seem to Harry otherwise than
he appears desirous of making me believe they appear to him now?
Perhaps. In any case, he can suffer no changed aspect in my heart,
and he is first in it, wherever the future finds me.

If ever you have leisure, a line from you is cordially appreciated. I
can always be addressed at "The Independent" or with the Harpers.

Ever yours sincerely
Edward I. Stevenson

5. Excerpt, letter from Edward Prime-Stevenson to George E. Woodberry.

Florence,
20 May 1921

My dear Sir:
   ... I have myself the pleasure of sending you a certain fat yellow-covered book of mine,[1] some ten or twelve months ago—(address-ing the parcel to the care of The Player's Club, N.Y.C.)—which I trust reached you, but of the fate of which postally, in these times of disturbed mails, I have as yet no idea. The volume would have a possible—and reminiscent—interest to you, I thought, because of at least one of its extremely heterogeneous inclusions.
With memories and regard,
Edward Prime-Stevenson

6. Excerpt, letter from Edward Prime-Stevenson to George E. Woodberry.

Hotel Minerva, Florence,
9 February 1922

Dear Mr. Woodberry:
   ... And bye the bye my dear Mr. Woodberry, I think that I ought not to forget just in the connection, this item to *you* ... For, while I write it, my mind slips back, back,—so far back indeed—to one or two fireside conversations in your old rooms in Seventeenth Street New York—conversations which left me your debtor psychically perhaps more than you could suppose. I have never, as far as I know, lost in all my life, other than one friend, unless the loss by death. And just that one friend whom I lost, so to say, and who—to me

---

[1]   EPS refers to *Her Enemy, Some Friends—and Other Personages* (1913) which contained "Once—But Not Twice," the story referred to in the letter's closing sentence. This reference clearly highlights the autobiographical origin of the tale.

(car le coeur a ses raisons[1]) was so profoundly more than "all the rest," no matter the whos and whys in their cases—I got back. In fact—had I lost him at all......?...

7. [This short story first appeared in *Her Enemy, Some Friends—and Other Personages: Stories and Studies Mostly of Human Hearts* (Florence: G.& R. Obsner, 1913; privately printed).]

ONCE: BUT NOT TWICE

"But was I false, or were you untrue,
Never was any friend like you!"
(Christian Burke)[2]

---

[1] For the heart has its reasons (French).The full quotation reads:"Le coeur a ses raisons, que la raison ne connaît point; on le sait en mille choses. Je dis que le coeur aime l'être universel naturellement, et soi-même naturellement, selon qu'il s'y adonne; et il se durcit contre l'un ou l'autre, à son choix.Vous avez rejeté l'un et conserve l'autre; est-ce par raison que vous vous aimez?" ["For the heart has its reasons, which reason does not know; one knows it in a thousand things. I say that the heart loves universal being naturally, and itself naturally, according as it devotes itself to it; and it hardens itself against one or the other, as its choice.You (the unbeliever) have rejected love for the universal being and have kept love of self; is it from reason that you love yourself?"]
—*Les Pensées*, number 24, of Blaise Pascal (1623–62)

[2] The epigraph is from the poem "Estranged" (1902), further quoted in the tale below. Christian Burke was a pen-name for the anonymous author of several books of poetry and religious tracts near the turn of the century.Though not particularly religious and claiming to disdain sentiment, EPS was nonetheless drawn to Burke's theme of bittersweet regret. Because the poem is somewhat misquoted, yet provides a thematic backbone to the story, it is worth reprinting here. Its publication date tells us that this story must have been penned between 1902 and 1913, several years after the quarrel between EPS and Flagler outlined in the Woodberry letters.

We were friends in the long ago—
    Now perchance when we pass or meet,
We hail each other across the street:
    And the wonder seems to grow
That either had sought or given more
    In those credulous days of yore!

Did you really suffice me then,
    Had I power your soul to move,
That we gave each other that silent love
    A man will share with men?
Yet were you false, or was I untrue?—
    Never was any friend like you!

(To Harry Harkness Flagler)

I.

The five o'clock evening-express from New York came swiftly into the little railroad-station at Marengo, with all the assurance marking its daily advent. The lamps in the cars twinkled for the train's length, in pale accord with a clear, yellowish December sky. Against that, the roofs of the little New Jersey town, so heroically named, and the black boughs and twigs of the leafless trees defined themselves in sharp silhouettes. The winter-moon was rising. Presently the bustle of the train's incoming diminished. The "commuting" husbands, their wives, full of the day's shopping or of the matinee—a traveling variety troupe, billed for Marengo's town-hall "for one night only"; dog-carts, phaetons and hacks,[1] they all filtered away presently. The last echoes of the receding train ceased among the hills.

"One minute, Mr. Jaques! Here's a letter for you," said Hampden, the postmaster, to a man stepping lightly across the station. Outside, a trap and a trim negro boy and a nervous Gordon setter awaited this last lingerer.

Jaques held the letter under the light looking at it sharply. Disbelief gave place to surprise. Oh, he recognized the handwriting on the envelope! An odd twist came to his thin lips as he opened it. So considerable a number of closely-written sheets anybody might be excused from reading in a draughty waiting-room. Whether this entered into Jaques's decision or not, it was plain, after an instant, that he was not going to read that letter till he chose to do so. He frowned—then

---

Had we parted in wrath and scorn,
    One might have sought the other's grace,
And meeting suddenly face to face
    A nobler love been born:
But vainly shall any seek for fruit
    When the tree's dying at its root!

Were you the man I thought of old?
    Are you the man I think to-day?
Is there perchance some word to say,
    A secret that's not yet told?
Dare I not hope—when this Life ends—
    Something again will make us friends!

(First published in *Temple Bar* 125 [May 1902]: 592.)

[1] Phaetons were light, four-wheeled carriages, with or without a top; hacks were carriages kept for hire.

laughed a little, quite to himself. Years had told lightly on his graceful, easy personality and harmonious youthfulness of face. Emotions were still easily reflected in it. At last, slipping the letter into his pocket, he hurried to his trap. He set the black horse into a swinging pace. He lived in solitary comfort, not to say luxury, out on "the old Jaques place," four miles from the railroad; his boyhood's home, inherited from his father. He was thirty-four. He was practically alone in the world.

Jaques laid the letter beside his uncompanioned dinner-plate, and then went upstairs to change his coat. Either he felt no curiosity now as to the letter's contents, or else he had made up his mind still to postpone, till certain surrounding conditions pleased him. But at last he sat down to dinner. Then he unfolded the communication. The servant came and went, with less and less attention from his master. Jaques laid leaf after leaf aside, now absolutely intent on their burden. And thus did the letter run:

II.

No.— West — Street,
December 12th, 189–

Dear Saladin:[1] [That old nickname from the writer made Jaques smile a trifle grimly.] It would be strange if you are not surprised at seeing, first, my handwriting, and second, at its flowing-out over so many pages as this communication is likely to cover. I have not written your name on an envelope, you have not addressed a line or two to me in—well, let us not reckon the unkindly period, especially tonight. Silence complete and mutual till now....

Has it been my fault or yours, old fellow? Has it been my folly or yours? That strange, that sudden difference between us! That sharp alteration in our intimacy, that I will not call a quarrel and that I dare not call a misunderstanding! At any rate, it has kept us from more than the casual bow in the street, or a few unemotional phrases, if face to face. How could it all have come about thus inflexibly? Yet stop! I do not want to ask that, or any other like enigma, tonight. Let the past be the past! Let what is bitter in it be sweetened! We still may find some talismanic bough to cast into current. Can we not try, at least?

---

[1] Saladin (1137-93), sultan of Egypt and Syria 1175-93, was known for his good faith, piety, justice, and chivalry. Interestingly, he died at Damascus (see Appendix A and EPS's mention of his own "Road to Damascus).

When last I met you—a year ago—you will remember that we agreed to consider our dispute closed, even if our intimacy was not to be renewed. We had separated for little, after all! ... It was understood that there was to be peace between us—a *salaam aleikoum*![1] Not a word about anything beyond peace, I think, at that time. Since our truce, I have not written to you, I know, by way of holding out the olive-branch further, though I have wished to do so. But I write tonight.

For tonight is an anniversary. I sit here remembering it, and listening to the rain that is sweeping across the deluged city. An anniversary of what? Dates were never a strong point with you or me during those days when, in college and out of it, you and I used to walk the highroad of life more closely together than do many near friends; crammed ourselves with law, history and political economy for occasional speeches at the primaries we now and then graced with our most sweet voices. You do not, I fancy, recall the significance of this remoter December day. Forgotten many a less auspicious hour, brushed away the separation that years have maintained, I say—God bless you, old fellow! I first met you twenty years ago! You were twenty, and I twenty-two;[2] each of us undergoing a special college-examination, in justifiable doubt of our respective "gettings through." Somehow we discerned, each the other, as a friend indeed; if emphatically a friend in need.

Twenty years, Saladin! A large slice out of the lives of any two mortals. "Painlessly and easily extracted," as say the dentists' signs. Yes, life is short, at its best, with a vengeance! It seems almost a pity to the man that childhood wastes so much of it. Is that brutal? Is it unkind to one's youth, I wonder? But oh, for living gaily and carelessly, quite as a cheery animal, the years seem ample!—while for doing what a man can do, for thinking what a man may think, for taking up what is worth the picking, for casting aside things not worthy our carriage, the space allowed is too brief! Childhood and boyhood shirk and shorten so much!

Twenty years! ... They have altered us little, I believe. At least you, whom I have rarely seen for seven of them I am assured, by common

---

[1] A salute of peace (Arabic).

[2] EPS confuses his mathematics, as on the previous page Jaques is 34 and by this arithmetic he should be 40. EPS was born in 1858 and Harry Harkness Flagler in 1870. EPS subtracted ten years from his birth date once he began his sojourn in Europe sometime after 1900 and kept up this lie thereafter; as a result even today there exists a confusion about his birth year in many records.

friends, luckier than I, are wonderfully unchanged in your outward self. A few lines in your face, a little deepening of the setting of your clear eyes, a trifle more girth to your figure—that seems to others' sight and to mine about all. So Harrison often tells me. Harrison was always jealous of you, including your good looks; and I venture to believe bears a little of that rankle today. As for me—well, my long illness of two years ago has thinned me—somewhat.[1] I haven't been able to take the world and fate so carelessly as you. Newspaper-work is not the easiest. A man ages in writing even love-stories.[2] Still, I believe my glass and—with a reasonable discount—my acquaintance, when they wag the finger at me also as one with whom Time has dealt somewhat delicately.[3] "By cracky, Macray!" exclaimed Lancaster, when I encountered that old chum of ours, the other evening—"By cracky! But *you* ain't changed a mite since we were all graduates together up town! Beats all!" I stood treat handsomely for Lancaster after this flattering unction. I quote that declaration of his (Lancaster is bald and just as gawky and shrewd and eccentric as to his cravats and deportment as of old) because it bears on—well, my forthcoming request.

Ah, my dear Saladin! What matters it whether our consulship of Plancus be very remote, or even if the almond tree's flourishing is imminent,[4] provided a friendship between a man and his brother-man stand unweakened [by] the test of time? It is much if one human heart, which we have long ago grappled to our own with hooks of steel, is still dear and still intelligible to us. "Nothing is better

---

1 Sometime after his remove to Europe EPS apparently had hurt himself in an Alpine climbing accident, and the recovery took a considerable time. His annotation in a copy of the one-act play "Amiability" (in *Her Enemy*) that he had donated to the Hotel Mirabeau (Lausanne) earmarks the comment of a character clearly modeled after EPS himself: "A bad mountain's one of my few pleasures left in this stale life! However, this summer may really be the last one at it. I'm not as clever at climbing as I used to be." Below this speech is the single word in his handwriting: "Prophetic" (Author's collection).

2 EPS was of course a journalist, and had published potboiler love stories such as "The Golden Moon" and "Mrs. Dee's Encore" in magazines such as *Harper's Bazar*.

3 Macray's humorous self-assessment finds its counterpart in EPS's own braggadocio about his youthful looks. He sent a photograph of himself to his cousins in 1928 when he was nearly seventy-one, noting that "It at least suggests what 200 miles of summer-walking and an hour of daily athletics in a gymnasium can do toward making 'a man not young' defy time and mock at physical decay!" (Coll. R. Biffi).

4 A Biblical reference to the passing of time; though EPS may well be remembering another Christian Burke poem, the title-piece from *The Flowering of the Almond-Tree, and Other Poems* (Edinburgh: Blackwood & Sons, 1896).

than love," says Swinburne's hapless leper.[1] I say amen to that, if it always means a regard so well-placed—a passionate, virile affection as sincere and tried, and a unity of ideas, of tastes, likes and dislikes as close as ours—was! Nothing *is* better than love!—when it can knit souls as happily, each for the other, as seemed our mutual fortune.

For, college-days over, and each of us reading law—rarely thinking it, I am sorry to believe—day by day in old Judge Gates's office, and spending our nights where and how we listed, what an inseparable "team" we made? We haunted the avenue, each fine afternoon. Our hats went off to the same acquaintances, who must have smiled at never greeting one of us without the other. Do you recall those regular Saturday nights at the theater, you paying conscientiously for the tickets one week, I for the next?—by which device we managed to see and criticize and grow enthusiastic or disgusted over pretty much everything in New York worth seeing. And over plenty that wasn't! How we sparred concerning favorite actors and actresses! How we strove to convert each other from aesthetic opinions that seemed fearfully erroneous! And our simple adventures! Do you remember the night when the young lady fainted while seeing Vera Hall as Alixe? You gallantly bore that sweet creature out into the lobby, with her father, afterward confessing to private concern if you weren't meeting the future Mrs. Jaques under such interestingly romantic circumstances? (Not so, however.) How exactly we used to follow the stage-business, tracing each detail of a performance from our favorite front-seats! We felt as if we were quite part of the piece, as if we represented that "special public" which comedians most devote themselves to entertaining. Oh those old theatrical nights! The worst play would go with a good grace under such auspices to-day. Theaters I seldom attend now; and I never come back from any in a tenth part of that satisfaction which you and I used to experience! But that, I suppose, is only natural, for it is—youth! How is it with you?

Certainly, vary as our tastes and predilections might where the plays and play-actors came into consideration, there was seldom a point of difference, an unshared like or dislike where music was concerned, during our long and enthusiastic servitude to it.[2] Almost

---

[1] "Nothing is better, I well think,/Than love; the hidden well-water/Is not so delicate to drink...."Thus begins Swinburne's poem "The Leper."

[2] EPS was a music critic of considerable standing in the 1890s, for *Harper's* and *The Independent*. Harry Flagler loved music and later would practically underwrite the New York Philharmonic-Symphony Orchestra.

a servitude it was! Was ever so omnivorous a musical craze? How we used to sit side by side, spell-bound through often, I fear, indifferent performances of our favorite operas! To walk slowly home, in starlight, softly whistling Gounod, or raving Verdi, or carried away headlong by the tide of Wagnerism! What endless musical jests and allusions and quotations we kept oscillating between us, each a little *Leitmotif* of our intimacy. It puzzles me to-day to tell just when we first took to calling a certain prima-donna, of impaired excellence, the Sweet Squealer! Or a baritone of note, whom it was our fortune to hear pretty often, "the good Adolf"—his personal reputation being so exactly the contrary to anything good. Rather diffidently, but with an innocent curiosity and much self-gratulation, we found our ways behind the aweful operatic curtain; and so flourishing our little Italian and French and German, we fairly penetrated Bohemia, with some misgivings but increasing delight; coming to know a few Fausts and Fidelios and Brünnhildes and Valentines—stalwart men of family, or matronly mothers.

But such musical evenings and the sweet sound of those orchestras and singers that fifteen years make into matter of *à travers chants*,[1] are less tenderly green in my thought than our quiet hours of duets and extemporizing and—oh, audacious word!—composing together, in that quiet roomy second floor back we shared. On rainy evenings it often held a great deal of happiness. What a pair we were to work our course together through Mozart's E Flat Symphony, *à quatre mains*![2]—or become most stupendously excited in storming through the finale of Beethoven's Fifth! Trembling with an ecstasy, that two high-strung young natures made no attempt to conceal, whole nights went to Schumann to Schubert, to Brahms, to Tschaikovsky, to Franck![3] To this day, I can never hear Brahms's noble Third Symphony but I am carried back to one evening when we first played it through together.[4] You jumped up from the stool in pure excitement, crying out that the slow movement was too wonderful!—you could play it no longer! I had to pacify your

---

[1] A musical medley (French).
[2] Four-handed duet (French).
[3] A not-so-surprising list of composers to choose. EPS names Beethoven, Brahms, and Tchaikovsky as showing evidence of "Uranian" leanings in *Intersexes* (396–397), and recent scholarship suggests the same of Schubert and Schumann.
[4] Not surprisingly, EPS says of Brahms and Bruckner that they have been characterized as "the ultimate voices in a homosexual message by symphonic music" (*Intersexes* 397).

strained nerves and regulate my own at the same time. Were we a pair of fools—or not? I think not.[1] Apropos I have always felt that you and I—thanks to our charming friend Kriesch, from Vienna, were among the earliest American converts to Bruckner, outside of discerning professional enthusiasts. By the by, we never were informed how the few other people in that house relished those long protracted *musicales*. I don't know. If they objected they never complained. If they suffered without complaint, let us give them the martyrs' crown of stoical patience, or of a vast civility.

The other day I came across that set of "Variations" you wrote, printed (at your own expense, of course) and dedicated to me. It was not dusty in the portfolio. By it lay some waltzes and songs we "collaborated." Upstairs, I am sure, rests in secure tranquility, our bold attempt at nothing less than an operetta; which however did not advance beyond its first act.

Do you "keep up your music" nowadays? There is always a piano in my rooms. Sometimes exceedingly good music is thence evolved by others; none, good or bad, by me. I have not touched a keyboard in two or three years, save one Sunday last summer. It was down at a little church, on Long Island. The organist asked me to "try" the instrument. First I said "no." Then I said "yes." So I played the collection-boxes up and down the narrow aisle, with the "Andante quasi Largo," in A Flat major, that you wrote down, one spring evening long ago. I was glad I did not have to use my eyes for any notes....

What an endless stock of other than artistic jokes and passwords we two kept current! Fragments of them recur to me, often enough; some that I can no longer establish with their trivial meanings. Do you remember how we always termed a dollar a "Rosina"; for some trivial and now—to me—unaccountable reason? Why should we never have alluded to a certain worthy elderly gentleman except as "The B-a-a-dger?" Or to an equally worthy hostess (whom we both heartily respected, but whose vagaries amused us) save as "the Old Angel"? Or why to dignified Miss Beatrice B— not otherwise than under that allegorical phrase, of stern significance, "Die Eiserne Jungfrau?"[2] To whom save you and me, could the geographic term "Cilician" possess so mirthful a significance? ...I should tremble for that intellect attempting to unravel the mazes of all our figures of

---

[1] A startlingly similar scene occurs in E.M. Forster's *Maurice*.

[2] "The Iron Virgin" (German).

speech, our bywords, *ad dementiam*! Foolish all these trifles. But all were follies much better than some that amuse other chums; and all of a sort that we can smile at to-day without a blush. And our music kept us from learning steps in sundry *danses macabres* that might make us limp nowadays.

Your singular tact, your simplicity of tastes and of nature kept your money from being the barrier between us that wealth is so often between friends. I had but just enough; you had so much![1] To the last, delicately, you were so like the gentlemen of the old days you used to delight to read of, that I never thought of your riches save as an accessory to yourself, the gilt frame that was nothing compared to the portrait it protected. Yet how gracefully, in a score of matters, here and there, did you smooth my way for me, week in and week out? You used to lighten this or that passing burden, bestowing now one now another pleasure, otherwise not for us both—as if from some vague source to which I could not even return my thanks.

It is said that in all friendship exists the leader and the led. Which led in ours? Who set the pattern oftenest, for thoughts or acts? I do not believe there was much precedence there. It seemed as if the same notions came to us at the same instants. Did ever two men come to understand one another as we did—words, looks, even thoughts, it often seemed—or get to catch the very elevation or depression of our emotional atmospheres, as if by an invisible barometer? Ah, I can see myself, once more, hurrying up town to our den, some afternoon when I was delayed!—or coming up the stairs late of an evening! As I opened the door, and caught sight of your face, of your attitude—presto! I looked toward life, as did your spirit, not a bit perhaps as mine had done a moment earlier! So was it with yourself, in your turn, I know well.

There is a little poem, by that graceful writer known as "Christian Burke" (a pseudonym, I believe) entitled, I think, "Estranged;" in which a man, soliloquizing earnestly, sadly, as to a broken friendship apostrophizes the absentee somewhat thus—I don't quote accurately, I have not the book at hand:

---

[1] Harry Harkness Flagler inherited considerable wealth as the son of Henry M. Flagler, the imposing oil baron who with John D. Rockefeller had originally founded the Standard Oil Company.

"Had we parted in wrath and scorn,
Each might have sought the other's grace,
And meeting suddenly, face to face,
A nobler love been born.
But vainly shall ye seek for fruit
When the tree's dying at the root!"

Saladin—our tree has never been in the way of dying! You know that—I know it. You feel that—I feel it ... It is always vigorous despite our proud neglect; evergreen and immortal as the Tree of Life! Friend, friend!—let us water it again, let us prune it again! Let us stir it again into leaf, flower and fruit—for the rest of our lives! It were a crime to do otherwise now. Come—be fellow-gardener with me again!— to rejoice under the shade of verdure so fair, and of apples surpassing those of the Hesperides,[1] or seen "in a picture of silver." Will you?

Every friendship worth while is an exchange. That is a psychical and social truism, of course. But the world forgets that in truisms we are likely to discover mainsprings of all human relationships. Yes, an exchange! For each friend gives something and receives some-thing—in instinctive counter-gift. That something must be suffi-cient, and it must be felt, even if unseen and unmeasured. Thus it comes that even the most unselfish friendship has need of the calm inquiry—"Granting all affections unequal, what do I get for what I give here? What do I give for what I get here?" And if two friends cannot answer—satisfactorily, swiftly, joyfully to themselves, and to each other, that question of equation, they are not to one another what they best could be. They are not true friends.

You and I could always answer such an interrogation—sentimen-tal. We knew that our friendship was not only of our hearts and lives but a thing of the logic of our hearts and lives. So many could have envied that double aspect of it, Saladin!

Then came your betrothal, and your wedding.[2] That calamity, for such it was to me, was not sudden. I foreknew it awhile. I faced it with a rigid philosophy. You divined that, but did not say so. I had always anticipated your marriage with your cousin. I admired her heartily. But when she and I regarded each other as rivals—for such

---

[1] One of the labors of Hercules is to steal the golden apples of the Hesperides, the daughters of the night.

[2] Flagler married in 1894.

we were—when I knew that another and more passionate emotion than our regard must push mine to the wall, must pass by rejoicing, I was heart-sore. I hated the world![1] Do many friends have such strange talks as was that last one of ours? "All shall be the same! Do you not see it?"You asked it half-apologetically, pleadingly. And then I answered sharply: "No, no nothing is the same! …You have always known my views as to that! I will not have *such* a friend's secondary intimacy. Spurious confidence! It is bound to be that forever henceforth. Divided heart!—I had rather have none! The day you marry, you go your ways and I mine; diverging step by step, but ever diverging. It is the end!"The end I made it, apace—I, not you. Love and pride are old yokemates.

That reason—yes, and the other reason. The other reason, too. But there!—*térjünk más tárgyra!*[2]

Well—why have I thus run through this story of our past, your story and mine, just this particular night?—while the rain falls in chill torrents over these New York's roofs, and you are, I dare say, reading Balzac or a London review, in the somber library at the Manor. (I remember the fine old house so clearly.[3] I dare say it is not changed by an article of furniture since I last saw it, nearly ten years ago.) I have written, first, because the tale has lengthened pleasantly under my hand, has surrounded my table here with such kindly ghosts of the past! It has so warmed away from my heart all disagreement, all torpor of long severance, that I fancy it may do the same for you. (Has it?) And, second, because I have a pertinent favor to ask of you—the last point in this long letter of retrospect.

This is the favor.

You are alone now—too much alone, I fear.[4] So am I. What sundered us—material or immaterial—has vanished…. Can we not make the psychologic experiment of reviving our old selves?—of leading them up from the past, at least in some measure?—of adapting them to the present? Can not we bring about once more some part of the harmony, the intimacy that, I am sure, has never been matched for either of us otherwise, and cannot be so? Come, Saladin!

---

[1] See the appended correspondence of EPS to George Woodberry regarding his estrangement from Flagler.

[2] Enough of that! Let's change the subject! (Hungarian).

[3] The Flagler mansion was actually located on Fifth Avenue and 54th Street in New York City.

[4] The real Mrs. Flagler did not die until 1939.

Let us be wise, in what yet is left of our time! The years have not been so many, after all. So much of our earlier identities holds good still that our imaginations, our wills, need not strongly be called into exercise. Surely never was there a more audacious hour for such a *redivivus*![1] ... Can we not begin to see each other much as once we did? Define how well we can pull together to-day? Beliefs, tastes, all the souvenirs of our former community of spirits—these are still our capital to draw upon in so piquant an experiment. Piquant? it is a frivolous word! Let it stand for my writing a more earnest one.

To be practical—can we not agree that, for some months to come, you and I will resume, so far as is possible—as it happens, it ought to be decidedly free for both—the old intimacy? You have good servants at the Manor. Leave the house more to them. Spend half of your week—every other day and night if you can (every day and night if you will) here with me, in our old roomy quarters, that I have merely widened and made yearly more habitable as beseems a prosperous journalist, like my present self. Or, a night or so in each week the Manor shall find me under its roof. Instead of the review or the newspaper, we will take up Mozart and Schumann and Saint-Säens, Debussy and Rachmaninoff and Macdowell and Wagner according to old or new lights. And even Society shall see us again, old man! If most of the fair-faced girls we used to bow to are married and become matriarchs, if many of the men be in portly fatherhood, *n'importe*![2] All the faces will not be strange to us, nor will we tread alone many deserted banquet halls. Come, then! Try this novel experiment with me! Try it, Saladin! It ought to succeed! Be it a true remainder of life to both of us—that new world which is our old, that old world which shall be our new!

Let us be business-like, and begin this happy intent with—an inaugural. Next Friday night's opera is "Aida."[3] Here is a ticket. Look at it. Do you recognize the check-number? Our old seats, Saladin! I induced the management to send me the same chairs in the same row. (One of them will be at your service for the rest of the season.) I have an unpostponable dinner with a business-friend early that evening, so I cannot ask you to meet me here. But I will not be seated late. At a few minutes before the curtain rises, I want

---

[1] Resurrection (Latin).
[2] No matter (French).
[3] Opera (1871) by Giuseppe Verdi (1813–1901).

you to come sauntering down the aisle, in your old way—looking as nearly as may be your old self—just as you used to do on evenings when we did not dine together before the opera. You will slip into your chair, you will clap your hand on my knee, exclaiming: "Well, old man, is it going to be good tonight, do you think? ..." And we will walk home together after the music is done, "talking it over together." Later—well, we will talk over, more or less—if it's worth while—we won't need to waste much time so, I think—whatever part of this letter, or of life, seems to need further reference. Anyhow the first step so will be taken to bring back to you and me a fellow-ship, a sunlight, a tranquility and a beauty that life has too long lacked! *So* long lacked, it seems to me! though it is only a matter of some years. To find it again ... will you come? As an experiment? As a proof that what has been once can be—twice? That what in our case has been once should be twice, *must* be twice? ...

(*Later*)

I was interrupted (*absit omen!*[1]) by an odd ill-turn—quite unim-portant—just as I was about to sign this long letter. So I scratch down my name—with my heart in it—an hour later. Has my hand-writing improved? Ever yours,

DOUGLAS MACRAY."

III.

Could one have watched the expressions that pursued one another on the face of the man who read this letter, seated in that quiet room by himself, he could have had little trouble in divining the effect. Jaques did not taste even a mouthful more, presently. He soon left the man to clear away the table. He walked into his library and shut the door. He sat down before his fire and thought and thought—looking into the bright flame that was burning now so warmingly and brilliantly—his head resting on his thin, firm hand.

Presently he rang the bell. "Telephone this message to the station at once, George," he said quietly. The man took the dispatch and withdrew. The telegram ran:

"Expect me Friday, without fail. The experiment must succeed. Once, twice, forever.

SALADIN."

---

[1]   May it bear no ill omen! Knock on wood! (Latin).

IV.

FROM "THE NEW YORK TIMES"
OF SATURDAY, DEC. —, 189–

"We regret to record the death of Mr. Douglas Macray, well known through the art and literary columns of the *Signal;* which sad incident occurred suddenly on Friday evening, as that gentleman was entering his cab to go from the Century Club to the Metropolitan Opera House. The malady that so unexpectedly closed Mr. Macray's busy career was *angina pectoris*, which Mr. Macray had anticipated might some day prove fatal to him, on the briefest notice. He was taken to his apartments, not very distant, but life was extinct. An old friend of Mr. Macray's, Mr. Bertram Jaques, of Marengo, was in town to meet the deceased at the opera, and awaited him at the performance; but by Mr. Macray's continued absence Mr. Jaques became anxious, and went to his friend's residence to inquire the cause of his delay. Mr. Jaques arrived at Mr. Macray's apartments, just as the body of his friend reached the house. He at once took the funeral-arrangements (elsewhere announced) in his personal charge. Mr. Macray was relatively a young man. He left no family."

Appendix F: "The Most Peculiar Friend I Have Ever Had"

1. Excerpt from *Semi-Centennial: Some of the Life and Part of the Opinions of Leonard Bacon*, by Leonard Bacon. New York: Harper & Brothers, 1939; pages 60–65.

In Geneva I made, under peculiar circumstances, the most peculiar friend I have ever had. As I entered the dining-room one evening I beheld a man engaged in what to me is the most enigmatic of amusements. Between mouthfuls he was reading the score of an opera. A cuneiform tablet would have seemed more entertaining to a person of my limitations, and accordingly I paid some attention to his appearance. In the midst of the table d'hôte propriety of the meal, an old English clergyman, whose white hair and beard gave him the look of an incompetent minor prophet, went quite literally mad at an adjoining table. Leaping to his feet, he delivered a passionate but incoherent jeremiad to the appalled guests of the Grand Hotel des Bergues. The sad-faced woman, wife, sister, daughter, who was his keeper, pulled him down by the coat-tails, and he sank into a volcanic silence that had promise of future eruptions. The scene was the extreme limit of the pathetic and the ludicrous. But the man with the opera score caught my eye at the high pitch of the excitement. Duly at the end of the meal he came over to our party and introduced himself to my father. So began an extraordinary part of my education. For reasons unnecessary to state, he shall be nameless, but he was in a great sense my teacher. And from that absurd origin, dated a long series of what still seem to me notable conversations and letters more notable still.

The man with the opera score had been a journalist at home, but now hung loose upon society abroad. He was small, thin, white-skinned, and *chétif*,[1] but he knew everything and everybody, and, as far as I was concerned, the mere fact that he existed was the essence of excitement and romance. For the moment to a boy of twenty he was the delight of the intellect. Without ostentation, for fun, by chance, he knew the right book, the play to see, the music to hear. Never did a man understand better the distinction between what is new and what

---

[1] Sickly (French).

appears to be so. For years his letters kept me abreast of odd tendencies in the European mind that I could never have found out for myself in any book. Sometimes he was penetrating, sometimes merely pleasantly peripheral. And I am glad I did not miss the delightful tangents on which he sent me off. Yet I think I knew from the first that there was something about the man with the opera score, and perhaps about me too, that of itself would make the relation transitory.

★ ★ ★ ★ ★

The man with the opera score turned up in Florence to comment and expatiate, as always charmingly. But he was still more effective in Rome. He belonged to the type for whom what we call Classic has more meaning than the Medieval or the Romantic. For this I cannot be sufficiently grateful, because I belong, as I suppose, to the opposed camp. With Tacitus and Suetonius and Gibbon at his tongue's end he made Rome, "that bad arrangement in yellow plaster," a place of unimaginable vitality. In the ruined corridors of the Palatine, he compelled me to feel the dagger through my side, when he spoke of the conspiracy against Commodus. A year later I understood, because of him, Roman jokes in the notes to Gibbon. I had not yet read the great passage in the *Autobiography* about the monks chanting vespers in the temple of Jupiter.[1] But the man with the opera score in our walks about the city fully prepared me to appreciate and taste "a stranger metamorphosis than any dreamed of by Ovid."[2] How should I forget looking out from the higher ruins over the Forum blazing white in the sun, while he poured into my ear droll stories of the Late Republic or the *chronique scandaleuse* of the exarchate of Ravenna? In spite of his Classic faith he was interested in the change of things. And next to my father I owe to the man with the opera score my interest in what has been called "the edges of history," Hellenistic Greece, the beginnings of the medieval darkness, the Byzantine Empire, which curiously enough has protected

---

[1] From the *Autobiography* (1796) of Edward Gibbon (1737–94): "It was at Rome, on the 15th of October 1764, as I sat musing amidst the ruins of the Capitol, while the barefooted friars were singing vespers in the temple of Jupiter, that the idea of writing the decline and fall of the city first started to my mind." The result was his masterpiece *Decline and Fall of the Roman Empire*.

[2] The influence of the *Metamorphosis* by Ovid (43 B.C.–A.D. 17) on Western art and literature cannot be exaggerated. The work is our best classical source of 250 myths, all based on the element of change.

me from boredom, when more sufficient men have turned first in despair and then with a sickly willingness—to bridge.

Anyhow one's first taste of Rome could not have had better auspices. He even exhibited to me the realities of the modern city so that the continuity of life that for three millennia has never ceased to cataract through those mean streets had meaning, vividness, and for all its bourgeois drabness, charm. I got from the man with the opera score some little sense of the difference between "blacks" and "whites," and why the opinions of a Prince Colonna were at variance with those of a free mason official in the admiralty. The types may be found in cities of the untrammeled West. And a member of the Union League Club is like one and Mr. Thomas Corcoran is like the other. No compliment to either is implied. Such divergencies in thought and feeling deserve more careful study than they are apt to get. If men thought of such matters at all, perhaps Italy would not be the intellectual hell-hole it is at present. And the United States would have more bread and fewer circuses. But at the moment, though I perceived some of the implications of the irrepressible conflict, I saw nothing fatally established by our stars.

It was my first intention to let the man with the opera score come across my little stage only at the proper chronological moments. But it seems better to polish him off all at once in spite of the dangers incurred in leaping ahead of the narrative. For years his ideas affected my life as Father Holt's affected Henry Esmond's.[1] But at length it was borne in upon me that I could not see eye to eye with him. I could give his serious notions such intellectual sympathy as I might be capable of, but I could not feel with him on various matters. And for the first time in my life I permitted a relationship to break. It is a hateful thing to have to do and caused me pain. If it caused him some, I regret that aspect. Yet I know it was necessary for me to take the line I took.

More than fifteen years later, I spoke with him for the last time in Florence. He was old, visibly sick, and, something to me not to be explained, if one considered his former views, violently addicted to what our ancestors called the errors of Rome.[2] Personally I greatly

---

[1]   Father Holt is the Jesuit priest who tutors the young Henry Esmond in the novel of the same name by William Makepeace Thackeray (1852).

[2]   The "errors of Rome" refers to the Protestant view of Roman Catholicism. In an undated letter (1907) in Yale University Library, EPS instructs the young Leonard Bacon: "Pray get and read carefully Zola's 'Rome,' both before you go to Rome *and* after. I know of no novel that is so cosmic as to a vast local subject; a milieu; the *polygonal* aspects of Rome." Zola's novel, placed on the Index of Forbidden Books by the Church, outlined Protestant dissatisfaction with the Vatican.

prefer Rome to Canterbury, and both are better than Geneva, but it is also true that I detest the lot. Accordingly the stereotyped arguments which he brought to bear against what he imagined to be my Protestant prejudices left me pretty cold, and that last meeting had nothing in it to remind me of our happier and earlier feasts of reason. In fact I was bored, and we parted with that extreme politeness which is the characteristic of unsuccessful encounters.

A few days later the dust and trampling of a multitude in the Via Bolognese excited my curiosity and I went to an upper window to see what it was all about. Below me a Corpus Domini procession, as long as a division and with more banners, was worming its way from Monte Morello back into the city. Almost directly under me in the "black blockade" marched the man with the opera score, hatless, and sharing his breviary with a fat bourgeois, doubtless of equal or greater faith. It made me shudder to think that that feeble body and sickly white bald head had been exposed to two hours of a blazing Florentine sun. Later I remembered Pascal's bitter sentence: "Saying your office will deaden your intellect and you will be happy." I intend no innuendo, when I say that I hope he found happiness in the stupefaction of prayer. The more I think of him the more I am grateful for the good he did me. But I am even more grateful that my notion of reality, whatever its deficiencies, was different from his, and, according to me, nearer, by planetary diameters, to life as it is.

I did not foresee writing the preceding sentence, or this one for that matter, when we left Italy after two more delightful months than most people have ever had....

2. [From the author's viewpoint: Letter from Edward Prime-Stevenson to Leonard Bacon. Courtesy Yale Collection of American Literature, Beinecke Rare Book and Manuscript Library, Yale University Library.]

Hotel Minerva, Florence
6 December 1907; afternoon

Dear Leonard:
There are many advantages, verily, of a psychic as well as a physic sort, in living over on this side—in having especially the Italian ambient about one. One of them is that if a man is heathenishly, shamelessly, convincedly, happily, often ecstatically human, on old lines that

are good and beautiful no matter what about them A or B or C in America or elsewhere think, or *say* they think—so often with a sigh—he can follow all sorts of nice little sentimental impulses. He yields himself, half-smiling half-seriously, to them, in the right *décor* for them. Your letter of the 29th was among my usual large contingent at "Cooks," this morning. I looked over some things in that unaesthetic locality. "No," said I to myself, "I will *not* read Leonard's letter here! *That* I firmly refuse to do! I know *quid decet quid non*, better than that!" So I walked slowly along the void, sunny Lung'arno. I went on—into the wide alley of the Cascine. Sitting down on one of those grey old stone-benches on the cross-road first met, I read what you write, where you will like it read. All about me was still and green.

I read it slowly. Then I read it again.... Leonard—Leonardo—take care—take care—You please me too much ... I fear a little. For, I say you please me too much.... Are you quite sure you mean all those charming things that you say? Are you quite "intelligent"—as runs the old commercial term—of what one reads? For, you see one *can* "read *into*" your lines, a temperament, and a nature, and a vision of human relationships that when one encounters them in an American, not very directly, very explicably, Latin or oriental seems a sort of anachronism. If you weren't "an American"—well, then one would not think twice before being made happy. Or, rather, if you weren't somehow or other—principally by the obligingness of your parents—a New-Englander born withal. But there—what rubbish I am writing in such parleyings with you—about you! Temperament so continuously defies all clear racialism, all nationality, all environment, all the distortions, the laboured artifices, the injunctions to think this to feel thus, to be so-and-so,—when our Ego says "This I seek—this I feel—this I believe—this I love—this I am! Not anything else." Why, one lives life through so, often and often, over there in that Cold Land, without having one human being, somehow—for it all depends on the currents of one's existence—to whom one can really *be oneself.* Speaking, feeling, showing, following oneself—to not even one! in a group of friends very fairly friends but still not-wholly such. Over here there's another sort of world as to that; as to so many other conditions of daily life. The clock keeps the old time, after all,—over this side.... *One has got back into the sun.* No wonder that so many of your compatriots and mine will rather live in a garret *au-deça*, than in a Commonwealth Avenue or Riverside-Drive palace *au-delà*. I know a legion of such deserters not small ... Into the sun ... into the sun!.... Good God—good

Sun-God!—how it shines here! —But what a tumultuous devil of—
I suppose you say it—rhapsodics—of inconsecutives of the purest *eau
folle*—I am writing! Yet really there is more coherency than you may
fancy ... I suppose that many letters from me are more chaotic, because
of my habit of never discarding a letter once begun, for new beginnings or middles or endings of it; and never "getting nerves" over letters
finished—unless in business correspondence, where I am almost
painfully attentive. But really, Leonard, it's not a bad resolution, when
you know your friend! When I profess and practice such sans-gêne,
you can judge how vigorously I rebuke your contrary ways: judging
from that remark in your last, about certain false starts, and backings,
and fillings in writing *me*!! Be a wise chap; and foolishly follow my
method. You'll feel a whole lot better for it! Do you fancy that there
is anything that you find in your mind to scratch down to me, oh,
Charmides, which startles, puzzles, antagonizes me. Rubbish. And again
rubbish is in such notions. I defy them. Do you, as well!

★   ★   ★   ★   ★

But at one graceful remark in your letter, alas! I found myself smiling rather bitterly, in thanking you for it. No, my dear boy,—no—
you didn't "fall in love" with me, and you could not do *that*. Not
unless in only an odd illusion, very charming to me, but very illog-
ical and out of the real key of your age and life. Yet—all the same,
Charmides,[1] you can possibly—just possibly—*come* to love such a
pis-aller Socrates, as I may be to you; with more or less of the vibra-
tion of the passional chord in the emotion. But I've past the time for
that to be my fortune "on sight," so to say, with the magnetism, the
unreasoned precipitancy toward your friend of say a decade or more
agone. Thanks to some god, I believe I still somehow *can* win a
heart—by gracious reflex ... A few years ago—or not so few—well,
I would then not challenge your phrase. —You see, I have known
well, what it is to be in Arcadia, and to walk along the Ilyssus.
Consequently—I haven't any flattering hallucinations as to myself
of—today. Besides, it was always the privilege of the grey and simian
sage to fall in love with any lad that liked him; but Greek aesthetics

---

[1]   Charmides, the subject of a dialogue (380 B.C.) by Plato, is a beautiful youth who
represents the ideal of Temperance. Socrates as his teacher speaks to him in the kindly
spirit of an elder. We are surprised to hear that Charmides afterwards became one of
the Thirty Tyrants of Athens.

didn't allow *him* to expect kind impossibilities in exchange! You see how romance humbles itself, before common-sense and a mirror and an almanac—in my case! I've happened to know a good many amiable and otherwise clear-headed men who haven't been as cool and wise in the foregoing respect as I wish to be; —as in ever desirable ...When a man gets to [a] certain time of life, even if he be lucky enough to find that men a lot younger than himself grow instinctively attached to him, on anywise, let him remember that he is— lucky; and that he is an ass to demand that the flame have the same colour and heat and endurance, as may have his own ...!

Oh, Leonard—the best thing in the world ever is youth! Nothing is worth *it*! Not merely internal, but external youth—beauty—! To feel oneself young, and to be young, under the sun! All the so called compensations for leaving *that* behind one, are *such* sorry matters!.... Nothing takes its place, nothing—at least nothing does so when one has been so happy as I have been! Not that I am unhappy now. Heavens above us, no!—not one man in a million faces his forties as happy-hearted as I do,—I expect. In large part because I believe our sex to be the best worth ever finding drawn to us; and to hold-to; and because somehow I still am not exactly a neglected moss-grown Hermes at the end of an ilex-walk. But—many times I am guilty of ingratitude and of *un*philosophy. I admit that 'tis very shabby behaviour. Only when one can say that he has not had his chances, that he has never had his day, that the gavottes have been few and the tables poor eating, and the rose-garlands of mediocre colour and scent, has he a right to grumble at quitting the ball-room; resigning his place to the new comers. I am about the last fellow to have any reason to repine on *that* sort of ground!—Mais, tout de même—?

In the name of all the Gods at once, what devil sets me to writing you so *en élégie*? Pardon, mon Alcibiade![1]

★　★　★　★　★

I came down from Paris, as far as Genève a month ago. You will be glad to know that before I came to the end of my two months in town there—that town which once meant so much to my intimate life, and which I had arbitrarily decided should never possess any such

---

[1] Alcibiades (450?–404 B.C.) was an Athenian general who as a teenager fell in love with Socrates and is portrayed as attempting a seduction of the older man in the *Symposium*.

interest for me again, and couldn't—you will be amused to know that any such attitude wholly was dismissed before I found even my last days drawing on. It was largely a sort of dépit amoureux.[1] We all know what tricks such antipathies play us. Adorable, irresistible place!—every corner, every aspect of which, once was so eloquent to me!—city in which I piqued myself on being plus parisien que les parisiens!—What a droll fatuity it was in me solemnly to renounce caring anything particular about it! Of course, part of my chilled emotions on this reversion to Paris, this returning to France, after a carefully deliberated and persisted absence of about ten years—in which I had broken off everything French—had transferred my existence so completely to German and Austro-Hungarian milieux—had much to do with my being so apathetic. And there have been so many changes in my old circle—là-bas. I said, "I will be disdainful, I will be indifferent. I will regard Paris simply in amiable intellectuality." I didn't even hunt up my relatives and friends. But all that changed before I left, I assure you. And people were so awfully kind withal, once I let the beaux restes of the old group know that I had slunk back....You see there was really something quite solemn about this reversion. So much has happened since I said "No more Paris! no more France!" But as matters are now in my mind, and have been for about two years, also in view of many plans connected with routes of travel lately available, I expect to be a considerable part of each year in France, and in Paris, again, after this. France and I—*we have made up*! By the way, you will be likewise gratified that I have recovered, and more than that, a most proper pride in what Coleridge (I think it was) once called "That detestable jargon, the French language" (!)—and in speaking and writing it at least decently. When I left Paris this time, in fact, so inevitable had that process been, that it was becoming almost easier for me to speak French than English; and certainly a lot pleasanter!.... I shall print in Geneva that bit of *blague* I finished there—"En Suisse, 1907: Impressions Nouvelles et Vielles." Also—I have had a good chance to "catch up," at last, pretty thoroughly with the movement of the contemporary Parisian stage. I have either seen or read, or both, nearly sixty pieces, since I said "Yes, I begin at this again, too." À-propos of that, you will find the special "Supplément Théâtrale" of "*L'Illustration*," if you can get hold of that excellent thing, very useful, to "keep the run" of the French theatre, month in

---

[1] Loving grudge (French).

and out. Twice a month, there appears, by special arrangement with the authours, whatever may be the leading piece of the hour: Donnay, Lavedan, Bernstein, Hermant, Sardou, Kistemaeckers, Mirbeau, de Flers, Capus, Coolus—everything that is the success of the moment.

I think I mentioned to you that the thing which impressed me the most as being any real "change" in Paris since I was last there—that is change of general aspect—were the Métro and the automobiles. I have become quite crazed in my enthusiasm for the Métro. I could *not* get used to flying about town in fifteen minutes, instead of taking hours. Especially it makes a difference to me, as my friends are mostly over Monceaux way, and down near the Bois. It seems to me the most perfect "*souterrain*" that could be made: though I believe that the New York one is considered admirable. I had only known the London one, which has too many steps to suit me, and its crowded "lifts" I dislike vastly. As for the autos, after I got my mind free from the agitation that every individual automobile in town was—as says King David— "seeking after my life to take it away," I highly esteemed them— platonically. Enter one I will not—no never! In spite of many blandishments and jeers, I have not; and I do not intend to.

★　★　★　★　★

I had two very enjoyable weeks in Genève. The "Bergues" seems unfailing in comfort and quiet. Most of the circle of last season was already réintégré. We had much comparing of summer experiences. The venerable Mr. Akers, crazy as ever, but (for the time) quiescent was back; with his wife: but made no *allocution* to me nor to any one else. (what a serio-comic episode was his breaking-out into that polemic, that evening, when you and your mother and your sister and I were at his mercy!) ... Coming down on the train from Paris, I had not only a coupé, but almost a whole carriage to myself. About an hour before we reached the Cornavin, I became aware of the presence, in another coupé, of a very good-looking young fellow of about 19. Presently he came in to my coupé, and in extremely English-French he ventured an inquiry as to the Customs. I set him right, in intelligible English. "Oh! you speak English" said he, with a most enormous and droll relief. He turned out to be the only son of a Bournemouth clergyman, coming to Switzerland for the first time, to pass the winter, and to study French—so as to prepare for a civil-service exam. He didn't know a soul in Genève; and he was far from

happy in mind. I forthwith took him under my protection.—
(immoral phrase!) I set him to rights as to Genève, during the fortnight; looked after his pension and French arrangements (he goes to
the École de Commerce)—presented him around town a bit—and
so on. We became quite intense friends. He said one thing about that,
so funny!—so "absolutely English"—the night before I was to quit
Genève. He happened to be in one of those vague emotional moods
that the Englishman rarely allows to reach full expression, even when
he would be anything but sorry to *know how* to do so. "Oh, you [have]
been so beastly, so absolutely *beastly* kind to me!" said he. That goes
Thackeray's young lieutenant one better.[1] The English are a most
curious study in "passionals." I am not partial to the race, I confess.
But they mean well. And they can be taught much, sometimes. Really.

★ ★ ★ ★ ★

The "Minerva" is about one-fourth full. Intensely quiet, day and
night, therefore. The circle of guests is not at all interesting. Except
for chatting with one American lady, a friend of my sister, —and a
specially intelligent and quiet-mannered individual—living on this
side during some twenty years—I have not said ten sentences to
anyone since I came; and have not been desirous to be more social.
My big room—which you may recall vaguely—has all been "done
over" new, in pale greens, and is vastly improved. I have had a carpen-
ter make me a biggish bookcase, to fit into a deep door-space, and
have had certain odds and ends in the way of my pictures and orna-
ments brought out of their deposits in the "magazzino." So the room
looks quite stately. All which sounds as if I were planning for a materially longer halt here than is the case. But everything goes into boxes
and trunks and closets as usual, in February when I go south.

★ ★ ★ ★ ★

The weather is dull, half-rainy, humid; good-for-nothing out of
doors, day by day. No cold yet. I oscillate between so many grades
of *completi* and *maglie* that I never know what is on my back—or to
stay there—for three hours together! I shall be rejoiced when the
weather settles itself and my attire.

---

1   Perhaps George Sedley Osborne in Thackeray's novel, *Vanity Fair.*

* * * * *

About your poem. You are right: it is emphatically better than the *Blonayade*. I have thought of only one considerable change in it,—which though not at all convincing may be of interest to you; and so I have ventured to *maneuver* its progress, in the alarming manner that you see. Also, I have queried, substituted, etc. here and there,—often without any essential reference to the change that I alluded to—the verbal effects, and choice of certain of the adjectives and sounds; matters of euphonics in verse—as they recur. But, you will kindly understand that I have made a quantity of pencillings that are largely matters of individual taste; and which you can readily reject, even undiscussed. The structural change that I speak particularly of, is this. Your poem makes "the Muse" *impersonal*; rather than personal to the poet, makes her death a matutinal one, which is rather out of sentimental "keeping," even if she *is* a morning-wanderer—and lessens (or rather does not attempt) what is so apposite through the poem—a sort of elegiac "progress" in the *history* of the Muse's career. Moreover, the limiting of her story and personality to the "morning," makes certain adjectives, certain tenses, and so on, difficult of clear use. Now, —to *my* mind—"the Muse" is more interesting and *individualized* if she has her day—like the rest of us! So I have gone over the lines, and not only made various suggestions and changes of words with reference to euphony or what else, but also with the wider idea of making the poem *emotionally and descriptively* a *progressive* one. The Muse *comes* with the morning. But her poet describes her, and their *entente cordiale*, not only through the morning, but through the day,—and she ends her life and any such days together, with your phrase about the "summer *sunset West*"—which otherwise has not any very clear propriety ... But this re-construction is not anything except a matter of taste, as I say, to which a poem so written, so easily lends itself. Besides, to write verse is one thing—to take a poem and turn it upside down and inside-out is another thing—a vast lot easier, and well, a universe more—impudent! So my unlimited excuses.

* * * * *

I read little except Italian or French. I go to Signora Bertini three times a week for Italian diction and writing. I have found that to "recur" to a good teacher every year or so, when the stay one makes in a place will allow it, is an excellent plan. Involuntarily one gets into such slovenly habits! I have decided to discontinue all my American periodicals, and to stick to the Continental group, which I find most useful or pleasurable. I have *held-on* to the "Atlantic Monthly" for many years: but it seems to me steadily lessening in quality. I take the "Mercure de France," which is invaluable, for knowing what is going on outside of the conventional lines of French, and other, letters. I now take pains to see *regularly* certain of the Paris journals; and of course some of the Italian reviews. But I really have not much time for reading. I do *not* intend to make it ... I mean to go through all Dr. Dill's books, however, presently; and in Rome I shall go through also a regular course in Boissier ... By the by, I met the other afternoon an American (living in Rome) who it seems knows, in flesh and blood, Xavier Mayne, the much queried authour of that remarkable little book "Imre: A Memorandum"—which you may have met—though being printed privately, it is now hard to come on,—even in Italy. So *that* settled the matter of the authourship ... *Item*, there is a man named *Mille*, who is writing, in the Paris "*Journal*," some extremely amusing and clever oriental sketches—quite a new note in matters of the sort. If I can get some together, I shall send them to you. I believe they will appear as a volume ultimately.

★ ★ ★ ★ ★

You somewhat amuse me—and certainly you perplex me admirably, my dear Leonard!—by intimating that I have "done" anything whatever "*for*" you since we encountered—be such "doing" intellectually, emotionally or what else. I am not *myope*, as to what I am to be charged with—credited with—of good, of bad, of indifferent—as a rule. But I'm d—d if I can see anything that you have as yet to refer to me, in an amiable acknowledgement! You are doing psychic algebra! Besides—besides—you put me in a sort of moral and intellectual embarrassment ... I am not at all a friend to be fully approved of, by any quantity of men and women. In fact, if only as to many social aspects of life and the world I am openly in a status of conviction, or of doubt—of negation, or affirmation, that makes me—I fear—a *demoralizing* sort of individuality, from ethical-conventional points of view. You yourself may not approve of me—you yourself may not l-l—l—l—ike me, after awhile, nearly so much as you do now—as you would wish to do, perhaps. I suppose that in "a nice sort of way" (as the man said [as] he wrung his wife's neck)—I am a Dangerous Being.... Think of that!—Ponder that!—Beware of that!—Are you prepared to make a Dangerous Being your Friend?—Well—at least you are warned. Also you may as well be warned of another thing; —that I am so intelligently and of perverse conviction a Dangerous Being, that I prefer to be such, —haven't a penny worth of fear in being such. In fact, the more I have gone about the world, the more I find that we Dangerous B-'s are in the right of many matters. Still—I arrogate naught. And if you don't continue to find me sympathetic,—well—I cannot change....

—I am to take, or to lose. If the latter, always saying—in Lady Morgan's graceful lines—

"C'est quitte à quitte—et bons amis!"

★　★　★　★　★

I laid my long letter down to receive a caller, who has stayed for God knows how long! At any rate, the letter is ended fatidically; for the afternoon is closing. I never write at nightfall, or night. Farewell. Write when you have time. I can understand that that is not too often your case. Buon capo d'anno! Pensieri augurii—stia felicissime! Vi abbraccio—[1]

Affectionately your friend,
Edward P-St.

---

[1]　Happy New Year! Best wishes—stay most happy! I embrace you—! (Italian).

Appendix G: A Contemporary Review of Imre

Raffalovich, André. Review of *Imre: A Memorandum*, by Xavier Mayne. *Chronique de l'unisexualité* in: *Archives d'anthropologie criminelle* 22.164/165 (15 Aug.–15 Sept. 1907): 628–30.[1]

Imré [*sic*] a memorandum by Xavier Mayne. The English Book Press. R. Rispoli, Naples. Calata Trinita Maggiora 53, 1906, privately printed est plutôt un document que de la littérature. C'est déplorablement écrit mais c'est *vécu*. L'auteur y raconte l'amitié-amour de deux uranistes supérieurs, mâles tous les deux, l'un viril, l'autre ultra-viril peut-être—invertis nés, ayant tous les deux souffers amèrement, appartenant à l'aristocratie morale et intellectuelle, l'un anglais de trente ans, l'autre officier Hongrois de vingt-cinq ans. Ils se rencontrent, se lient d'amitié, s'aiment, ne se devinent pas (les invertis ne se reconnaissant pas, comme on l'a faussement prétendu), se démasquent successivement (ce qui fournit au récit du mouvement et de l'émotion), et se donnent l'un à l'autre pour la vie, corps et coeur, loyalement, tendrement, passionnément.

Un lecteur qui ne cherche ni le style ni le romanesque, et qui n'est pas *un sombre et ignorant persécuteur de ses frères* non conformiste, lira *Imré* non sans intérêt. Il y reconnaîtra l'aspiration vers un idéal viril, la haine de l'effémination et de la luxure, la haine des corrupteurs de l'enfance, des satyres qui hantent les latrines; il en appréciera l'ambition de réagir contre les préjugés des hétérosexuals aveugles, aveuglés et cruels, et contre les invertis depravés, ou insignifiants ou compromettants. Même en admettant la véracité des confessions que les deux héros se font l'un à l'autre, même en admettant que leur liaison sera durable et heureuse, le lecteur sans préjugés, s'il se met au même diapason mystique que Xavier Mayne, se demande si ce n'est pas une perversion de l'amour céleste de chercher l'ami suprême dans un homme, une déviation de l'amour de l'homme pour Dieu.

Et puis quelle confusion d'idées, quel désordre, est indiqué par la liste de grands uranistes Thémistocle, Agésilas, Aristide, Cléomène, Socrate, Platon, Saint-Augustin, Servet, Beza, Alexandre, Jules César, Auguste, Adrien, Eugène, Charles XII, Frédéric, Tilly, Skobeleff, Gordon, Hector Macdonald, Shakespeare, Marlowe, Platen,

---

[1] For this review I am grateful to Raimondo Biffi.

Grillparzer, Hölderin, Newton, Michel Ange, Liebig, Sodoma, Whitman, Jérôme Duquesnoy, Winckelmann, Mirabeau, Beethoven, Louis de Bavière! Pourquoi jeter les chastes ou les dépravés parmi les grands invertis, de quel droit? Est-ce pour les opposer théâtralement à Héliogabale, Gilles de Rais, Henri III, le marquis de Sade, aux prostitués, aux artistes, aux musiciens, aux jeunes esthètes parfumés comme des cocottes—est-ce pour pouvoir s'écrier sommes—nous, or ou excréments?

[*Imre* a memorandum by Xavier Mayne. The English Book Press. R. Rispoli, Naples. Calata Tinita Maggiora 53. 1906, privately printed is above all a document more than literature. It is deplorably written but it is *lived*. The author tells of the love-friendship of two superior uranians, both males, one virile, the other ultra-virile perhaps—born inverts, both having suffered bitterly, belonging to the moral and intellectual aristocracy, one a thirty-year-old Englishman, the other a Hungarian officer of twenty-five. They meet, strike up a friendship, fall in love, don't find out about each other (inverts not recognizing each other, as is falsely presumed), unmask themselves successively (which furnishes the parade of movement and emotion), and give themselves each to the other for life, body and heart, loyally, tenderly, passionately.

A reader who looks for neither style nor romance, and who is not *a dark and ignorant persecutor of his nonconformist brothers*, will read *Imre* not without interest. He will meet there the aspiration towards a virile ideal, hatred for effeminacy and luxury, hate for the corrupters of youth, for satyrs who haunt the latrines; he will value there the daring to react against the prejudiced among heterosexuals and unisexuals. The superior uranian, according to the thesis of *Imre*, must defend himself all at once against himself, against blind heterosexuals, blinded and cruel, and against depraved inverts, be they insignificant or compromising. Even in allowing the truth of the confessions which the two heroes make to one another, even allowing that their liaison will be lasting and happy, the reader without prejudices, if he is in the same mystical key as Xavier Mayne, asks himself if it's not a perversion of celestial love to find the supreme friend in a man, a deviation from the love of man for God.

And then what a confusion of ideas, what disorder, is shown by the list of great uranians: Themistocles, Agesilaus, Aristides, Kleomenes, Socrates, Plato, St. Augustine, Servetus, Beza, Alexander,

Julius Caesar, Augustus, Hadrian, Eugene, Charles XII, Frederic, Tilly, Skobeleff, Gordon, Hector Macdonald, Shakespeare, Marlowe, Platen, Grillparzer, Hölderlin, Newton, Michelangelo, Liebig, Sodoma, Whitman, Jérôme Duquesnoy, Winckelmann, Mirabeau, Beethoven, Louis de Bavière! Why throw the chaste or the depraved among the great inverts, by what right? Is it to theatrically set them in opposition to Heliogabalus, Gilles de Rais, Henri III, the Marquis de Sade, to the prostitutes, the artists, the musicians, the young aesthetes perfumed like cocottes—is it just to be able to shout out numbers—we, the gold or the excrement?]

Works Cited and Recommended Reading

Works by Edward Prime-Stevenson

Dramatic Stories to Read Aloud. Privately printed. Florence: The Italian
  Mail, 1924.

*Her Enemy, Some Friends—and Other Personages: Stories and Studies Mostly
  of Human Hearts.* Privately printed. Florence: G. and R. Obsner, 1913.

"*Il Trovatore:* An Essay on the History of the Opera." Introductory essay.
  Il Trovatore: An Opera in Four Acts. By Giuseppe Verdi. New York: G.
  Schirmer, 1926.

Imre: A Memorandum. Privately printed. Naples: English Book-Press/R.
  Rispoli, 1906. [as Xavier Mayne] Reprinted: New York: Arno
  Press, 1975.

The Intersexes. Privately printed. Rome [?], 1908/1909. [as Xavier
  Mayne] Reprinted: New York: Arno Press, 1975.

Janus [*A Matter of Temperament*]. Chicago: Belford, Clarke, 1889.

Left to Themselves, Being the Ordeal of Philip and Gerald [*Philip and Gerald*].
  New York: Hunt and Easton, 1891.

Letter to C.-F. Ramuz. 11 October 1912. Bibliothèque Cantonale et
  Universitaire. Lausanne, Switzerland.

Letter to Robert Schauffler. 28 August 1934. Harry Ransom
  Humanities Research Center. U of Texas at Austin.

Letters to George Woodberry. 1892–1922. Houghton Library. Harvard
  University, Cambridge, MA: bMS Am 1587 (237).

Letters to Leonard Bacon. 1907–1927. Leonard Bacon Collection. Yale
  Collection of American Literature, Beinecke Rare Book and
  Manuscript Library. Yale University Library. New Haven, CT.

Letters to Mrs. William A. Prime. 1927–1930. Collection Raimondo
  Biffi. Rome, Italy.

Letters to Paul Elmer More. 1906–1921. More Papers, Manuscripts
  Division, Department of Rare Books and Special Collections.
  Princeton University Library. Princeton, NJ.

"A Little Owl of Florence." *The Independent* 59 (28 September 1905):
  742–746.

Long-Haired Iopas: Old Chapters from Twenty-five Years of Music-Criticism.
  Privately printed. Florence: The Italian Mail, 1927.

"Madame Clerc." *Vignettes: Real and Ideal; Stories by American Authors.*
  Ed. Frederic Edward McKay. Boston: DeWolfe, Fiske, 1890.

"(A Man's) Preface." *The Evolution of Woman.* By Harry Whitney McVickar. New York: Harper and Brothers, 1896.

Mrs. Dee's Encore [*You Will, Will You?*]. *Harper's Bazar* 29: 5–12 (1 February–28 March 1896).

"The Political Crisis in Hungary: 1903." *The Independent* 55 (30 July 1903): 1803–1807.

A Repertory of One Hundred Symphonic Programmes, for Public Auditions of the Orthophonic Phonograph-Gramophone. Privately printed. Florence: The Giuntina Press, 1932.

"The Revolt of the Holidays: A Christmas Gambol." *Harper's Book of Little Plays for Children.* New York: Harper and Brothers, 1910.

The Square of Sevens: An Authoritative System of Cartomancy. New York: Harper and Brothers, 1896. [as Robert Antrobus]

Those Restless Pilgrimages [Selected travel writings]. Ed. Tom Sargant. North Pomfret, VT: Elysium, 2002.

White Cockades: An Incident of the 'Forty-Five'. New York: Scribner, 1887.

In addition, many critical essays, biographical sketches, poems, articles, and reviews appear throughout the 1880s and especially 1890s in *Harper's Weekly* and *The Independent*, as well as *The Atlantic Monthly*, *Scribner's*, and *Life*.

Untraced Works

Alciphron and Clelia: A Narrative Poem
"Charles Brockden Brown: A Pioneer in American Romance"
"En Suisse, 1907: Impressions Nouvelles et Vielles."
The Golden Moon (*The Firebrand Secret*) [juvenile]
"La Casaccia: un Racconto"
"The Parting Guest: A Drama" [series of metrical translations from Racine, Molière, and others]
Red William's Wood
Sébastien au Plus Bel Age
Some Men, and Women, and Music
"Un Tout Petit Carnet Suisse"

Background Works: Edward Prime-Stevenson

Austen, Roger. *Playing the Game: The Homosexual Novel in America.* Indianapolis: Bobbs-Merrill, 1977.

Bacon, Leonard. *Semi-Centennial: Some of the Life and Part of the Opinions of Leonard Bacon.* New York: Harper, 1939.

Bergman, David. *Gaiety Transfigured: Gay Self-Representation in American Literature*. Madison: U of Wisconsin P, 1991.

Féray, Jean-Claude, and Raimondo Biffi. "Xavier Mayne (Edward I. Prime-Stevenson), Romancier Français?" *Inverses: Littératures, Arts, Homosexualités* 1 (2001): 47–57.

Fone, Byrne R.S. *A Road to Stonewall: Male Homosexuality and Homophobia in English and American Literature, 1750–1969*. New York: Twayne, 1995.

————, ed. *The Columbia Anthology of Gay Literature: Readings from Western Antiquity to the Present Day*. New York: Columbia UP, 1998.

————. "This Other Eden: Arcadia and the Homosexual Imagination." *Essays on Gay Literature*. Ed. Stuart Kellogg. New York: Harrington Park Press, 1985. 13–34.

Garde, Noel I. (Edgar Leoni). "The First Native American 'Gay' Novel," *One Institute Quarterly of Homophile Studies* 9 (Spring 1960): 185–190.

————. "The Mysterious Father of American Homophile Literature," *One Institute Quarterly of Homophile Studies* 3 (Fall 1958): 94–98.

Gifford, James. *Dayneford's Library: American Homosexual Writing 1900–1913*. Amherst: U of Massachusetts P, 1995.

————. "Left to Themselves: The Subversive Boys Books of Edward Prime-Stevenson." *Journal of American and Comparative Cultures* 24. 3/4 (Fall/Winter 2001): 113–116.

Herzer, Manfred. "'The Very Rubbish of Humanity'—Prime-Stevenson und der Schwulen Kitsch in der Literatur am Beginn des zwanzwigsten Jahrbunderts." *Capri* 32 (2002): 10–14.

Hubert, Philip G., Jr. "Some of Our Music Critics." *The Book Buyer* 18.4 (May 1899): 303–307.

Livesey, Matthew Jerald. "From This Moment On: The Homosexual Origins of the Gay Novel in America." Diss. U of Wisconsin, Madison, 1997.

Miller, Philip Lieson. "Edward Prime-Stevenson: Expatriate Opera Critic." *The Opera Quarterly* 6 (Autumn 1988): 37–51.

Mitchell, Mark, and David Leavitt, eds. *Pages Passed from Hand to Hand: The Hidden Tradition of Homosexual Literature in English from 1748 to 1914*. Boston: Mariner, 1997.

"Mr. Stevenson." *Musical Courier* 60.2 (12 January 1910): 23–24.

"Prime-Stevenson Publication." *Musical Courier* 68.8 (25 February 1914): 24.

Setz, Wolfram. Afterword: "Ein literarischer Fall" [A Literary Case]. *Imre: Eine Psychologische Romanze*. By Xavier Mayne (Edward Irenaeus

Prime-Stevenson). Trans. D.G. Ed. Wolfram Setz. Berlin: Bibliothek rosa Winkel, 1997. 143–160.

Summers, Claude J., ed. *The Gay and Lesbian Literary Heritage: A Reader's Companion to the Writers and Their Works, from Antiquity to the Present.* New York: Henry Holt, 1995.

Background Works: General Studies

Aldrich, Robert, and Garry Wotherspoon, eds. *Who's Who in Gay and Lesbian History: From Antiquity to World War II.* New York: Routledge, 2001.

Chandler, David Leon. *Henry Flagler: The Astonishing Life and Times of the Visionary Robber Baron Who Founded Florida.* New York: Macmillan, 1986.

Chauncey, George. *Gay New York: Gender, Urban Culture, and the Making of the Gay Male World 1890–1940.* New York: Basic Books, 1994.

Ellis, Havelock. *Sexual Inversion.* 3rd ed. New York: Random, 1936.

——— and John Addington Symonds. *Sexual Inversion.* 1897. New York: Ayer, 1994.

Éri, Gyöngyi, and Zsuzsa Jobbágyi. *A Golden Age: Art and Society in Hungary 1896–1914.* 3rd ed. Budapest: Corvina, 1997.

Katz, Jonathan Ned. *Gay American History: Lesbians and Gay Men in the U.S.A.* New York: Avon, 1976.

Koestenbaum, Wayne. *Double Talk: The Erotics of Male Literary Collaboration.* New York: Routledge, 1989.

Lázár, István. *An Illustrated History of Hungary.* 6th ed. Budapest: Corvina, 1999.

———. *A Brief History of Hungary.* 3rd ed. Budapest: Corvina, 1999.

Lukacs, John. *Budapest 1900: A Historical Portrait of a City and Its Culture.* New York: Grove, 1988.

Martin, Sidney Walter. *Henry Flagler: Visionary of the Gilded Age.* Lake Buena Vista, FL: Tailored Tours, 1998.

Mondimore, Francis Mark. *A Natural History of Homosexuality.* Baltimore: Johns Hopkins UP, 1996.

Sargant, Tom. *Bugger's Talk; Volume One: Why the Invert Swings His Hips.* London: Gay Men's Press, 2002.

Symonds, John Addington. *The Memoirs of John Addington Symonds: The Secret Homosexual Life of a Leading Nineteenth-Century Man of Letters.* Ed. Phyllis Grosskurth. Chicago: U of Chicago P, 1984.